ZU...

Max Beerbohm (1872–1956) was born
in London and educated at Charter-
house and Merton College, Oxford.
ZULEIKA DOBSON was his only novel,
written in 1911. He also wrote short
stories and was the drama critic of the
*Saturday Review*. He lived in Italy from
1910 onwards apart from the duration
of the two Wars.

# MAX BEERBOHM

# Zuleika Dobson

Minerva

**A Minerva Paperback**
ZULEIKA DOBSON

First published in Great Britain 1911
by William Heinemann Ltd
This Minerva edition published 1991
by Mandarin Paperbacks
an imprint of Reed Consumer Books Ltd
Michelin House, 81 Fulham Road, London SW3 6RB
and Auckland, Melbourne, Singapore and Toronto

Reprinted 1992, 1995

Copyright © 1911 by Dodd, Mead & Company, Inc.
Copyright © 1939 by Max Beerbohm

A CIP catalogue record for this title
is available from the British Library
ISBN 0 7493 9916 3

Printed and bound in Great Britain
by Cox & Wyman Ltd, Reading, Berkshire

*ILLI ALMAE MATRI*

## NOTE

*When, in 1911, this book was first published, some people seemed to think it was intended as a satire on such things as the herd instinct, as feminine coquetry, as snobbishness, even as legerdemain; whereas I myself had supposed it was just a fantasy; and as such, I think, it should be regarded by others.   But all fantasy should have a solid basis in reality; and to any young readers of the book it may seem that my presentment of Oxford life was a wild infraction of that law.   Let me assure them that my fantasy was far more like to the old Oxford than was the old Oxford like to the place now besieged and invaded by Lord Nuffield's armies.*

*M.B.*   1946

# I

THAT old bell, presage of a train, had just sounded through Oxford station; and the undergraduates who were waiting there, gay figures in tweed or flannel, moved to the margin of the platform and gazed idly up the line. Young and careless, in the glow of the afternoon sunshine, they struck a sharp note of incongruity with the worn boards they stood on, with the fading signals and grey eternal walls of that antique station, which, familiar to them and insignificant, does yet whisper to the tourist the last enchantments of the Middle Age.

At the door of the first-class waiting-room, aloof and venerable, stood the Warden of Judas. *College* An ebon pillar of tradition seemed he, in his garb of old-fashioned cleric. Aloft, between the wide brim of his silk hat and the white extent of his shirt-front, appeared those eyes which hawks, that nose which eagles, had often envied. He supported his years on an ebon stick. He alone was worthy of the background.

Came a whistle from the distance. The breast of an engine was descried, and a long train curving after it, under a flight of smoke. It grew and grew. Louder and louder, its noise foreran it. It became a furious, enormous monster, and, with an instinct for safety, all men receded from the platform's margin. (Yet came there with it, unknown to them, a danger far more terrible than itself.) Into the station it came blustering, with cloud and clangour. Ere it had yet stopped, the door of one carriage flew open, and from it, in a white travelling-dress, in a toque a-twinkle with fine diamonds, a lithe and radiant creature slipped nimbly down to the platform.

A cynosure indeed! A hundred eyes were fixed on her, and half as many hearts lost to her. The Warden of Judas himself had mounted on his nose a pair of black-rimmed glasses. Him espying, the nymph darted in his direction. The throng made way for her. She was at his side.

"Grandpapa!" she cried, and kissed the old man on either cheek. (Not a youth there but would have bartered fifty years of his future for that salute.)

"My dear Zuleika," he said, "welcome to Oxford! Have you no luggage?"

"Heaps!" she answered. "And a maid who will find it."

"Then," said the Warden, "let us drive straight to College." He offered her his arm, and they proceeded slowly to the entrance. She chatted gaily, blushing not in the long avenue of eyes she passed through. All the youths, under her spell, were now quite oblivious of the relatives they had come to meet. Parents, sisters, cousins, ran unclaimed about the platform. Undutiful, all the youths were forming a serried suite to their enchantress. In silence they followed her. They saw her leap into the Warden's landau, they saw the Warden seat himself upon her left. Nor was it until the landau was lost to sight that they turned—how slowly, and with how bad a grace!—to look for their relatives.

Through those slums which connect Oxford with the world, the landau rolled on towards Judas. Not many youths occurred, for nearly all—it was the Monday of Eights Week—were down by the river, cheering the crews. There did, however, come spurring by, on a polo-pony, a very splendid youth. His straw hat was encircled with a riband of blue and white, and he raised it to the Warden.

"That," said the Warden, "is the Duke of Dorset, a member of my College. He dines at my table to-night."

Zuleika, turning to regard his Grace, saw that he had not

2

reined in and was not even glancing back at her over his shoulder. She gave a little start of dismay, but scarcely had her lips pouted ere they curved to a smile—a smile with no malice in its corners.

As the landau rolled into "the Corn", another youth—a pedestrian, and very different—saluted the Warden. He wore a black jacket, rusty and amorphous. His trousers were too short, and he himself was too short: almost a dwarf. His face was as plain as his gait was undistinguished. He squinted behind spectacles.

"And who is that?" asked Zuleika.

A deep flush overspread the cheek of the Warden. "That," he said, "is also a member of Judas. His name, I believe, is Noaks."

"Is he dining with us to-night?" asked Zuleika.

"Certainly not," said the Warden. "Most decidedly not."

Noaks, unlike the Duke, had stopped for an ardent retrospect. He gazed till the landau was out of his short sight; then, sighing, resumed his solitary walk.

The landau was rolling into "the Broad", over that ground which had once blackened under the faggots lit for Latimer and Ridley. It rolled past the portals of Balliol and of Trinity, past the Ashmolean. From those pedestals which intersperse the railing of the Sheldonian, the high grim busts of the Roman Emperors stared down at the fair stranger in the equipage. Zuleika returned their stare with but a casual glance. The inanimate had little charm for her.

A moment later, a certain old don emerged from Blackwell's, where he had been buying books. Looking across the road, he saw, to his amazement, great beads of perspiration glistening on the brows of those Emperors. He trembled, and hurried away. That evening, in Common Room, he told what he had seen; and no amount of polite scepticism would convince him that it was but the hallucination of one who had been reading too much Mommsen. He persisted that he had seen what he described. It was not until two days had elapsed that some credence was accorded him.

Yes, as the landau rolled by, sweat started from the brows of the Emperors. They, at least, foresaw the peril that was overhanging Oxford, and they gave such warning as they could. Let that be remembered to their credit. Let that incline us to think more gently of them. In their lives we know, they were infamous, some of them—"nihil non commiserunt stupri, saevitiae, impietatis." But are they too little punished, after all? Here in Oxford, exposed eternally and inexorably to heat and frost, to the four winds that lash them and the rains that wear them away, they are expiating, in effigy, the abominations of their pride and cruelty and lust. Who were lechers, they are without bodies; who were tyrants, they are crowned never but with crowns of snow; who made themselves even with the gods, they are by American visitors frequently mistaken for the Twelve Apostles. It is but a little way down the road that the two Bishops perished for their faith, and even now we do never pass the spot without a tear for them. Yet how quickly they died in the flames! To these Emperors, for whom none weeps, time will give no surcease. Surely, it is sign of some grace in them that they rejoiced not, this bright afternoon, in the evil that was to befall the city of their penance.

## II

THE sun streamed through the bay-window of a "best" bedroom in the Warden's house, and glorified the pale crayon-portraits on the wall, the dimity curtains, the old fresh chintz. He invaded the many trunks which—all painted Z. D.—gaped, in various stages of excavation, around the room. The doors of the huge wardrobe stood, like the doors of Janus's temple in time of war, majestically open; and the sun seized this opportunity of exploring the mahogany recesses. But the carpet, which had faded under his immemorial visitations, was now almost entirely hidden from him, hidden under layers of fair fine linen, layers of silk, brocade, satin, chiffon, muslin. All the colours of the rainbow, materialised by modistes, were there. Stacked on chairs were I know not what of sachets, glove-cases, fan-cases. There were innumerable packages in silver-paper and pink ribands. There was a pyramid of band-boxes. There was a virgin forest of boot-trees. And rustling quickly hither and thither, in and out of this profusion, with armfuls of finery, was an obviously French maid. Alert, unerring, like a swallow she dipped and darted. Nothing escaped her, and she never rested. She had the air of the born unpacker— swift and firm, yet withal tender. Scarce had her arms been laden but their loads were lying lightly between shelves or tightly in drawers. To calculate, catch, distribute, seemed to her but a single process. She was one of those who are born to make chaos cosmic.

Insomuch that ere the loud chapel clock tolled another hour all the trunks had been sent empty away. The carpet

5

was unflecked by any scrap of silver-paper. From the mantelpiece, photographs of Zuleika surveyed the room with a possessive air. Zuleika's pincushion, a-bristle with new pins, lay on the dimity-flounced toilet-table, and round it stood a multitude of multiform glass vessels, domed, all of them, with dull gold, on which Z. D., in zianites and diamonds, was encrusted. On a small table stood a great casket of malachite, initialled in like fashion. On another small table stood Zuleika's library. Both books were in covers of dull gold. On the back of one cover BRADSHAW, in beryls, was encrusted; on the back of the other, A.B.C. GUIDE, in amethysts, beryls, chrysoprases, and garnets. And Zuleika's great cheval-glass stood ready to reflect her. Always it travelled with her, in a great case specially made for it. It was framed in ivory, and of fluted ivory were the slim columns it swung between. Of gold were its twin sconces, and four tall tapers stood in each of them.

The door opened, and the Warden, with hospitable words, left his grand-daughter at the threshold.

Zuleika wandered to her mirror. "Undress me, Mélisande," she said. Like all who are wont to appear by night before the public, she had the habit of resting towards sunset.

Presently Mélisande withdrew. Her mistress, in a white peignoir tied with a blue sash, lay in a great chintz chair, gazing out of the bay-window. The quadrangle below was very beautiful, with its walls of rugged grey, its cloisters, its grass carpet. But to her it was of no more interest than if it had been the rattling court-yard to one of those hotels in which she spent her life. She saw it, but heeded it not. She seemed to be thinking of herself, or of something she desired, or of someone she had never met. There was ennui, and there was wistfulness, in her gaze. Yet one would have guessed these things to be transient—to be no more than the little shadows that sometimes pass between a bright mirror and the brightness it reflects.

Zuleika was not strictly beautiful. Her eyes were a trifle large, and their lashes longer than they need have been. An anarchy of small curls was her chevelure, a dark upland of misrule, every hair asserting its rights over a not discreditable brow. For the rest, her features were not at all original. They seemed to have been derived rather from a gallimaufry of familiar models. From Madame la Marquise de Saint-Ouen came the shapely tilt of the nose. The mouth was a mere replica of Cupid's bow, lacquered scarlet and strung with the littlest pearls. No apple-tree, no wall of peaches, had not been robbed, nor any Tyrian rose-garden, for the glory of Miss Dobson's cheeks. Her neck was imitation-marble. Her hands and feet were of very mean proportions. She had no waist to speak of.

Yet, though a Greek would have railed at her asymmetry, and an Elizabethan have called her "gipsy," Miss Dobson now, in the midst of the Edwardian Era, was the toast of two hemispheres. Late in her 'teens, she had become an orphan and a governess. Her grandfather had refused her appeal for a home or an allowance, on the ground that he would not be burdened with the upshot of a marriage which he had once forbidden and not yet forgiven. Lately, however, prompted by curiosity or by remorse, he had asked her to spend a week or so of his declining years with him. And she, "resting" between two engagements—one at Hammerstein's Victoria, N.Y.C., the other at the Folies Bergères, Paris—and having never been in Oxford, had so far let bygones be bygones as to come and gratify the old man's whim.

It may be that she still resented his indifference to those early struggles which, even now, she shuddered to recall. For a governess's life she had been, indeed, notably unfit. Hard she had thought it, that penury should force her back into the school-room she was scarce out of, there to champion the sums and maps and conjugations she had never tried to master. Hating her work, she had failed signally to pick up

7

any learning from her little pupils, and had been driven from house to house, a sullen and most ineffectual maiden. The sequence of her situations was the swifter by reason of her pretty face. Was there a grown-up son, always he fell in love with her, and she would let his eyes trifle boldly with hers across the dinner-table. When he offered her his hand, she would refuse it—not because she "knew her place", but because she did not love him. Even had she been a good teacher, her presence could not have been tolerated thereafter. Her corded trunk, heavier by another packet of billets-doux and a month's salary in advance, was soon carried up the stairs of some other house.

It chanced that she came, at length, to be governess in a large family that had Gibbs for its name and Notting Hill for its background. Edward, the eldest son, was a clerk in the city, who spent his evenings in the practice of amateur conjuring. He was a freckled youth, with hair that bristled in places where it should have lain smooth, and he fell in love with Zuleika duly, at first sight, during high-tea. In the course of the evening, he sought to win her admiration by a display of all his tricks. These were familiar to this household, and the children had been sent to bed, the mother was dozing, long before the séance was at an end. But Miss Dobson, unaccustomed to any gaieties, sat fascinated by the young man's sleight of hand, marvelling that a top-hat could hold so many gold-fish, and a handkerchief turn so swiftly into a silver florin. All that night, she lay wide awake, haunted by the miracles he had wrought. Next evening, when she asked him to repeat them: "Nay," he whispered, "I cannot bear to deceive the girl I love. Permit me to explain the tricks." So he explained them. His eyes sought hers across the bowl of gold-fish, his fingers trembled as he taught her to manipulate the magic canister. One by one, she mastered the paltry secrets. Her respect for him waned with every revelation. He complimented her on her skill. "I

8

could not do it more neatly myself!" he said. "Oh, dear Miss Dobson, will you but accept my hand, all these things shall be yours—the cards, the canister, the gold-fish, the demon egg-cup—all yours!" Zuleika, with ravishing coyness, answered that if he would give her them now, she would "think it over". The swain consented, and at bed-time she retired with the gift under her arm. In the light of her bedroom candle Marguerite hung not in greater ecstasy over the jewel-casket than hung Zuleika over the box of tricks. She clasped her hands over the tremendous possibilities it held for her—manumission from her bondage, wealth, fame, power. Stealthily, so soon as the house slumbered, she packed her small outfit, embedding therein the precious gift. Noiselessly, she shut the lid of her trunk, corded it, shouldered it, stole down the stairs with it. Outside—how that chain had grated! and her shoulder, how it was aching!— she soon found a cab. She took a night's sanctuary in some railway hotel. Next day, she moved into a small room in a lodging-house off the Edgware Road, and there for a whole week she was sedulous in the practice of her tricks. Then she inscribed her name on the books of a "Juvenile Party Entertainments Agency".

The Christmas holidays were at hand, and before long she got an engagement. It was a great evening for her. Her repertory was, it must be confessed, old and obvious; but the children, in deference to their hostess, pretended not to know how the tricks were done, and assumed their prettiest airs of wonder and delight. One of them even pretended to be frightened, and was led howling from the room. In fact, the whole thing went off splendidly. The hostess was charmed, and told Zuleika that a glass of lemonade would be served to her in the hall. Other engagements soon followed. Zuleika was very, very happy. I cannot claim for her that she had a genuine passion for her art. The true conjurer finds his guerdon in the consciousness of work done perfectly and for its own sake. Lucre and applause are not necessary to him. If he were set down, with the materials of his art, on a desert island, he would yet be quite happy. He would not cease to produce the barber's-pole from his mouth. To the indifferent winds he would still speak his patter, and even in the last throes of starvation would not eat his live rabbit or his gold-fish. Zuleika, on a desert island, would have spent most of her time in looking for a man's foot-print. She was, indeed, far too human a creature to care much for art. I do not say that she took her work lightly. She thought she had genius, and she liked to be told that this was so. But mainly she loved her work as a means of mere self-display. The frank admiration which, into whatsoever house she entered, the grown-up sons flashed on her; their eagerness to see her to the door; their impressive way of putting her into her omnibus—those were the things she revelled in. She was a nymph to whom men's admiration was the greatest part of life. By day, whenever she went into the streets, she was conscious that no man passed her without a stare; and this consciousness gave a sharp zest to her outings. Sometimes she was followed to her door—crude flattery which she was too innocent to fear. Even when she went into the haberdasher's to make some little purchase of tape or riband, or into the grocer's—for she was an epicure in her humble way—to buy a tin of potted meat for her supper, the homage of the young men behind the counter did flatter and exhilarate her. As the homage of men became for her, more and more, a matter of course, the more subtly necessary was it to her happiness. The more she won of it, the more she treasured it. She was alone in the world, and it saved her from any moment of regret that she had neither home nor friends. For her the streets that lay around her had no squalor, since she paced them always in the golden nimbus of her fascinations. Her bedroom seemed not mean nor lonely to her, since the little square of glass, nailed above the washstand, was ever there to reflect her face. Thereinto, indeed, she was ever peering. She would droop her head from side to side, she would bend it forward and see herself from beneath her eyelashes, then tilt it back and watch herself over her supercilious chin. And she would smile, frown, pout, languish—let all the emotions hover upon her face; and always she seemed to herself lovelier than she had ever been.

Yet was there nothing Narcissine in her spirit. Her love for her own image was not cold æstheticism. She valued that image not for its own sake, but for sake of the glory it always won for her. In the little remote music-hall, where she was soon appearing nightly as an "early turn", she reaped glory in a nightly harvest. She could feel that all the gallery-boys, because of her, were scornful of the sweethearts wedged between them, and she knew that she had but to say "Will any gentleman in the audience be so good as to lend me his hat?" for the stalls to rise as one man and rush towards the platform. But greater things were in store for her. She was engaged at two halls in the West End. Her horizon was fast receding and expanding. Homage became nightly tangible in bouquets, rings, brooches—things acceptable and (luckier than their donors) accepted. Even Sunday was not barren for Zuleika: modish hostesses gave her postprandially to their guests. Came that Sunday night, *notanda candidissimo calculo!* when she received certain guttural compliments which made absolute her vogue and enabled her to command, thenceforth, whatever terms she asked for.

Already, indeed, she was rich. She was living at the most exorbitant hotel in all Mayfair. She had innumerable gowns and no necessity to buy jewels; and she also had, which pleased her most, the fine cheval-glass I have described. At the close of the Season, Paris claimed her for a month's engagement. Paris saw her and was prostrate. Boldini did a portrait of her. Jules Bloch wrote a song about her; and this,

for a whole month, was howled up and down the cobbled
alleys of Montmartre. And all the little dandies were mad for
"la Zuleika". The jewellers of the Rue de la Paix soon had
nothing left to put in their windows—everything had been
bought for "la Zuleika". For a whole month, baccarat was
not played at the Jockey Club—every member had suc-
cumbed to a nobler passion. For a whole month, the whole
demi-monde was forgotten for one English virgin. Never,
even in Paris, had a woman triumphed so. When the day
came for her departure, the city wore such an air of sullen
mourning as it had not worn since the Prussians marched to
its Elysée. Zuleika, quite untouched, would not linger in the
conquered city. Agents had come to her from every capital
in Europe, and, for a year, she ranged, in triumphal nomady,
from one capital to another. In Berlin, every night, the
students escorted her home with torches. Prince Vierfünf-
sechs-Siebenachtneun offered her his hand, and was condemned by the Kaiser to six months' confinement in his
little castle. In Yildiz Kiosk, the tyrant who still throve there
conferred on her the Order of Chastity, and offered her the
central couch in his seraglio. She gave her performance in
the Quirinal, and, from the Vatican, the Pope launched
against her a Bull which fell utterly flat. In Petersburg, the
Grand Duke Salamander Salamandrovitch fell enamoured of
her. Of every article in the apparatus of her conjuring-tricks
he caused a replica to be made in finest gold. These treasures
he presented to her in that great malachite casket which now
stood on the little table in her room; and thenceforth it was
with these that she performed her wonders. They did not
mark the limit of the Grand Duke's generosity. He was for
bestowing on Zuleika the half of his immensurable estates.
The Grand Duchess appealed to the Tzar. Zuleika was
conducted across the frontier, by an escort of love-sick
Cossacks. On the Sunday before she left Madrid, a great
bull-fight was held in her honour. Fifteen bulls received the

*coup de grâce*, and Alvarez, the matador of matadors, died in the arena with her name on his lips. He had tried to kill the last bull without taking his eyes off *la divina señorita*. A prettier compliment had never been paid her, and she was immensely pleased with it. For that matter, she was immensely pleased with everything. She moved proudly to the incessant music of a pæan, aye! of a pæan that was always *crescendo*.

Its echoes followed her when she crossed the Atlantic, till they were lost in the louder, deeper, more blatant pæan that rose for her from the shores beyond. All the stops of that "mighty organ, many-piped", the New York Press, were pulled out simultaneously, as far as they could be pulled, in Zuleika's honour. She delighted in the din. She read every line that was printed about her, tasting her triumph as she had never tasted it before. And how she revelled in the Brobdingnagian drawings of her, which, printed in nineteen colours, towered between the columns or sprawled across them! There she was, measuring herself back to back with the Statue of Liberty; scudding through the firmament on a comet, whilst a crowd of tiny men in evening-dress stared up at her from the terrestrial globe; peering through a microscope held by Cupid over a diminutive Uncle Sam; teaching the American Eagle to stand on its head; and doing a hundred-and-one other things—whatever suggested itself to the fancy of native art. And through all this iridescent maze of symbolism were scattered many little slabs of realism. At home, on the street, Zuleika was the smiling target of all snap-shooters, and all the snap-shots were snapped up by the Press and reproduced with annotations: Zuleika Dobson walking on Broadway in the sables gifted her by Grand Duke Salamander—she says "You can bounce blizzards in them"; Zuleika Dobson yawning over a love-letter from millionaire Edelweiss; relishing a cup of clam-broth—she says "They don't use clams out there"; ordering her maid to fix her a warm bath; finding a split in the gloves she has just drawn on before starting for the musicale given in her honour by Mrs. Suetonius X. Meistersinger, the most exclusive woman in New York; chatting at the telephone to Miss Camille Van Spook, the best-born girl in New York; laughing over the recollection of a compliment made her by George Abimelech Post, the best-groomed man in New York; meditating a new trick; admonishing a waiter who has upset a cocktail over her skirt; having herself manicured; drinking tea in bed. Thus was Zuleika enabled daily to be, as one might say, a spectator of her own wonderful life. On her departure from New York, the papers spoke no more than the truth when they said she had had "a lovely time". The further she went West—millionaire Edelweiss had loaned her his private car— the lovelier her time was. Chicago drowned the echoes of New York; final Frisco dwarfed the headlines of Chicago. Like one of its own prairie-fires, she swept the country from end to end. Then she swept back, and sailed for England. She was to return for a second season in the coming autumn. At present, she was, as I have said, "resting".

As she sat here in the bay-window of her room, she was not reviewing the splendid pageant of her past. She was a young person whose reveries never were in retrospect. For her the past was no treasury of distinct memories, all hoarded and classified, some brighter than others and more highly valued. All memories were for her but as the motes in one fused radiance that followed her and made more luminous the pathway of her future. She was always looking forward. She was looking forward now—that shade of ennui had passed from her face—to the week she was to spend in Oxford. A new city was a new toy to her, and—for it was youth's homage that she loved best—this city of youths was a toy after her own heart.

Aye, and it was youths who gave homage to her most freely. She was of that high-stepping and flamboyant type that captivates youth most surely. Old men and men of middle age admired her, but she had not that flower-like quality of shyness and helplessness, that look of innocence, so dear to men who carry life's secrets in their heads. Yet Zuleika *was* very innocent, really. She was as pure as that young shepherdess Marcella, who, all unguarded, roved the mountains and was by all the shepherds adored. Like Marcella, she had given her heart to no man, had preferred none. Youths were reputed to have died for love of her, as Chrysostom died for love of the shepherdess; and she, like the shepherdess, had shed no tear. When Chrysostom was lying on his bier in the valley, and Marcella looked down from the high rock, Ambrosio, the dead man's comrade, cried out on her, upbraiding her with bitter words—"Oh basilisk of our mountains!" Nor do I think Ambrosio spoke too strongly. Marcella cared nothing for men's admiration, and yet, instead of retiring to one of those nunneries which are founded for her kind, she chose to rove the mountains, causing despair to all the shepherds. Zuleika, with her peculiar temperament, would have gone mad in a nunnery. "But," you may argue, "ought not she to have taken the veil, even at the cost of her reason, rather than cause so much despair in the world? If Marcella was a basilisk, as you seem to think, how about Miss Dobson?" Ah, but Marcella knew quite well, boasted even, that she never would or could love any man. Zuleika, on the other hand, was a woman of really passionate fibre. She may not have had that conscious, separate, and quite explicit desire to be a mother with which modern playwrights credit every unmated member of her sex. But she did know that she could love. And, surely, no woman who knows that of herself can be rightly censured for not recluding herself from the world: it is only women without the power to love who have no right to provoke men's love.

Though Zuleika had never given her heart, strong in her

were the desire and the need that it should be given. Whithersoever she had fared, she had seen nothing but youths fatuously prostrate to her—not one upright figure which she could respect. There were the middle-aged men, the old men, who did not bow down to her; but from middle-age, as from old, she had a sanguine aversion. She could love none but a youth. Nor—though she herself, womanly, would utterly abase herself before her ideal—could she love one who fell prone before her. And before her all youths always did fall prone. She was an empress, and all youths were her slaves. Their bondage delighted her, as I have said. But no empress who has any pride can adore one of her slaves. Whom, then, could proud Zuleika adore? It was a question which sometimes troubled her. There were even moments when, looking into her cheval-glass, she cried out against that arrangement in comely lines and tints which got for her the dulia she delighted in. To be able to love once—would not that be better than all the homage in the world? But would she ever meet whom, looking up to him, she could love—she, the omnisubjugant? Would she ever, ever meet him?

It was when she wondered thus, that the wistfulness came into her eyes. Even now, as she sat by the window, that shadow returned to them. She was wondering shyly, had she met him at length? That young equestrian who had not turned to look at her; whom she was to meet at dinner to-night . . . was it he? The ends of her blue sash lay across her lap, and she was lazily unravelling their fringes. "Blue and white!" she remembered. "They were the colours he wore round his hat." And she gave a little laugh of coquetry. She laughed, and, long after, her lips were still parted in a smile.

So did she sit, smiling, wondering, with the fringes of her sash between her fingers, while the sun sank behind the opposite wall of the quadrangle, and the shadows crept out across the grass, thirsty for the dew.

## III

THE clock in the Warden's drawing-room had just struck eight, and already the ducal feet were beautiful on the white bearskin hearthrug. So slim and long were they, of instep so nobly arched, that only with a pair of glazed ox-tongues on a breakfast-table were they comparable. Incomparable quite, the figure and face and vesture of him who ended in them.

The Warden was talking to him, with all the deference of elderly commoner to patrician boy. The other guests—an Oriel don and his wife—were listening with earnest smile and submissive droop, at a slight distance. Now and again, to put themselves at their ease, they exchanged in undertone a word or two about the weather.

"The young lady whom you may have noticed with me," the Warden was saying, "is my orphaned grand-daughter." (The wife of the Oriel don discarded her smile, and sighed, with a glance at the Duke, who was himself an orphan.) "She has come to stay with me." (The Duke glanced quickly round the room.) "I cannot think why she is not down yet." (The Oriel don fixed his eyes on the clock, as though he suspected it of being fast.) "I must ask you to forgive her. She appears to be a bright, pleasant young woman."

"Married?" asked the Duke.

"No," said the Warden; and a cloud of annoyance crossed the boy's face. "No; she devotes her life entirely to good works."

"A hospital nurse?" the Duke murmured.

"No, Zuleika's appointed task is to induce delightful

wonder rather than to alleviate pain. She performs conjuring-tricks."

"Not—not Miss Zuleika Dobson?" cried the Duke.

"Ah yes. I forgot that she had achieved some fame in the outer world. Perhaps she has already met you?"

"Never," said the young man coldly. "But of course I have heard of Miss Dobson. I did not know she was related to you."

The Duke had an intense horror of unmarried girls. All his vacations were spent in eluding them and their chaperons. That he should be confronted with one of them—with such an one of them!—in Oxford, seemed to him sheer violation of sanctuary. The tone, therefore, in which he said "I shall be charmed," in answer to the Warden's request that he would take Zuleika into dinner, was very glacial. So was his gaze when, a moment later, the young lady made her entry.

"She did not look like an orphan," said the wife of the Oriel don, subsequently, on the way home. The criticism was a just one. Zuleika would have looked singular in one of those lowly double-files of straw-bonnets and drab cloaks which are so steadying a feature of our social system. Tall and lissom, she was sheathed from the bosom downwards in flamingo silk, and she was liberally festooned with emeralds. Her dark hair was not even strained back from her forehead and behind her ears, as an orphan's should be. Parted somewhere at the side, it fell in an avalanche of curls upon one eyebrow. From her right ear drooped heavily a black pearl, from her left a pink; and their difference gave an odd, bewildering witchery to the little face between.

Was the young Duke bewitched? Instantly, utterly. But none could have guessed as much from his cold stare, his easy and impassive bow. Throughout dinner, none guessed that his shirt-front was but the screen of a fierce warfare waged between pride and passion. Zuleika, at the foot of the table, fondly supposed him indifferent to her. Though he sat on her right, not one word or glance would he give her. All his conversation was addressed to the unassuming lady who sat on his other side, next to the Warden. Her he edified and flustered beyond measure by his insistent courtesy. Her husband, alone on the other side of the table, was mortified by his utter failure to engage Zuleika in small-talk. Zuleika was sitting with her profile turned to him—the profile with the pink pearl—and was gazing full at the young Duke. She was hardly more affable than a cameo. "Yes," "No," "I don't know," were the only answers she would vouchsafe to his questions. A vague "Oh really?" was all he got for his timid little offerings of information. In vain he started the topic of modern conjuring-tricks as compared with the conjuring-tricks performed by the ancient Egyptians. Zuleika did not even say "Oh really?" when he told her about the metamorphosis of the bulls in the Temple of Osiris. He primed himself with a glass of sherry, cleared his throat. "And what," he asked, with a note of firmness, "did you think of our cousins across the water?" Zuleika said "Yes;" and then he gave in. Nor was she conscious that he ceased talking to her. At intervals throughout the rest of dinner, she murmured "Yes," and "No," and "Oh really?" though the poor little don was now listening silently to the Duke and the Warden.

She was in a trance of sheer happiness. At last, she thought her hope was fulfilled—that hope which, although she had seldom remembered it in the joy of her constant triumphs, had been always lurking in her, lying near to her heart and chafing her, like the shift of sackcloth which that young brilliant girl, loved and lost of Giacopone di Todi, wore always in secret submission to her own soul, under the fair soft robes and the rubies men saw on her. At last, here was the youth who would not bow down to her; whom, looking up to him, she could adore. She ate and drank automatically, never taking her gaze from him. She felt not one touch of pique at his behaviour. She was tremulous with a joy that was new to her, greater than any joy she had known. Her soul was as a flower in its opetide. She was in love. Rapt, she studied every lineament of the pale and perfect face—the brow from which bronze-coloured hair rose in tiers of burnished ripples; the large steel-coloured eyes, with their carven lids; the carven nose, and the plastic lips. She noted how long and slim were his fingers, and how slender his wrists. She noted the glint cast by the candles upon his shirt-front. The two large white pearls there seemed to her symbols of his nature. They were like two moons: cold, remote, radiant. Even when she gazed at the Duke's face, she was aware of them in her vision.

Nor was the Duke unconscious, as he seemed to be, of her scrutiny. Though he kept his head averse, he knew that always her eyes were watching him. Obliquely, he saw them; saw, too, the contour of the face, and the black pearl and the pink; could not blind himself, try as he would. And he knew that he was in love.

Like Zuleika herself, this young Duke was in love for the first time. Wooed though he had been by almost as many maidens as she by youths, his heart, like hers, had remained cold. But he had never felt, as she had, the desire to love. He was not now rejoicing, as she was, in the sensation of first love; nay, he was furiously mortified by it, and struggled with all his might against it. He had always fancied himself secure against any so vulgar peril; always fancied that by him at least, the proud old motto of his family—"*Pas si bête*"—would not be belied. And I daresay, indeed, that had he never met Zuleika, the irresistible, he would have lived, and at a very ripe old age died, a dandy without reproach. For in him the dandiacal temper had been absolute hitherto, quite untainted and unruffled. He was too much concerned with his own perfection ever to think of admiring anyone else.

Different from Zuleika, he cared for his wardrobe and his toilet-table not as a means to making others admire him the more, but merely as a means through which he could intensify, a ritual in which to express and realise, his own idolatry. At Eton he had been called "Peacock", and this nickname had followed him up to Oxford. It was not wholly apposite, however. For, whereas the peacock is a fool even among birds, the Duke had already taken (besides a particularly brilliant First in Mods) the Stanhope, the Newdigate, the Lothian, and the Gaisford Prize for Greek Verse. And these things he had achieved *currente calamo*, "wielding his pen," as Scott said of Byron, "with the easy negligence of a nobleman." He was now in his third year of residence, and was reading, a little, for Literae Humaniores. There is no doubt that but for his untimely death he would have taken a particularly brilliant First in that school also.

For the rest, he had many accomplishments. He was adroit in the killing of all birds and fishes, stags and foxes. He played polo, cricket, racquets, chess, and billiards as well as such things can be played. He was fluent in all modern languages, had a very real talent in water-colour, and was accounted, by those who had had the privilege of hearing him, the best amateur pianist on this side of the Tweed. Little wonder, then, that he was idolised by the undergraduates of his day. He did not, however, honour many of them with his friendship. He had a theoretic liking for them as a class, as the "young barbarians all at play" in that little antique city; but individually they jarred on him, and he saw little of them. Yet he sympathised with them always, and, on occasion, would actively take their part against the dons. In the middle of his second year, he had gone so far that a College Meeting had to be held, and he was sent down for the rest of term. The Warden placed his own landau at the disposal of the illustrious young exile, who therein was driven to the station, followed by a long, vociferous procession of undergraduates in cabs. Now, it happened that this was a time of political excitement in London. The Liberals, who were in power, had passed through the House of Commons a measure more than usually socialistic; and this measure was down for its second reading in the Lords on the very day that the Duke left Oxford, an exile. It was but a few weeks since he had taken his seat in the Lords; and this afternoon, for the want of anything better to do, he strayed in. The Leader of the House was already droning his speech for the bill, and the Duke found himself on one of the opposite benches. There sat his compeers, sullenly waiting to vote for a bill which every one of them detested. As the speaker subsided, the Duke, for the fun of the thing, rose. He made a long speech against the bill. His gibes at the Government were so scathing, so utterly destructive his criticism of the bill itself, so lofty and so irresistible the flights of his eloquence, that, when he resumed his seat, there was only one course left to the Leader of the House. He rose and, in a few husky phrases, moved that the bill "be read this day six months." All England rang with the name of the young Duke. He himself seemed to be the one person unmoved by his exploit. He did not re-appear in the Upper Chamber, and was heard to speak in slighting terms of its architecture, as well as of its upholstery. Nevertheless, the Prime Minister became so nervous that he procured for him, a month later, the Sovereign's offer of a Garter which had just fallen vacant. The Duke accepted it. He was, I understand, the only undergraduate on whom this Order had ever been conferred. He was very much pleased with the insignia, and when, on great occasions, he wore them, no one dared say that the Prime Minister's choice was not fully justified. But you must not imagine that he cared for them as symbols of achievement and power. The dark blue riband, and the star scintillating to eight points, the heavy mantle of blue velvet, with its lining of taffeta and shoulder-knots of white satin, the crimson surcoat, the great embullioned tassels, and the chain of linked gold, and the plumes of ostrich and heron uprising from the black velvet hat—these things had for him little significance save as a fine setting, a finer setting than the most elaborate smoking-suit, for that perfection of respect which the gods had given him. This was indeed the gift he valued beyond all others. He knew well, however, that women care little for a man's appearance, and that what they seek in a man is strength of character, and rank, and wealth. These three gifts the Duke had in a high degree, and he was by women much courted because of them. Conscious that every maiden he met was eager to be his Duchess, he had assumed always a manner of high austerity among maidens, and even if he had wished to flirt with Zuleika he would hardly have known how to do it. But he did not wish to flirt with her. That she had bewitched him did but make it the more needful that he should shun all converse with her. It was imperative that he should banish her from his mind, quickly. He must not dilute his own soul's essence. He must not surrender to any passion his dandihood. The dandy must be celibate, cloistral; is, indeed, but a monk with a mirror for beads and breviary—an anchorite, mortifying his soul that his body may be perfect. Till he met Zuleika, the Duke had not known the meaning of temptation. He fought now, a St. Anthony, against the apparition. He would not look at her, and he hated her. He loved her, and he could not help seeing her. The black pearl and the pink seemed to dangle ever nearer and clearer to him, mocking him and beguiling. Inexpellible was her image.

So fierce was the conflict in him that his outward nonchalance gradually gave way. As dinner drew to its close, his conversation with the wife of the Oriel don flagged and halted. He sank, at length, into a deep silence. He sat with downcast eyes, utterly distracted.

Suddenly, something fell, plump! into the dark whirlpool

of his thoughts. He started. The Warden was leaning forward, had just said something to him.

"I beg your pardon?" asked the Duke. Dessert, he noticed, was on the table, and he was paring an apple. The Oriel don was looking at him with sympathy, as at one who had swooned and was just "coming to".

"Is it true, my dear Duke," the Warden repeated, "that you have been persuaded to play to-morrow evening at the Judas concert?"

"Ah yes, I am going to play something."

Zuleika bent suddenly forward, addressed him. "Oh," she cried, clasping her hands beneath her chin, "will you let me come and turn over the leaves for you?"

He looked her full in the face. It was like seeing suddenly at close quarters some great bright monument that one has long known only as a sun-caught speck in the distance. He saw the large violet eyes open to him, and their lashes curling to him; the vivid parted lips; and the black pearl, and the pink.

"You are very kind," he murmured, in a voice which sounded to him quite far away. "But I always play without notes."

Zuleika blushed. Not with shame, but with delirious pleasure. For that snub she would just then have bartered all the homage she had hoarded. This, she felt, was the climax. She would not outstay it. She rose, smiling to the wife of the Oriel don. Everyone rose. The Oriel don held open the door, and the two ladies passed out of the room.

The Duke drew out his cigarette case. As he looked down at the cigarettes, he was vaguely conscious of some strange phenomenon somewhere between them and his eyes. Foredone by the agitation of the past hour, he did not at once realise what it was that he saw. His impression was of something in bad taste, some discord in his costume . . . a black pearl and a pink pearl in his shirt-front!

Just for a moment, absurdly over-estimating poor Zuleika's skill, he supposed himself a victim of legerdemain. Another moment, and the import of the studs revealed itself. He staggered up from his chair, covering his breast with one arm, and murmured that he was faint. As he hurried from the room, the Oriel don was pouring out a tumbler of water and suggesting burnt feathers. The Warden, solicitous, followed him into the hall. He snatched up his hat, gasping that he had spent a delightful evening—was very sorry—was subject to these attacks. Once outside, he took frankly to his heels.

At the corner of the Broad, he looked back over his shoulder. He had half expected a scarlet figure skimming in pursuit. There was nothing. He halted. Before him, the Broad lay empty beneath the moon. He went slowly, mechanically, to his rooms.

The high grim busts of the Emperors stared down at him, their faces more than ever tragically cavernous and distorted. They saw and read in that moonlight the symbols on his breast. As he stood on his doorstep, waiting for the door to be opened, he must have seemed to them a thing for infinite compassion. For were they not privy to the doom that the morrow, or the morrow's morrow, held for him—held not indeed for him alone, yet for him especially, as it were, and for him most lamentably?

## IV

THE breakfast things were not yet cleared away. A plate
freaked with fine strains of marmalade, an empty toast-rack,
a broken roll—these and other things bore witness to a day
inaugurated in the right spirit.

Away from them, reclining along his window-seat, was the
Duke. Blue spirals rose from his cigarette, nothing in the
still air to trouble them. From their railing, across the road,
the Emperors gazed at him.

For a young man, sleep is a sure solvent of distress. There
whirls not for him in the night any so hideous a phantas-
magoria as will not become, in the clarity of next morning, a
spruce procession for him to lead. Brief the vague horror of
his awakening; memory sweeps back to him, and he sees
nothing dreadful after all. "Why not?" is the sun's bright
message to him, and "Why not indeed?" his answer. After
hours of agony and doubt prolonged to cock-crow, sleep had
stolen to the Duke's bed-side. He awoke late, with a heavy
sense of disaster; but lo! when he remembered, everything
took on a new aspect. He was in love. "Why not?" He
mocked himself for the morbid vigil he had spent in probing
and vainly binding the wounds of his false pride. The old
life was done with. He laughed as he stepped into his bath.
Why should the disseizin of his soul have seemed shameful
to him? He had had no soul till it passed out of his keeping.
His body thrilled to the cold water, his soul as to a new
sacrament. He was in love, and that was all he wished
for . . . There, on the dressing-table, lay the two studs,
visible symbols of his love. Dear to him, now, the colours

26

of them? He took them in his hand, one by one, fondling them. He wished he could wear them in the day-time; but this, of course, was impossible. His toilet finished, he dropped them into the left pocket of his waistcoat.

Therein, near to his heart, they were lying now, as he looked out at the changed world—the world that had become Zuleika. "Zuleika!" his recurrent murmur, was really an apostrophe to the whole world.

Piled against the wall were certain boxes of black japanned tin, which had just been sent to him from London. At any other time he would certainly not have left them unopened. For they contained his robes of the Garter. Thursday, the day after to-morrow, was the date fixed for the investiture of a foreign king who was now visiting England: and the full chapter of Knights had been commanded to Windsor for the ceremony. Yesterday the Duke had looked keenly forward to his excursion. It was only in those too rarely required robes that he had the sense of being fully dressed. But to-day not a thought had he of them.

Some clock clove with silver the stillness of the morning. Ere came the second stroke, another and nearer clock was striking. And now there were others chiming in. The air was confused with the sweet babel of its many spires, some of them booming deep, measured sequences, some tinkling impatiently and outwitting others which had begun before them. And when this anthem of jealous antiphonies and uneven rhythms had dwindled quite away and fainted in one last solitary note of silver, there started somewhere another sequence; and this, almost at its last stroke, was interrupted by yet another, which went on to tell the hour of noon in its own way, quite slowly and significantly, as though none knew it.

And now Oxford was astir with footsteps and laughter— the laughter and quick footsteps of youths released from lecture-rooms. The Duke shifted from the window.

Somehow, he did not care to be observed, though it was usually at this hour that he showed himself for the setting of some new fashion in costume. Many an undergraduate, looking up, missed the picture in the window-frame.

The Duke paced to and fro, smiling ecstatically. He took the two studs from his pocket and gazed at them. He looked in the glass, as one seeking the sympathy of a familiar. For the first time in his life, he turned impatiently aside. It was a new kind of sympathy he needed to-day.

The front door slammed, and the staircase creaked to the ascent of two heavy boots. The Duke listened, waited irresolute. The boots passed his door, were already clumping up the next flight. "Noaks!" he cried. The boots paused, then clumped down again. The door opened and disclosed that homely figure which Zuleika had seen on her way to Judas.

Sensitive reader, start not at the apparition! Oxford is a plexus of anomalies. These two youths were (odd as it may seem to you) subject to the same Statutes, affiliated to the same College, reading for the same School; aye! and though the one had inherited half a score of noble and castellated roofs, whose mere repairs cost him annually thousands and thousands of pounds, and the other's people had but one little mean square of lead, from which the fireworks of the Crystal Palace were clearly visible every Thursday evening, in Oxford one roof sheltered both of them. Furthermore, there was even some measure of intimacy between them. It was the Duke's whim to condescend further in the direction of Noaks than in any other. He saw in Noaks his own foil and antithesis, and made a point of walking up the High with him at least once in every term. Noaks, for his part, regarded the Duke with feelings mingled of idolatry and disapproval. The Duke's First in Mods oppressed him (who, by dint of dogged industry, had scraped a Second) more than all the other differences between them. But the dullard's envy of brilliant men is always assuaged by the suspicion that they will come to a bad end. Noaks may have regarded the Duke as a rather pathetic figure, on the whole.

"Come in, Noaks," said the Duke. "You have been to a lecture?"

"Aristotle's Politics," nodded Noaks.

"And what were they?" asked the Duke. He was eager for sympathy in his love. But so little used was he to seeking sympathy that he could not unburden himself. He temporised. Noaks muttered something about getting back to work, and fumbled with the door-handle.

"Oh, my dear fellow, don't go," said the Duke. "Sit down. Our Schools don't come on for another year. A few minutes can't make a difference in your Class. I want to—to tell you something, Noaks. Do sit down."

Noaks sat down on the edge of a chair. The Duke leaned against the mantelpiece, facing him. "I suppose, Noaks," he said, "you have never been in love."

"Why shouldn't I have been in love?" asked the little man, angrily.

"I can't imagine you in love," said the Duke, smiling.

"And I can't imagine *you*. You're too pleased with yourself," growled Noaks.

"Spur your imagination, Noaks," said his friend. "I *am* in love."

"So am I," was an unexpected answer, and the Duke (whose need of sympathy was too new to have taught him sympathy with others) laughed aloud. "Whom do you love?" he asked, throwing himself into an arm-chair.

"I don't know who she is," was another unexpected answer.

"When did you meet her?" asked the Duke. "Where? What did you say to her?"

"Yesterday. In the Corn. I didn't *say* anything to her."

"Is she beautiful?"

"Yes. What's that to you?"

"Dark or fair?"

"She's dark. She looks like a foreigner. She looks like—like one of those photographs in the shop windows."

"A rhapsody, Noaks! What became of her? Was she alone?"

"She was with the old Warden, in his carriage."

Zuleika—Noaks! The Duke started, as at an affront, and glared. Next moment, he saw the absurdity of the situation. He relapsed into his chair, smiling. "She's the Warden's grand-daughter," he said. "I dined at the Warden's last night."

Noaks sat still, peering across at the Duke. For the first time in his life, he was resentful of the Duke's great elegance and average stature, his high lineage and incomputable wealth. Hitherto, these things had been too remote for envy. But now, suddenly, they seemed near to him—nearer and more overpowering than the First in Mods had ever been. "And of course she's in love with you?" he snarled.

Really, this was for the Duke a new issue. So salient was his own passion that he had not had time to wonder whether it were returned. Zuleika's behaviour during dinner . . . But that was how so many young women had behaved. It was no sign of disinterested love. It might mean merely . . . Yet no! Surely, looking into her eyes, he had seen there a radiance finer than could have been lit by common ambition. Love, none other, must have lit in those purple depths the torches whose clear flames had leapt out to him. She loved him. She, the beautiful, the wonderful, had not tried to conceal her love for him. She had shown him all—had shown all, poor darling! only to be snubbed by a prig, driven away by a boor, fled from by a fool. To the nethermost corner of his soul, he cursed himself for what he had done, and for all he had left undone. He would go to her on his knees. He would implore her to impose on him insufferable penances. There was no penance, how bittersweet soever, could make him a little worthy of her.

"Come in!" he cried mechanically. Entered the landlady's daughter.

"A lady downstairs," she said, "asking to see your Grace. Says she'll step round again later if your Grace is busy."

"What is her name?" asked the Duke, vacantly. He was gazing at the girl with pain-shot eyes.

"Miss Zuleika Dobson," pronounced the girl.

He rose.

"Show Miss Dobson up," he said.

Noaks had darted to the looking-glass and was smoothing his hair with a tremulous, enormous hand.

"Go!" said the Duke, pointing to the door. Noaks went, quickly. Echoes of his boots fell from the upper stairs and met the ascending susurrus of a silk skirt.

The lovers met. There was an interchange of ordinary greetings: from the Duke, a comment on the weather; from Zuleika, a hope that he was well again—they had been so sorry to lose him last night. Then came a pause. The landlady's daughter was clearing away the breakfast things. Zuleika glanced comprehensively at the room, and the Duke gazed at the hearthrug. The landlady's daughter clattered out with her freight. They were alone.

"How pretty!" said Zuleika. She was looking at his star of the Garter, which sparkled from a litter of books and papers on a small side-table.

"Yes," he answered. "It is pretty, isn't it?"

"Awfully pretty!" she rejoined.

This dialogue led them to another hollow pause. The Duke's heart beat violently within him. Why had he not asked her to take the star and keep it as a gift? Too late now! Why could he not throw himself at her feet? Here were two beings, lovers of each other, with none by. And yet . . .

She was examining a water-colour on the wall, seemed to be absorbed by it. He watched her. She was even lovelier than he had remembered; or rather her loveliness had been, in some subtle way, transmuted. Something had given to her a graver, nobler beauty. Last night's nymph had become the Madonna of this morning. Despite her dress, which was of a tremendous tartan, she diffused the pale authentic radiance of a spirituality most high, most simple. The Duke wondered where lay the change in her. He could not understand. Suddenly she turned to him, and he understood. No longer the black pearl and the pink, but two white pearls! . . . He thrilled to his heart's core.

"I hope," said Zuleika, "you aren't awfully vexed with me for coming like this?"

"Not at all," said the Duke. "I am delighted to see you." How inadequate the words sounded, how formal and stupid!

"The fact is," she continued, "I don't know a soul in Oxford. And I thought perhaps you'd give me luncheon, and take me to see the boat-races. Will you?"

"I shall be charmed," he said, pulling the bell-rope. Poor fool! he attributed the shade of disappointment on Zuleika's face to the coldness of his tone. He would dispel that shade. He would avow himself. He would leave her no longer in this false position. So soon as he had told them about the meal, he would proclaim his passion.

The bell was answered by the landlady's daughter.

"Miss Dobson will stay to luncheon," said the Duke. The girl withdrew. He wished he could have asked her not to.

He steeled himself. "Miss Dobson," he said, "I wish to apologise to you."

Zuleika looked at him eagerly. "You can't give me luncheon? You've got something better to do?"

"No. I wish to ask you to forgive me for my behaviour last night."

"There is nothing to forgive."

"There is. My manners were vile. I know well what happened. Though you, too, cannot have forgotten, I won't spare myself the recital. You were my hostess, and I ignored you. Magnanimous, you paid me the prettiest compliment woman ever paid to man, and I insulted you. I left the house in order that I might not see you again. To the doorsteps down which he should have kicked me, your grandfather followed me with words of kindliest courtesy. If he had sped me with a kick so skilful that my skull had been shattered on the kerb, neither would he have outstepped those bounds set to the conduct of English gentlemen, nor would you have garnered more than a trifle on account of your proper reckoning. I do not say that you are the first person whom I have wantonly injured. But it is a fact that I, in whom pride has ever been the topmost quality, have never expressed sorrow to anyone for anything. Thus, I might urge that my present abjectness must be intolerably painful to me, and should incline you to forgive. But such an argument were specious merely. I will be quite frank with you. I will confess to you that, in this humbling of myself before you, I take a pleasure as passionate as it is strange. A confusion of feelings? Yet you, with a woman's instinct, will have already caught the clue to it. It needs no mirror to assure me that the clue is here for you, in my eyes. It needs no dictionary of quotations to remind me that the eyes are the windows of the soul. And I know that from two open windows my soul has been leaning and signalling to you, in a code far more definitive and swifter than words of mine, that I love you."

Zuleika, listening to him, had grown gradually paler and paler. She had raised her hands and cowered as though he were about to strike her. And then, as he pronounced the last three words, she had clasped her hands to her face and with a wild sob darted away from him. She was leaning now against the window, her head bowed and her shoulders quivering.

The Duke came softly behind her. "Why should you cry?

Why should you turn away from me? Did I frighten you with the suddenness of my words? I am not versed in the tricks of wooing. I should have been more patient. But I love you so much that I could hardly have waited. A secret hope that you loved me too emboldened me, compelled me. You *do* love me. I know it. And, knowing it, I do but ask you to give yourself to me, to be my wife. Why should you cry? Why should you shrink from me? Dear, if there were anything . . . any secret . . . if you had ever loved and been deceived, do you think I should honour you the less deeply, should not cherish you the more tenderly? Enough for me, that you are mine. Do you think I should ever reproach you for anything that may have——"

Zuleika turned on him. "How dare you?" she gasped. "How dare you speak to me like that?"

The Duke reeled back. Horror had come into his eyes. "You do not love me!" he cried.

"*Love* you?" she retorted. "*You?*"

"You no longer love me. Why? Why?"

"What do you mean?"

"You loved me. Don't trifle with me. You came to me loving me with all your heart."

"How do you know?"

"Look in the glass." She went at his bidding. He followed her. "You see them?" he said, after a long pause. Zuleika nodded. The two pearls quivered to her nod.

"They were white when you came to me," he sighed. "They were white because you loved me. From them it was that I knew you loved me even as I loved you. But their old colours have come back to them. That is how I know that your love for me is dead."

Zuleika stood gazing pensively, twitching the two pearls between her fingers. Tears gathered in her eyes. She met the reflection of her lover's eyes, and her tears brimmed over. She buried her face in her hands, and sobbed like a child.

Like a child's, her sobbing ceased quite suddenly. She groped for her handkerchief, angrily dried her eyes, and straightened and smoothed herself.

"Now I'm going," she said.

"You came here of your own accord, because you loved me," said the Duke. "And you shall not go till you have told me why you have left off loving me."

"How did you know I loved you?" she asked after a pause. "How did you know I hadn't simply put on another pair of ear-rings?"

The Duke, with a melancholy laugh, drew the two studs from his waistcoat-pocket. "These are the studs I wore last night," he said.

Zuleika gazed at them. "I see," she said; then looking up, "when did they become like that?"

"It was when you left the dining-room that I saw the change in them."

"How strange! It was when I went into the drawing-room that I noticed mine. I was looking in the glass, and——" She started. "Then you were in love with me last night?"

"I began to be in love with you from the moment I saw you."

"Then how could you have behaved as you did?"

"Because I was a pedant. I tried to ignore you, as pedants always do try to ignore any fact they cannot fit into their pet system. The basis of my pet system was celibacy. I don't mean the mere state of being a bachelor. I mean celibacy of the soul—egoism, in fact. You have converted me from that. I am now a confirmed tuist."

"How dared you insult me?" she cried, with a stamp of her foot. "How dared you make a fool of me before those people? Oh, it is too infamous!"

"I have already asked you to forgive me for that. You said there was nothing to forgive."

"I didn't dream that you were in love with me."

"What difference can that make?"

"All the difference! All the difference in life!"

"Sit down! You bewilder me," said the Duke. "Explain yourself!" he commanded.

"Isn't that rather much for a man to ask of a woman?"

"I don't know. I have no experience of women. In the abstract, it seems to me that every man has a right to some explanation from the woman who has ruined his life."

"You are frightfully sorry for yourself," said Zuleika, with a bitter laugh. "Of course it doesn't occur to you that *I* am at all to be pitied. No! you are blind with selfishness. You love me—I don't love you: that is all you can realise. Probably you think you are the first man who has ever fallen on such a plight."

Said the Duke, bowing over a deprecatory hand: "If there were to pass my window one tithe of them whose hearts have been lost to Miss Dobson, I should win no solace from that interminable parade."

Zuleika blushed. "Yet," she said more gently, "be sure they would all be not a little envious of *you!* Not one of them ever touched the surface of my heart. You stirred my heart to its very depths. Yes, you made me love you madly. The pearls told you no lie. You were my idol—the one thing in the wide world to me. You were so different from any man I had ever seen except in dreams. You did not make a fool of yourself. I admired you. I respected you. I was all afire with adoration of you. And now," she passed her hand across her eyes, "now it is all over. The idol has come sliding down its pedestal to fawn and grovel with all the other infatuates in the dust about my feet."

The Duke looked thoughtfully at her. "I thought," he said, "that you revelled in your power over men's hearts. I had always heard that you lived for admiration."

"Oh," said Zuleika, "of course I like being admired.

Oh yes, I like all that very much indeed. In a way, I suppose, I'm even pleased that *you* admire me. But oh, what a little miserable pleasure that is in comparison with the rapture I have forfeited! I had never known the rapture of being in love. I had longed for it, but I had never guessed how wonderfully wonderful it was. It came to me. I shuddered and wavered like a fountain in the wind. I was more helpless and flew lightlier than a shred of thistledown among the stars. All night long, I could not sleep for love of you; nor had I any desire of sleep, save that it might take me to you in a dream. I remember nothing that happened to me this morning before I found myself at your door."

"Why did you ring the bell? Why didn't you walk away?"

"Why? I had come to see you, to be near you, to be *with* you."

"To force yourself on me."

"Yes."

"You know the meaning of the term 'effective occupation'? Having marched in, how could you have held your position, unless——"

"Oh, a man doesn't necessarily drive a woman away because he isn't in love with her."

"Yet that was what you thought I had done to you last night."

"Yes, but I didn't suppose you would take the trouble to do it again. And if you had, I should have only loved you the more. I thought you would most likely be rather amused, rather touched, by my importunity. I thought you would take a listless advantage, make a plaything of me—the diversion of a few idle hours in summer, and then, when you had tired of me, would cast me aside, forget me, break my heart. I desired nothing better than that. That is what I must have been vaguely hoping for. But I had no definite scheme. I wanted to be with you, and I came to you. It seems years ago, now! How my heart beat as I waited on the doorstep! 'Is his Grace at home?' 'I don't know. I'll inquire. What name shall I say?' I saw in the girl's eyes that she, too, loved you. Have *you* seen that?"

"I have never looked at her," said the Duke.

"No wonder, then, that she loves you," sighed Zuleika. "She read my secret at a glance. Women who love the same man have a kind of bitter freemasonry. We resented each other. She envied me my beauty, my dress. I envied the little fool her privilege of being always near to you. Loving you, I could conceive no life sweeter than hers—to be always near you; to black your boots, carry up your coals, scrub your doorstep; always to be working for you, hard and humbly and without thanks. If you had refused to see me, I would have bribed that girl with all my jewels to cede me her position."

The Duke made a step towards her. "You would do it still," he said in a low voice.

Zuleika raised her eyebrows. "I would not offer her one garnet," she said, "now."

"You *shall* love me again," he cried. "I will force you to. You said just now that you had ceased to love me because I was just like other men. I am not. My heart is no tablet of mere wax, from which an instant's heat can dissolve whatever impress it may bear, leaving it blank and soft for another impress, and another, and another. My heart is a bright hard gem, proof against any die. Came Cupid, with one of his arrow-points for graver, and what he cut on the gem's surface never can be effaced. There, deeply and for ever, your image is intagliated. No years, nor fires, nor cataclysm of total Nature, can efface from that great gem your image."

"My dear Duke," said Zuleika, "don't be so silly. Look at the matter sensibly. I know that lovers don't try to regulate their emotions according to logic; but they do, nevertheless, unconsciously conform with some sort of logical system. I left off loving you when I found that you loved me. There is the premiss. Very well! Is it likely that I shall begin to love you again because you can't leave off loving me?"

The Duke groaned. There was a clatter of plates outside, and she whom Zuleika had envied came to lay the table for luncheon.

A smile flickered across Zuleika's lips; and "Not one garnet!" she murmured.

# V

LUNCHEON passed in almost unbroken silence. Both
Zuleika and the Duke were ravenously hungry, as people
always are after the stress of any great emotional crisis.
Between them, they made very short work of a cold chicken, a
salad, a gooseberry-tart and a Camembert. The Duke
filled his glass again and again. The cold classicism of his
face had been routed by the new romantic movement which
had swept over his soul. He looked two or three months
older than when first I showed him to my reader.

He drank his coffee at one draught, pushed back his chair,
threw away the cigarette he had just lit. "Listen!" he said.

Zuleika folded her hands on her lap.

"You do not love me. I accept as final your hint that you
never will love me. I need not say—could not, indeed, ever
say—how deeply, deeply you have pained me. As lover, I
am rejected. But that rejection," he continued, striking the
table, "is no stopper to my suit. It does but drive me to the
use of arguments. My pride shrinks from them. Love,
however, is greater than pride; and I, John, Albert, Edward,
Claude, Orde, Angus, Tankerton,* Tanville-Tankerton,†
fourteenth Duke of Dorset, Marquis of Dorset, Earl of
Grove, Earl of Chastermaine, Viscount Brewsby, Baron
Grove, Baron Petstrap, and Baron Wolock, in the Peerage of
England, offer you my hand. Do not interrupt me. Do not
toss your head. Consider well what I am saying. Weigh the
advantages you would gain by acceptance of my hand.
Indeed, they are manifold and tremendous. They are also

* Pronounced as Tacton. † Pronounced as Tavvle-Tacton

obvious: do not shut your eyes to them. You, Miss Dobson, what are you? A conjurer, and a vagrant; without means, save such as you can earn by the sleight of your hand; without position; without a home; all unguarded but by your own self-respect. That you follow an honourable calling, I do not for one moment deny. I do, however, ask you to consider how great are its perils and hardships, its fatigues and inconveniences. From all these evils I offer you instant refuge. I offer you, Miss Dobson, a refuge more glorious and more augustly gilded than you, in your airiest flights of fancy, can ever have hoped for or imagined. I own about 340,000 acres. My town residence is in St. James's Square. Tankerton, of which you may have seen photographs, is the chief of my country seats. It is a Tudor house, set on the ridge of a valley. The valley, its park, is halved by a stream so narrow that the deer leap across. The gardens are estraded upon the slope. Round the house runs a wide paven terrace. There are always two or three peacocks trailing their sheathed feathers along the balustrade, and stepping how stiffly! as though they had just been unharnessed from Juno's chariot. Two flights of shallow steps lead down to the flowers and fountains. Oh, the gardens are wonderful. There is a Jacobean garden of white roses. Between the ends of two pleached alleys, under a dome of branches, is a little lake, with a Triton of black marble, and with water-lilies. Hither and thither under the archipelago of water-lilies, dart gold-fish—tongues of flame in the dark water. There is also a long strait alley of clipped yew. It ends in an alcove for a pagoda of painted porcelain which the Prince Regent—peace be to his ashes!—presented to my great-grandfather. There are many twisting paths, and sudden aspects, and devious, fantastic arbours. Are you fond of horses? In my stables of pinewood and plated-silver seventy are installed. Not all of them together could vie in power with one of the meanest of my motor-cars."

"Oh, I never go in motors," said Zuleika. "They make one look like nothing on earth, and like everybody else."

"I myself," said the Duke, "use them little for that very reason. Are you interested in farming? At Tankerton there is a model farm which would at any rate amuse you, with its heifers and hens and pigs that are like so many big new toys. There is a tiny dairy, which is called 'Her Grace's'. You could make, therein, real butter with your own hands, and round it into little pats, and press every pat with a different device. The boudoir that would be yours is a blue room. Four Watteaus hang in it. In the dining-hall hang portraits of my forefathers—*in petto*, your forefathers-in-law—by many masters. Are you fond of peasants? My tenantry are delightful creatures, and there is not one of them who remembers the bringing of the news of the Battle of Waterloo. When a new Duchess is brought to Tankerton, the oldest elm in the park must be felled. That is one of many strange old customs. As she is driven through the village, the children of the tenantry must strew the road with daisies. The bridal chamber must be lighted with as many candles as years have elapsed since the creation of the Dukedom. If you came into it, there would be"—and the youth, closing his eyes, made a rapid calculation—"exactly three hundred and eighty-eight candles. On the eve of the death of a Duke of Dorset two black owls come and perch on the battlements. They remain there through the night, hooting. At dawn they fly away, none knows whither. On the eve of the death of any other Tanville-Tankerton, comes (no matter what be the time of year) a cuckoo. It stays for an hour, cooing, then flies away, none knows whither. Whenever this portent occurs, my steward telegraphs to me, that I, as head of the family, be not unsteeled against the shock of a bereavement, and that my authority be sooner given for the unsealing and garnishing of the family vault. Not every forefather of mine rests quiet beneath his escutcheoned marble. There are they

who revisit, in their wrath or their remorse, the places
wherein erst they suffered or wrought evil. There is one
who, every Halloween, flits into the dining-hall, and hovers
before the portrait which Hans Holbein made of him, and
flings his diaphanous grey form against the canvas, hoping,
maybe, to catch from it the fiery flesh-tints and the solid
limbs that were his, and so to be reincarnate. He flies
against the painting, only to find himself t'other side of the
wall it hangs on. There are five ghosts permanently residing
in the right wing of the house, two in the left, and eleven in
the park. But all are quite noiseless and quite harmless. My
servants, when they meet them in the corridors or on the
stairs, stand aside to let them pass, thus paying them the
respect due to guests of mine; but not even the rawest
housemaid ever screams or flees at sight of them. I, their
host, often waylay them and try to commune with them; but
always they glide past me. And how gracefully they glide,
these ghosts! It is a pleasure to watch them. It is a lesson in
deportment. May they never be laid! Of all my household
pets, they are the dearest to me. I am Duke of Strathsporran
and Cairngorm, Marquis of Sorby, and Earl Cairngorm, in
the Peerage of Scotland. In the glens of the hills about
Strathsporran are many noble and nimble stags. But I have
never set foot in my house there, for it is carpeted throughout
with the tartan of my clan. You seem to like tartan. What
tartan is it you are wearing?"

Zuleika looked down at her skirt. "I don't know," she
said. "I got it in Paris."

"Well," said the Duke, "it is very ugly. The Dalbraith
tartan is harmonious in comparison, and has, at least, the
excuse of history. If you married me, you would have the
right to wear it. You would have many strange and fascinat-
ing rights. You would go to Court. I admit that the
Hanoverian Court is not much. Still, it is better than
nothing. At your presentation, moreover, you would be given

the *entrée*. Is that nothing to you? You would be driven to
Court in my state-coach. It is swung so high that the street-
sters can hardly see its occupant. It is lined with rose-silk;
and on its panels, and on its hammer-cloth, my arms are
emblazoned—no one has ever been able to count the
quarterings. You would be wearing the family jewels,
reluctantly surrendered to you by my aunt. They are many
and marvellous, in their antique settings. I don't want to
brag. It humiliates me to speak to you as I am speaking.
But I am heart-set on you, and to win you there is not a
precious stone I would leave unturned. Conceive a *parure*
all of white stones—diamonds, white sapphires, white
topazes, tourmalines. Another, of rubies and amethysts, set
in gold filigree. Rings that once were poison-combs on
Florentine fingers. Red roses for your hair—every petal a
hollowed ruby. Amulets and ape-buckles, zones and
fillets. Aye! know that you would be weeping for wonder
before you had seen a tithe of these gauds. Know, too, Miss
Dobson, that in the Peerage of France I am Duc d'Etretat
et de la Roche Guillaume. Louis Napoleon gave the title to
my father for not cutting him in the Bois. I have a house in
the Champs Elysées. There is a Swiss in its court-yard. He
stands six-foot-seven in his stockings, and the chasseurs are
hardly less talll than he. Wherever I go, there are two chefs
in my retinue. Both are masters in their art, and furiously
jealous of each other. When I compliment either of them on
some dish, the other challenges him. They fight with
rapiers, next morning, in the garden of whatever house I am
occupying. I do not know whether you are greedy? If so, it
may interest you to learn that I have a third chef, who makes
only soufflés, and an Italian pastry-cook; to say nothing of a
Spaniard for salads, an Englishwoman for roasts, and an
Abyssinian for coffee. You found no trace of their handiwork
in the meal you have just had with me? No; for in Oxford it
is a whim of mine—I may say a point of honour—to lead the

44

ordinary life of an undergraduate. What I eat in this room is cooked by the heavy and unaided hand of Mrs. Batch, my landlady. It is set before me by the unaided and—or are you in error?—loving hand of her daughter. Other ministers have I none here. I dispense with my private secretaries. I am unattended by a single valet. So simple a way of life repels you? You would never be called upon to share it. If you married me, I should take my name off the books of my College. I propose that we should spend our honeymoon at Baiae. I have a villa at Baiae. It is there that I keep my grandfather's collection of majolica. The sun shines there always. A long olive-grove secretes the garden from the sea. When you walk in the garden, you know the sea only in blue glimpses through the vacillating leaves. White-gleaming from the bosky shade of this grove are several goddesses. Do you care for Canova? I don't myself. If you do, these figures will appeal to you: they are in his best manner. Do you love the sea? This is not the only house of mine that looks out on it. On the coast of County Clare—am I not Earl of Enniskerry and Baron Shandrin in the Peerage of Ireland?—I have an ancient castle. Sheer from a rock stands it, and the sea has always raged up against its walls. Many ships lie wrecked under that loud implacable sea. But mine is a brave strong castle. No storm affrights it; and not the centuries, clustering houris, with their caresses can seduce it from its hard austerity. I have several titles which for the moment escape me. Baron Llffthwchl am I, and . . . and . . . but you can find them for yourself in Debrett. In me you behold a Prince of the Holy Roman Empire, and a Knight of the Most Noble Order of the Garter. Look well at me! I am Hereditary Comber of the Queen's Lap-Dogs. I am young. I am handsome. My temper is sweet, and my character without blemish. In fine, Miss Dobson, I am a most desirable *parti*."

"But," said Zuleika, "I don't love you."

45

The Duke stamped his foot. "I beg your pardon," he said hastily. "I ought not to have done that. But—you seem to have entirely missed the point of what I was saying."

"No, I haven't," said Zuleika.

"Then what," cried the Duke, standing over her, "what is your reply?"

Said Zuleika, looking up at him, "My reply is that I think you are an awful snob."

The Duke turned on his heel, and strode to the other end of the room. There he stood for some moments, his back to Zuleika.

"I think," she resumed in a slow, meditative voice, "that you are, with the possible exception of a Mr. Edelweiss, *the* most awful snob I have ever met."

The Duke looked back over his shoulder. He gave Zuleika the stinging reprimand of silence. She was sorry, and showed it in her eyes. She felt she had gone too far. True, he was nothing to her now. But she had loved him once. She could not forget that.

"Come!" she said. "Let us be good friends. Give me your hand!" He came to her, slowly. "There!"

The Duke withdrew his fingers before she unclasped them. That twice-flung taunt rankled still. It was monstrous to have been called a snob. A snob!—he, whose readiness to form what would certainly be regarded as a shocking mis-alliance ought to have stifled the charge, not merely vin-dicated him from it! He had forgotten, in the blindness of his love, how shocking the misalliance would be. Perhaps she, unloving, had not been so forgetful? Perhaps her refusal had been made, generously, for his own sake. Nay, rather for her own. Evidently, she had felt that the high sphere from which he beckoned was no place for the likes of her. Evidently, she feared she would pine away among those strange splendours, never be acclimatised, always be un-worthy. He had thought to overwhelm her, and he had done his work too thoroughly. Now he must try to lighten the load he had imposed.

Seating himself opposite to her: "You remember," he said, "that there is a dairy at Tankerton?"

"A dairy? Oh yes."

"Do you remember what it is called?"

Zuleika knit her brows.

He helped her out. "It is called 'Her Grace's'."

"Oh, of course!" said Zuleika.

"Do you know *why* it is called so?"

"Well, let's see . . . I know you told me."

"Did I? I think not. I will tell you now. . . . That cool out-house dates from the middle of the eighteenth century. My great-great-grandfather, when he was a very old man, married *en troisièmes noces* a dairy-maid on the Tankerton estate. Meg Speedwell was her name. He had seen her walking across a field, not many months after the interment of his second Duchess, Maria, that great and gifted lady. I know not whether it was that her bonny mien fanned in him some embers of his youth, or that he was loth to be outdone in gracious eccentricity by his crony the Duke of Dewlap, who himself had just taken a bride from a dairy. (You have read Meredith's account of that affair? No? You should.) Whether it was veritable love or mere modishness that formed my ancestor's resolve, presently the bells were ringing out, and the oldest elm in the park was being felled, in Meg Speedwell's honour, and the children were strewing daisies on which Meg Speedwell trod, a proud young hoyden of a bride, with her head in the air and her heart in the seventh heaven. The Duke had given her already a horde of fine gifts; but these, he had said, were nothing—trash in comparison with the gift that was to ensure for her a perdurable felicity. After the wedding-breakfast, when all the squires had ridden away on their cobs, and all the squires' ladies in their coaches, the Duke led his bride forth

47

from the hall, leaning on her arm, till they came to a little edifice of new white stone, very spick and span, with two lattice-windows and a bright green door between. This he made her enter. A flutter with excitement, she turned the handle. In a moment she flounced back red with shame and anger—flounced forth from the fairest, whitest, dapperest dairy, wherein was all of the best that the keenest dairy-maid might need. The Duke bade her dry her eyes, for that it ill-befitted a great lady to be weeping on her wedding-day. 'As for gratitude,' he chuckled, 'zounds! that is a wine all the better for the keeping.' Duchess Meg soon forgot this unworthy wedding-gift, such was her rapture in the other, the so august, appurtenances of her new life. What with her fine silk gowns and farthingales, and her powder-closet, and the canopied bed she slept in—a bed bigger far than the room she had slept in with her sisters, and standing in a room far bigger than her father's cottage; and what with Betty, her maid, who had pinched and teased her at the village school, but now waited on her so meekly and trembled so fearfully at a scolding; and what with the fine hot dishes that were set before her every day, and the gallant speeches and glances of the fine young gentlemen whom the Duke invited from London, Duchess Meg was quite the happiest Duchess in all England. For a while, she was like a child in a hay-rick. But anon, as the sheer delight of novelty wore away, she began to take a more serious view of her position. She began to realise her responsibilities. She was determined to do all that a great lady ought to do. Twice every day she assumed the vapours. She schooled herself in the mysteries of Ombre, of Macao. She spent hours over the tambour-frame. She rode out on horse-back, with a riding-master. She had a music-master to teach her the spinet; a dancing-master, too, to teach her the Minuet and the Triumph and the Gaudy. All these accomplishments she found mighty hard. She was afraid of her horse. All the morning, she dreaded the hour when it would be brought round from the stables. She dreaded her dancing lesson. Try as she would, she could but stamp her feet flat on the parquet, as though it had been the village green. She dreaded her music lesson. Her fingers, disobedient to her ambition, clumsily thumped the keys of the spinet, and by the notes of the score propped up before her she was as cruelly perplexed as by the black and red pips of the cards she conned at the gaming-table, or by the red and gold threads that were always straying and snapping on her tambour-frame. Still she persevered. Day in, day out, sullenly, she worked hard to be a great lady. But skill came not to her, and hope dwindled; only the dull effort remained. One accomplishment she did master—to wit, the vapours: they became for her a dreadful reality. She lost her appetite for the fine hot dishes. All night long she lay awake, restless, tearful, under the fine silk canopy, till dawn stared her into slumber. She seldom scolded Betty. She who had been so lusty and so blooming saw in her mirror that she was pale and thin now; and the fine young gentlemen, seeing it too, paid more heed now to their wine and their dice than to her. And always, when she met him, the Duke smiled the same mocking smile. Duchess Meg was pining slowly and surely away. . . . One morning, in spring-time, she altogether vanished. Betty, bringing the cup of chocolate to the bedside, found the bed empty. She raised the alarm among her fellows. They searched high and low. Nowhere was their mistress. The news was broken to their master, who, without comment, rose, bade his man dress him, and presently walked out to the place where he knew he would find her. And there, to be sure, she was, churning, churning for dear life. Her sleeves were rolled above her elbows, and her skirt was kilted high; and, as she looked back over her shoulder and saw the Duke, there was the flush of roses in her cheeks, and the light of a thousand thanks in her eyes. 'Oh,' she cried, 'what a curtsey

I would drop you, but that to let go the handle were to spoil all!' And every morning, ever after, she woke when the birds woke, rose when they rose, and went singing through the dawn to the dairy, there to practise for her pleasure that sweet and lowly handicraft which she had once practised for her need. And every evening, with her milking-stool under her arm, and her milk-pail in her hand, she went into the field and called the cows to her, as she had been wont to do. To those other, those so august, accomplishments she no more pretended. She gave them the go-by. And all the old zest and joyousness of her life came back to her. Soundlier than ever slept she, and sweetlier dreamed, under the fine silk canopy, till the birds called her to her work. Greater than ever was her love of the fine furbelows that were hers to flaunt in, and sharper her appetite for the fine hot dishes, and more tempestuous her scolding of Betty, poor maid. She was more than ever now the cynosure, the adored, of the fine young gentlemen. And as for her husband, she looked up to him as the wisest, kindest man in all the world."

"And the fine young gentlemen," said Zuleika, "did she fall in love with any of them?"

"You forget," said the Duke coldly, "she was married to a member of my family."

"Oh, I beg your pardon. But tell me: did they *all* adore her?"

"Yes. Every one of them, wildly, madly."

"Ah," murmured Zuleika, with a smile of understanding. A shadow crossed her face. "Even so," she said, with some pique, "I don't suppose she had so very many adorers. She never went out into the world."

"Tankerton," said the Duke dryly, "is a large house, and my great-great-grandfather was the most hospitable of men. However," he added, marvelling that she had again missed the point so utterly, "my purpose was not to confront you with a past rival in conquest, but to set at rest a fear which I had, I think, roused in you by my somewhat full description of the high majestic life to which you, as my bride, would be translated."

"A fear? What sort of a fear?"

"That you would not breathe freely—that you would starve (if I may use a somewhat fantastic figure) among those strawberry-leaves. And so I told you the story of Meg Speedwell, and how she lived happily ever after. Nay, hear me out! The blood of Meg Speedwell's lord flows in my veins. I think I may boast that I have inherited something of his sagacity. In any case, I can profit by his example. Do not fear that I, if you were to wed me, should demand a metamorphosis of your present self. I should take you as you are, gladly. I should encourage you to be always exactly as you are—a radiant, irresistible member of the upper middle-class, with a certain freedom of manner acquired through a life of peculiar liberty. Can you guess what would be my principal wedding gift to you? Meg Speedwell had her dairy. For you, would be built another out-house—a neat hall wherein you would perform your conjuring tricks, every evening except Sunday, before me and my tenants and my servants, and before such of my neighbours as might care to come. None would respect you the less, seeing that I approved. Thus in you would the pleasant history of Meg Speedwell repeat itself. You, practising for your pleasure— nay, hear me out!—that sweet and lowly handicraft which——"

"I won't listen to another word!" cried Zuleika. "You are the most insolent person I have ever met. I happen to come of a particularly good family. I move in the best society. My manners are absolutely perfect. If I found myself in the shoes of twenty Duchesses simultaneously, I should know quite well how to behave. As for the one pair you can offer me, I kick them away—so. I kick them back at you. I tell you——"

"Hush," said the Duke, "hush! You are over-excited. There will be a crowd under my window. There, there! I am sorry. I thought——"

"Oh, I know what you thought," said Zuleika, in a quieter tone. "I am sure you meant well. I am sorry I lost my temper. Only, you might have given me credit for meaning what I said: that I would not marry you, because I did not love you. I daresay there would be great advantages in being your Duchess. But the fact is, I have no worldly wisdom. To me, marriage is a sacrament. I could no more marry a man about whom I could not make a fool of myself than I could marry one who made a fool of himself about me. Else had I long ceased to be a spinster. Oh my friend, do not imagine that I have not rejected, in my day, a score of suitors quite as eligible as you."

"As eligible? Who were they?" frowned the Duke.

"Oh, Archduke this, and Grand Duke that, and His Serene Highness the other. I have a wretched memory, for names."

"And my name, too, will soon escape you, perhaps?"

"No. Oh, no. I shall always remember yours. You see, I was in love with you. You deceived me into loving you . . ." She sighed. "Oh, had you but been as strong as I thought you . . . Still, a swain the more. That is something." She leaned forward, smiling archly. "Those studs—show me them again."

The Duke displayed them in the hollow of his hand. She touched them lightly, reverently, as a tourist touches a sacred relic in a church.

At length: "Do give me them," she said. "I will keep them in a little secret partition of my jewel-case." The Duke had closed his fist. "Do!" she pleaded. "My other jewels—they have no separate meanings for me. I never remember who gave me this one or that. These would be quite different. I should always remember their history . . . Do!"

"Ask me for anything else," said the Duke. "These are the one thing I could not part with—even to you, for whose sake they are hallowed."

Zuleika pouted. On the verge of persisting, she changed her mind, and was silent.

"Well!" she said abruptly, "how about these races? Are you going to take me to see them?"

"Races? What races?" murmured the Duke. "Oh yes. I had forgotten. Do you really mean that you want to see them?"

"Why, of course! They are great fun, aren't they?"

"And you are in a mood for great fun? Well, there is plenty of time. The Second Division is not rowed till half-past four."

"The Second Division? Why not take me to the First?"

"That is not rowed till six."

"Isn't this rather an odd arrangement?"

"No doubt. But Oxford never pretended to be strong in mathematics."

"Why, it's not yet three!" cried Zuleika, with a woebegone stare at the clock. "What is to be done in the meantime?"

"Am not I sufficiently diverting?" asked the Duke bitterly.

"Quite candidly, no. Have you any friend lodging with you here?"

"One, overhead. A man named Noaks."

"A small man, with spectacles?"

"Very small, with very large spectacles."

"He was pointed out to me yesterday, as I was driving from the Station. . . . No, I don't think I want to meet him. What can you have in common with him?"

"One frailty, at least: he, too, Miss Dobson, loves you."

"But of course he does. He saw me drive past. Very few of the others," she said, rising and shaking herself, "have set eyes on me. Do let us go out and look at the Colleges. I do need change of scene. If you were a doctor, you would have prescribed that long ago. It is very bad for me to be here, a kind of Cinderella, moping over the ashes of my love for you. Where is your hat?"

Looking round, she caught sight of herself in the glass. "Oh," she cried, "what a fright I do look! I must never be seen like this!"

"You look very beautiful."

"I don't. That is a lover's illusion. You yourself told me that this tartan was perfectly hideous. There was no need to tell me that. I came thus because I was coming to see you. I chose this frock in the deliberate fear that you, if I made myself presentable might succumb at second sight of me. I would have sent out for a sack and dressed myself in that. I would have blacked my face all over with burnt cork, only I was afraid of being mobbed on the way to you."

"Even so, you would but have been mobbed for your incorrigible beauty."

"My beauty! How I hate it!" sighed Zuleika. "Still, here it is, and I must needs make the best of it. Come! Take me to Judas. I will change my things. Then I shall be fit for the races."

As these two emerged side by side, into the street, the Emperors exchanged stony sidelong glances. For they saw the more than normal pallor of the Duke's face, and something very like desperation in his eyes. They saw the tragedy progressing to its foreseen close. Unable to stay its course, they were grimly fascinated now.

## VI

"The evil that men do lives after them; the good is oft interred with their bones." At any rate, the sinner has a better chance than the saint of being hereafter remembered. We, in whom original sin preponderates, find him easier to understand. He is near to us, clear to us. The saint is remote, dim. A very great saint may, of course, be remembered through some sheer force or originality in him; and then the very mystery that involves him for us makes him the harder to forget: he haunts us the more surely because we shall never understand him. But the ordinary saints grow faint to posterity; whilst quite ordinary sinners pass vividly down the ages.

Of the disciples of Jesus, which is he that is most often remembered and cited by us? Not the disciple whom Jesus loved; neither of the Boanerges, nor any other of them who so steadfastly followed Him and served Him; but the disciple who betrayed Him for thirty pieces of silver. Judas Iscariot it is who outstands, over-shadowing those other fishermen. And perhaps it was by reason of this precedence that Christopher Whitrid, Knight in the reign of Henry VI, gave the name of Judas to the College which he had founded. Or perhaps it was because he felt that in a Christian community not even the meanest and basest of men should be accounted beneath contempt, beyond redemption.

At any rate, thus he named his foundation. And, though for Oxford men the savour of the name itself has long evaporated through its local connection, many things show that for the Founder himself it was no empty vocable. In a niche above the gate stands a rudely carved statue of Judas, holding a money-bag in his right hand. Among the original statutes of the College is one by which the Bursar is enjoined to distribute in Passion Week thirty pieces of silver among the needier scholars "for saike of atonynge". The meadow adjoining the back of the College has been called from time immemorial "the Potter's Field". And the name of Salt Cellar is not less ancient and significant.

Salt Cellar, that grey and green quadrangle visible from the room assigned to Zuleika, is very beautiful, as I have said. So tranquil is it as to seem remote not merely from the world, but even from Oxford, so deeply is it hidden away in the core of Oxford's heart. So tranquil is it, one would guess that nothing had ever happened in it. For five centuries these walls have stood, and during that time have beheld, one would say, no sight less seemly than the good work of weeding, mowing, rolling, that has made, at length, so exemplary the lawn. These cloisters that grace the south and east sides—five centuries have passed through them, leaving in them no echo, leaving on them no sign, of all that the outer world, for good or evil, has been doing so fiercely, so raucously.

And yet, if you are versed in the antiquities of Oxford, you know that this small, still quadrangle has played its part in the rough-and-tumble of history, and has been the background of high passions and strange fates. The sun-dial in its midst has told the hours to more than one bygone King. Charles I lay for twelve nights in Judas; and it was here, in this very quadrangle, that he heard from the lips of a breathless and blood-stained messenger the news of Chalgrove Field. Sixty years later, James, his son, came hither, black with threats, and from one of the hind-windows of the Warden's house—maybe, from the very room where now Zuleika was changing her frock—addressed the Fellows, and presented to them the Papist by him chosen to be their

Warden, instead of the Protestant whom they had elected. They were not of so stern a stuff as the Fellows of Magdalen, who, despite His Majesty's menaces, had just rejected Bishop Farmer. The Papist was elected, there and then, *al fresco*, without dissent. Cannot one see them, these Fellows of Judas, huddled together round the sun-dial, like so many sheep in a storm? The King's wrath, according to a contemporary record, was so appeased by their pliancy that he deigned to lie for two nights in Judas, and at a grand refection in Hall "was gracious and merrie". Perhaps it was in lingering gratitude for such patronage that Judas remained so pious to his memory even after smug Herrenhausen had been dumped down on us for ever. Certainly, of all the Colleges none was more ardent than Judas for James Stuart. Thither it was that young Sir Harry Esson led, under cover of night, three-score recruits whom he had enlisted in the surrounding villages. The cloisters of Salt Cellar were piled with arms and stores; and on its grass—its sacred grass!—the squad was incessantly drilled, against the good day when Ormond should land his men in Devon. For a whole month Salt Cellar was a secret camp. But somehow, at length—woe to "lost causes and impossible loyalties"—Herrenhausen had wind of it; and one night, when the soldiers of the white cockade lay snoring beneath the stars, stealthily the white-faced Warden unbarred his postern—that very postern through which now Zuleika had passed on the way to her bedroom—and stealthily through it, one by one on tiptoe, came the King's foot-guards. Not many shots rang out, nor many swords clashed, in the night air, before the trick was won for law and order. Most of the rebels were over-powered in their sleep; and those who had time to snatch arms were too dazed to make good resistance. Sir Harry Esson himself was the only one who did not live to be hanged. He had sprung up alert, sword in hand, at the first alarm, setting his back to the cloisters. There he fought calmly, ferociously, till a bullet went through his chest. "By God, this College is well-named!" were the words he uttered as he fell forward and died.

Comparatively tame was the scene now being enacted in this place. The Duke, with bowed head, was pacing the path between the lawn and the cloisters. Two other undergraduates stood watching him, whispering to each other, under the archway that leads to the Front Quadrangle. Presently, in a sheepish way, they approached him. He halted and looked up.

"I say," stammered the spokesman.

"Well?" asked the Duke. Both youths were slightly acquainted with him; but he was not used to being spoken to by those whom he had not first addressed. Moreover, he was loth to be thus disturbed in his sombre reverie. His manner was not encouraging.

"Isn't it a lovely day for the Eights?" faltered the spokesman.

"I conceive," the Duke said, "that you hold back some other question."

The spokesman smiled weakly. Nudged by the other, he muttered "Ask him yourself!"

The Duke diverted his gaze to the other, who, with an angry look at the one, cleared his throat, and said "I was going to ask if you thought Miss Dobson would come and have luncheon with me to-morrow?"

"A sister of mine will be there," explained the one, knowing the Duke to be a precisian.

"If you are acquainted with Miss Dobson, a direct invitation should be sent to her," said the Duke. "If you are not——" The aposiopesis was icy.

"Well, you see," said the other of the two, "that is just the difficulty. I *am* acquainted with her. But is she acquainted with *me*? I met her at breakfast this morning, at the Warden's."

"So did I," added the one.

"But she—well," continued the other, "she didn't take much notice of us. She seemed to be in a sort of dream."

"Ah!" murmured the Duke, with melancholy interest.

"The only time she opened her lips," said the other, "was when she asked us whether we took tea or coffee."

"She put hot milk in my tea," volunteered the one, "and upset the cup over my hand, and smiled vaguely."

"And smiled vaguely," sighed the Duke.

"She left us long before the marmalade stage," said the one.

"Without a word," said the other.

"Without a glance?" asked the Duke. It was testified by the one and the other that there had been not so much as a glance.

"Doubtless," the disingenuous Duke said, "she had a headache . . . Was she pale?"

"Very pale," answered the one.

"A healthy pallor," qualified the other, who was a constant reader of novels.

"Did she look," the Duke inquired, "as if she had spent a sleepless night?"

That was the impression made on both.

"Yet she did not seem listless or unhappy?"

No, they would not go so far as to say that.

"Indeed, were her eyes of an almost unnatural brilliance?"

"Quite unnatural," confessed the one.

"Twin stars," interpolated the other.

"Did she, in fact, seem to be consumed by some inward rapture?"

Yes, now they came to think of it, this was exactly how she *had* seemed.

It was sweet, it was bitter, for the Duke. "I remember," Zuleika had said to him, "nothing that happened to me this morning till I found myself at your door." It was bittersweet to have that outline filled in by these artless pencils. No, it was only bitter, to be, at his time of life, living in the past.

"The purpose of your tattle?" he asked coldly.

The two youths hurried to the point from which he had diverted them. "When she went by with you just now," said the one, "she evidently didn't know us from Adam."

"And I had so hoped to ask her to luncheon," said the other.

"Well?"

"Well, we wondered if you would re-introduce us. And then perhaps . . ."

There was a pause. The Duke was touched to kindness for these fellow-lovers. He would fain preserve them from the anquish that beset himself. So humanising is sorrow.

"You are in love with Miss Dobson?" he asked.

Both nodded.

"Then," said he, "you will in time be thankful to me for not affording you further traffic with that lady. To love and be scorned—does Fate hold for us a greater inconvenience? You think I beg the question? Let me tell you that I, too, love Miss Dobson, and that she scorns me."

To the implied question "What chance would there be for you?" the reply was obvious.

Amazed, abashed, the two youths turned on their heels.

"Stay!" said the Duke. "Let me, in justice to myself, correct an inference you may have drawn. It is not by reason of any defect in myself, perceived or imagined, that Miss Dobson scorns me. She scorns me simply because I love her. All who love her she scorns. To see her is to love her. Therefore shut your eyes to her. Strickly exclude her from your horizon. Ignore her. Will you do this?"

"We will try," said the one, after a pause.

"Thank you very much," added the other.

The Duke watched them out of sight. He wished he

could take the good advice he had given them. . . . Suppose
he did take it! Suppose he went to the Bursar, obtained an
exeat, fled straight to London! What just humiliation for
Zuleika to come down and find her captive gone! He
pictured her staring round the quadrangle, ranging the
cloisters, calling to him. He pictured her rustling to the
gate of the College, inquiring at the porter's lodge. "His
Grace, Miss, he passed through a minute ago. He's going
down this afternoon."

Yet, even while his fancy luxuriated in this scheme, he well
knew that he would not accomplish anything of the kind—
knew well that he would wait here humbly, eagerly, even
though Zuleika lingered over her toilet till crack o' doom.
He had no desire that was not centred in her. Take away his
love for her, and what remained? Nothing—though only in
the past twenty-four hours had this love been added to him.
Ah, why had he ever seen her? He thought of his past, its
cold splendour and insouciance. But he knew that for him
there was no returning. His boats were burnt. The
Cytherean babes had set their torches to that flotilla, and it
had blazed like match-wood. On the isle of the enchantress
he was stranded for ever. For ever stranded on the isle of an
enchantress who would have nothing to do with him!
What, he wondered, should be done in so piteous a quandary?
There seemed to be two courses. One was to pine slowly and
painfully away. The other . . .

Academically, the Duke had often reasoned that a man for
whom life holds no chance of happiness cannot too quickly
shake life off. Now, of a sudden, there was for that theory a
vivid application.

"Whether 'tis nobler in the mind to suffer," was not a
point by which he, "more an antique Roman than a Dane,"
was at all troubled. Never had he given ear to that cackle
which is called Public Opinion. The judgment of his peers—
this, he had often told himself, was the sole arbitrage he

could submit to; but then, who was to be on the bench? Peerless, he was irresponsible—the captain of his soul, the despot of his future. No injunction but from himself would he bow to; and his own injunctions—so little Danish was he —had always been peremptory and lucid. Lucid and peremptory, now, the command he issued to himself.

"So sorry to have been so long," carolled a voice from above. The Duke looked up. "I'm all but ready," said Zuleika at her window.

That brief apparition changed the colour of his resolve. He realised that to die for love of this lady would be no mere measure of precaution, or counsel of despair. It would be in itself a passionate indulgence—a fiery rapture, not to be foregone. What better could he ask than to die for his love? Poor indeed seemed to him now the sacrament of marriage beside the sacrament of death. Death was incomparably the greater, the finer seal. Death was the one true bridal.

He flung back his head, spread wide his arms, quickened his pace almost to running speed. Ah, he would win his bride before the setting of the sun. He knew not by what means he would win her. Enough that even now, full-hearted, fleet-footed, he was on his way to her, and that she heard him coming.

When Zuleika, a vision in vaporous white, came out through the postern, she wondered why he was walking at so remarkable a pace. To him, wildly expressing in his movement the thought within him, she appeared as his awful bride. With a cry of joy, he bounded towards her, and would have caught her in his arms, had she not stepped nimbly aside.

"Forgive me!" he said, after a pause. "It was a mistake— an idiotic mistake of identity. I thought you were . . ."

Zuleika, rigid, asked: "Have I many doubles?"

"You know well that in all the world is none so blest as to be like you. I can only say that I was over-wrought. I can only say that it shall not occur again."

She was very angry indeed. Of his penitence there could be no doubt. But there are outrages for which no penitence can atone. This seemed to be one of them. Her first impulse was to dismiss the Duke forthwith and for ever. But she wanted to show herself at the races. And she could not go alone. And except the Duke there was no one to take her. True, there was the concert to-night; and she could show herself there to advantage; but she wanted *all* Oxford to see her—see her *now*.

"I am forgiven?" he asked. In her, I am afraid, self-respect outweighed charity. "I will try," she said merely, "to forget what you have done." Motioning him to her side, she opened her parasol, and signified her readiness to start.

They passed together across the vast gravelled expanse of the Front Quadrangle. In the porch of the College there were, as usual, some chained-up dogs, patiently awaiting their masters. Zuleika, of course, did not care for dogs. One has never known a good man to whom dogs were not dear; but many of the best women have no such fondness. You will find that the woman who is really kind to dogs is always one who has failed to inspire sympathy in men. For the attractive woman, dogs are mere dumb and restless brutes—possibly dangerous, certainly soulless. Yet will coquetry teach her to caress any dog in the presence of a man enslaved by her. Even Zuleika, it seems, was not above this rather obvious device for awaking envy. Be sure she did not at all like the look of the very big bull-dog who was squatting outside the porter's lodge. Perhaps, but for her present anger, she would not have stooped endearingly down to him, as she did, cooing over him and trying to pat his head. Alas, her pretty act was a failure. The bulldog cowered away from her, horrifically grimacing. This was strange. Like the majority of his breed, Corker (for such was his name) had ever been wistful to be noticed by anyone—effusively grateful for every word or pat, an ever-ready wagger and nuzzler, to none ineffable. No begger, no burglar, had ever been rebuffed by this catholic beast. But he drew the line at Zuleika.

Seldom is even a fierce bulldog heard to growl. Yet Corker growled at Zuleika.

# VII

THE Duke did not try to break the stony silence in which
Zuleika walked. Her displeasure was a luxury to him, for it
was so soon to be dispelled. A little while, and she would be
hating herself for her pettiness. Here was he, going to die
for her; and here was she, blaming him for a breach of
manners. Decidedly, the slave had the whip-hand. He stole
a sidelong look at her, and could not repress a smile. His
features quickly composed themselves. The Triumph of
Death must not be handled as a cheap score. He wanted to
die because he would thereby so poignantly consummate his
love, express it so completely, once and for all . . . And
she—who could say that she, knowing what he had done,
might not, illogically, come to love him? Perhaps she would
devote her life to mourning him. He saw her bending over
his tomb, in beautiful humble curves, under a starless sky,
watering the violets with her tears.

Shades of Novalis and Friedrich Schlegel and other
despicable maunderers! He brushed them aside. He would
be practical. The point was, when and how to die? Time:
the sooner the better. Manner . . . less easy to determine.
He must not die horribly, nor without dignity. The manner
of the Roman philosophers? But the only kind of bath
which an undergraduate can command is a hip-bath. Stay!
there was the river. Drowning (he had often heard) was a
rather pleasant sensation. And to the river he was even now
on his way.

It troubled him that he could swim. Twice, indeed, from
his yacht, he had swum the Hellespont. And how about the

animal instinct of self-preservation, strong even in despair? No matter! His soul's set purpose would subdue that. The law of gravitation that brings one to the surface? There his very skill in swimming would help him. He would swim under water, along the river-bed, swim till he found weeds to cling to, weird strong weeds that he would coil round him, exulting faintly . . .

As they turned into Radcliffe Square, the Duke's ear caught the sound of a far-distant gun. He started, and looked up at the clock of St. Mary's. Half-past four! The boats had started.

He had heard that whenever a woman was to blame for a disappointment, the best way to avoid a scene was to inculpate oneself. He did not wish Zuleika to store up yet more material for penitence. And so "I am sorry," he said. "That gun—did you hear it? It was the signal for the race. I shall never forgive myself."

"Then we shan't see the race at all?" cried Zuleika.

"It will be over, alas, before we are near the river. All the people will be coming back through the meadows."

"Let us meet them."

"Meet a torrent? Let us have tea in my rooms and go down quietly for the other Division."

"Let us go straight on."

Through the square, across the High, down Grove Street, they passed. The Duke looked up at the tower of Merton, ὡς οὔποτ᾽ αὖθις ἀλλὰ νῦν πανύστατον. Strange that to-night it would still be standing here, in all its sober and solid beauty—still be gazing, over the roofs and chimneys, at the tower of Magdalen, its rightful bride. Through untold centuries of the future it would stand thus, gaze thus. He winced. Oxford walls have a way of belittling us; and the Duke was loth to regard his doom as trivial.

Aye, by all minerals we are mocked. Vegetables, yearly deciduous, are far more sympathetic. The lilac and laburnum, making lovely now the railed pathway to Christ Church meadow, were all a-swaying and a-nodding to the Duke as he passed by. "Adieu, adieu, your Grace," they were whispering. "We are very sorry for you—very sorry indeed. We never dared suppose you would predecease us. We think your death a very great tragedy. Adieu! Perhaps we shall meet in another world—that is, if the members of the animal kingdom have immortal souls, as we have."

The Duke was little versed in their language: yet, as he passed between these gently garrulous blooms, he caught at least the drift of their salutation, and smiled a vague but courteous acknowledgment, to the right and the left alternately, creating a very favourable impression.

No doubt, the young elms lining the straight way to the barges had seen him coming; but any whispers of their leaves were lost in the murmur of the crowd returning from the race. Here, at length, came the torrent of which the Duke had spoken; and Zuleika's heart rose at it. Here was Oxford! From side to side the avenue was filled with a dense procession of youths—youths interspersed with maidens whose parasols were as flotsam and jetsam on a seething current of straw hats. Zuleika neither quickened nor slackened her advance. But brightlier and brightlier shone her eyes.

The vanguard of the procession was pausing now, swaying, breaking at sight of her. She passed, imperial, through the way cloven for her. All a-down the avenue, the throng parted as though some great invisible comb were being drawn through it. The few youths who had already seen Zuleika, and by whom her beauty had been bruited throughout the University, were lost in a new wonder, so incomparably fairer was she than the remembered vision. And the rest hardly recognised her from the descriptions, so incomparably fairer was the reality than the hope.

She passed among them. None questioned the worthiness of her escort. Could I give you better proof of the awe in

which our Duke was held? Any man is glad to be seen
escorting a very pretty woman. He thinks it adds to his
prestige. Whereas, in point of fact, his fellow-men are
saying merely: "Who's that appalling fellow with her?" or
"Why does she go about with that ass So-and-So?" Such
cavil may in part be envy. But it is a fact that no man,
howsoever graced, can shine in juxtaposition to a very pretty
woman. The Duke himself cut a poor figure beside Zuleika.
Yet not one of all the undergraduates felt she could have
made a wiser choice.

She swept among them. Her own intrinsic radiance was
not all that flashed from her. She was a moving reflector and
refractor of all the rays of all the eyes that mankind had
turned on her. Her mien told the story of her days. Bright
eyes, light feet—she trod erect from a vista whose glare was
dazzling to all beholders. She swept among them, a miracle,
overwhelming, breath-bereaving. Nothing at all like her had
ever been seen in Oxford.

Mainly architectural, the beauties of Oxford. True, the
place is no longer one-sexed. There are the virguncules of
Somerville and Lady Margaret's Hall; but beauty and the
lust for learning have yet to be allied. There are the innumerable wives and daughters around the Parks, running in
and out of their little red-brick villas; but the indignant
shade of celibacy seems to have called down on the dons a
Nemesis which precludes them from either marrying beauty
or begetting it. (From the Warden's son, that unhappy
curate, Zuleika inherited no tittle of her charm. Some of it,
there is no doubt, she did inherit from the circus-rider who
was her mother.)

But the casual feminine visitors? Well, the sisters and
cousins of an undergraduate seldom seem more passable to
his comrades than to himself. Altogether, the instinct of sex
is not pandered to in Oxford. It is not, however, as it may
once have been, dormant. The modern importation of

samples of femininity serves to keep it alert, though not to gratify it. A like result is achieved by another modern development—photography. The undergraduate may, and usually does, surround himself with photographs of pretty ladies known to the public. A phantom harem! Yet the houris have an effect on their sultan. Surrounded both by plain women of flesh and blood and by beauteous women on pasteboard, the undergraduate is the easiest victim of living loveliness—is as a fire ever well and truly laid, amenable to a spark. And if the spark be such a flaring torch as Zuleika?— marvel not, reader, at the conflagration.

Not only was the whole throng of youths drawing asunder before her: much of it, as she passed, was forming up in her wake. Thus, with the confluence of two masses—one coming away from the river, the other returning to it—chaos seethed around her and the Duke before they were half-way along the avenue. Behind them, and on either side of them, the people were crushed inextricably together, swaying and surging this way and that. "Help!" cried many a shrill feminine voice. "Don't push!" "Let me out!" "You brute!" "Save me, save me!" Many ladies fainted, whilst their escorts, supporting them and protecting them as best they could, peered over the heads of their fellows for one glimpse of the divine Miss Dobson. Yet for her and the Duke, in the midst of the terrific compress, there was space enough. In front of them, as by a miracle of deference, a way still cleared itself. They reached the end of the avenue without a pause in their measured progress. Nor even when they turned to the left, along the rather narrow path beside the barges, was there any obstacle to their advance. Passing evenly forward, they alone were cool, unhustled, undishevelled.

The Duke was so rapt in his private thoughts that he was hardly conscious of the strange scene. And as for Zuleika, she, as well she might be, was in the very best of good humours.

"What a lot of house-boats!" she exclaimed. "Are you going to take me on to one of them?"

The Duke started. Already they were alongside the Judas barge. "Here," he said, "is our goal."

He stepped through the gate of the railings, out upon the plank, and offered her his hand.

She looked back. The young men in the vanguard were crushing their shoulders against the row behind them, to stay the oncoming host. She had half a mind to go back through the midst of them; but she really did want her tea, and she followed the Duke on to the barge, and under his auspices climbed the steps to the roof.

It looked very cool and gay, this roof under its awning of red and white stripes. Nests of red and white flowers depended along either side of it. Zuleika moved to the side which commanded a view of the bank. She leaned her arms on the balustrade, and gazed down.

The crowd stretched as far as she could see—a vista of faces upturned to her. Suddenly it hove forward. Its vanguard was swept irresistibly past the barge—swept by the desire of the rest to see her at closer quarters. Such was the impetus that the vision for each man was but a lightning-flash: he was whirled past, struggling, almost before his brain took the message of his eyes.

Those who were Judas men made frantic efforts to board the barge, trying to hurl themselves through the gate in the railings; but they were swept vainly on.

Presently the torrent began to slacken, became a mere river, a mere procession of youths staring up rather shyly.

Before the last stragglers had marched by, Zuleika moved away to the other side of the roof, and, after a glance at the sunlit river, sank into one of the wicker chairs, and asked the Duke to look less disagreeable and to give her some tea.

Among others hovering near the little buffet were the two youths whose parley with the Duke I have recorded.

Zuleika was aware of the special persistency of their gaze. When the Duke came back with her cup, she asked him who they were. He replied, truthfully enough, that their names were unknown to him.

"Then," she said, "ask them their names, and introduce them to me."

"No," said the Duke, sinking into the chair beside her. "That I shall not do. I am your victim: not your pander. Those two men stand on the threshold of a possibly useful and agreeable career. I am not going to trip them up for you."

"I am not sure," said Zuleika, "that you are very polite. Certainly you are foolish. It is natural for boys to fall in love. If these two are in love with me, why not let them talk to me? It were an experience on which they would always look back with romantic pleasure. They may never see me again. Why grudge them this little thing?" She sipped her tea. "As for tripping them up on a threshold—that is all nonsense. What harm has unrequited love ever done to anybody?" She laughed. "Look at *me!* When I came to your rooms this morning, thinking I loved in vain, did I seem one jot the worse for it? Did I look different?"

"You looked, I am bound to say, nobler, more spiritual."

"More spiritual?" she exclaimed. "Do you mean I looked tired or ill?"

"No, you seemed quite fresh. But then, you are singular. You are no criterion."

"You mean you can't judge those two young men by me? Well, I am only a woman, of course. I have heard of women, no longer young, wasting away because no man loved them. I have often heard of a young woman fretting because some particular young man didn't love her. But I never heard of her wasting away. Certainly a young man doesn't waste away for love of some particular young woman. He very soon makes love to some other one. If his be an ardent nature, the quicker his transition. All the most ardent of my past adorers have married. Will you put my cup down, please?"

"Past?" echoed the Duke, as he placed her cup on the floor. "Have any of your lovers ceased to love you?"

"Ah no, no; not in retrospect. I remain their ideal, and all that, of course. They cherish the thought of me. They see the world in terms of me. But I am an inspiration, not an obsession; a glow, not a blight."

"You don't believe in the love that corrodes, the love that ruins?"

"No," laughed Zuleika.

"You have never dipped into the Greek pastoral poets, nor sampled the Elizabethan sonneteers?"

"No, never. You will think me lamentably crude: my experience of life has been drawn from life itself."

"Yet often you talk as though you had read rather much. Your way of speech has what is called 'the literary flavour'."

"Ah, that is an unfortunate trick which I caught from a writer, a Mr. Beerbohm, who once sat next to me at dinner somewhere. I can't break myself of it. I assure you I hardly ever open a book. Of life, though, my experience has been very wide. Brief? But I suppose the soul of man during the past two or three years has been much as it was in the reign of Queen Elizabeth and of—whoever it was that reigned over the Greek pastures. And I daresay the modern poets are making the same old silly distortions. But forgive me," she added gently, "perhaps you yourself are a poet?"

"Only since yesterday," answered the Duke (not less unfairly to himself than to Roger Newdigate and Thomas Gaisford). And he felt he was especially a dramatic poet. All the while that she had been sitting by him here, talking so glibly, looking so straight into his eyes, flashing at him so many pretty gestures, it was the sense of tragic irony that prevailed in him—that sense which had stirred in him, and been repressed, on the way from Judas. He knew that she was making her effect consciously for the other young men by whom the roof of the barge was now thronged. Him alone she seemed to observe. By her manner, she might have seemed to be making love to him. He envied the men she was so deliberately making envious—the men whom, in her undertone to him, she was really addressing. But he did take comfort in the irony. Though she used him as a stalking-horse, he, after all, was playing with her as a cat plays with a mouse. While she chattered on, without an inkling that he was no ordinary lover, and coaxing him to present two quite ordinary young men to her, he held over her the revelation that he for love of her was about to die.

And, while he drank in the radiance of her beauty, he heard her chattering on. "So you see," she was saying, "it couldn't do those young men any harm. Suppose un-requited love *is* anguish: isn't the discipline wholesome? Suppose I *am* a sort of furnace: shan't I purge, refine, temper? Those two boys are but scorched from here. That is horrid; and what good will it do them?" She laid a hand on his arm. "Cast them into the furnace for their own sake, dear Duke! Or cast one of them, or," she added, glancing round at the throng, "any one of these others!"

"For their own sake?" he echoed, withdrawing his arm. "If you were not, as the whole world knows you to be, perfectly respectable, there might be something in what you say. But as it is, you can but be an engine for mischief; and your sophistries leave me unmoved. I shall certainly keep you to myself."

"I hate you," said Zuleika, with an ugly petulance that crowned the irony.

"So long as I live," uttered the Duke, in a level voice, "you will address no man but me."

"If your prophecy is to be fulfilled," laughed Zuleika, rising from her chair, "your last moment is at hand."

"It is," he answered, rising too.

"What do you mean?" she asked, awed by something in his tone.

"I mean what I say: that my last moment is at hand." He withdrew his eyes from hers, and, leaning his elbows on the balustrade, gazed thoughtfully at the river. "When I am dead," he added, over his shoulder, "you will find these fellows rather coy of your advances."

For the first time since his avowal of his love for her, Zuleika found herself genuinely interested in him. A suspicion of his meaning had flashed through her soul.— But no! surely he could not mean *that*! It must have been a metaphor merely. And yet, something in his eyes . . . She leaned beside him. Her shoulder touched his. She gazed questioningly at him. He did not turn his face to her. He gazed at the sunlit river.

The Judas Eight had just embarked for their voyage to the starting-point. Standing on the edge of the raft that makes a floating platform for the barge, William, the hoary bargee, was pushing them off with his boat-hook, wishing them luck with deferential familiarity. The raft was thronged with Old Judasians—mostly clergymen—who were shouting hearty hortations, and evidently trying not to appear so old as they felt—or rather, not to appear so startlingly old as their contemporaries looked to them. It occurred to the Duke as a strange thing, and a thing to be glad of, that he, in this world, would never be an Old Judasian. Zuleika's shoulder pressed his. He thrilled not at all. To all intents, he was dead already.

The enormous eight young men in the thread-like skiff— the skiff that would scarce have seemed an adequate vehicle for the tiny "cox" who sat facing them—were staring up at Zuleika with that uniformity of impulse which, in another direction, had enabled them to bump a boat on two of the previous "nights". If to-night they bumped the next boat,

Univ., then would Judas be three places "up" on the river; and to-morrow Judas would have a Bump Supper. Furthermore, if Univ. were bumped to-night, Magdalen might be bumped to-morrow. Then would Judas, for the first time in history, be head of the river. Oh tremulous hope! Yet, for the moment, these eight young men seemed to have forgotten the awful responsibility that rested on their over-developed shoulders. Their hearts, already strained by rowing, had been transfixed this afternoon by Eros' darts. All of them had seen Zuleika as she came down to the river; and now they sat gaping up at her, fumbling with their oars. The tiny cox gaped too; but he it was who first recalled duty. With piping adjurations he brought the giants back to their senses. The boat moved away down stream, with a fairly steady stroke.

Not in a day can the traditions of Oxford be sent spinning. From all the barges the usual punt-loads of young men were being ferried across to the towing-path—young men naked of knee, armed with rattles, post-horns, motor-hooters, gongs, and other instruments of clangour. Though Zuleika filled their thoughts, they hurried along the towing-path, as by custom, to the starting-point.

She, meanwhile, had not taken her eyes off the Duke's profile. Nor had she dared, for fear of disappointment, to ask him just what he had meant.

"All these men," he repeated dreamily, "will be coy of your advances." It seemed to him a good thing that his death, his awful example, would disinfatuate his fellow alumni. He had never been conscious of public spirit. He had lived for himself alone. Love had come to him yesternight, and to-day had waked in him a sympathy with mankind. It was a fine thing to be a saviour. It was splendid to be human. He looked quickly round to her who had wrought this change in him.

But the loveliest face in all the world will not please you if you see it suddenly, eye to eye, at a distance of half an inch from your own. It was thus that the Duke saw Zuleika's: a monstrous deliquium a-glare. Only for the fraction of an instant, though. Recoiling, he beheld the loveliness that he knew—more adorably vivid now in its look of eager questioning. And in his every fibre he thrilled to her. Even so had she gazed at him last night, this morning. Aye, now as then, her soul was full of him. He had recaptured, not her love, but his power to please her. It was enough. He bowed his head; and *Moriturus te saluto* were the words formed silently by his lips. He was glad that his death would be a public service to the University. But the salutary lesson of what the newspapers would call his "rash act" was, after all, only a side-issue. The great thing, the prospect that flushed his cheek, was the consummation of his own love, for its own sake, by his own death. And, as he met her gaze, the question that had already flitted through his brain found a faltering utterance; and "Shall you mourn me?" he asked her.

But she would have no ellipses. "What are you going to do?" she whispered.

"Do you not know?"

"Tell me."

"Once and for all: you cannot love me?"

Slowly she shook her head. The black pearl and the pink, quivering, gave stress to her ultimatum. But the violet of her eyes was all but hidden by the dilation of her pupils.

"Then," whispered the Duke, "when I shall have died, deeming life a vain thing without you, will the gods give you tears for me? Miss Dobson, will your soul awaken? When I shall have sunk for ever beneath these waters whose supposed purpose here this afternoon is but that they be ploughed by the blades of these young oarsmen, will there be struck from that flint, your heart, some late and momentary spark of pity for me?"

"Why of course, of *course!*" babbled Zuleika, with clasped hands and dazzling eyes. "But," she curbed herself "it is—it would—oh, you mustn't *think* of it! I couldn't allow it! I—I should never forgive myself!"

"In fact, you would mourn me always?"

"Why yes! . . . Y-es—always." What else could she say? But would his answer be that he dared not condemn her to lifelong torment?

"Then," his answer was, "my joy in dying for you is made perfect."

Her muscles relaxed. Her breath escaped between her teeth. "You are utterly resolved?" she asked. "Are you?"

"Utterly."

"Nothing I might say could change your purpose?"

"Nothing."

"No entreaty, howsoever piteous, could move you?"

"None."

Forthwith she urged, entreated, cajoled, commanded, with infinite prettiness of ingenuity and of eloquence. Never was such a cascade of dissuasion as hers. She only didn't say she could love him. She never hinted that. Indeed, throughout her pleading rang this recurrent *motif*: that he must live to take to himself as mate some good, serious, clever woman who would be a not unworthy mother of his children.

She laid stress on his youth, his great position, his brilliant attainments, the much he had already achieved, the splendid possibilities of his future. Though of course she spoke in undertones, not to be overheard by the throng on the barge, it was almost as though his health were being floridly proposed at some public banquet—say, at a Tenants' Dinner. Insomuch that, when she ceased, the Duke half expected Jellings, his steward, to bob up uttering, with lifted hands, a stentorian "For-or," and all the company to take up the chant: "*he's*—a *jolly* good—*fellow*." His brief reply, on those occasions, seemed always to indicate that, whatever

77

else he might be, a jolly good fellow he was not. But by Zuleika's eulogy he really was touched. "Thank you—thank you," he gasped; and there were tears in his eyes. Dear the thought that she so revered him, so wished him not to die. But this was no more than a rush-light in the austere radiance of his joy in dying for her.

And the time was come. Now for the sacrament of his immersion in infinity.

"Good-bye," he said simply, and was about to swing himself on to the ledge of the balustrade. Zuleika, divining his intention, made way for him. Her bosom heaved quickly, quickly. All colour had left her face; but her eyes shone as never before.

Already his foot was on the ledge, when hark! the sound of a distant gun. To Zuleika, with all the chords of her soul strung to the utmost tensity, the effect was as if she herself had been shot; and she clutched at the Duke's arm, like a frightened child. He laughed. "It was the signal for the race," he said, and laughed again, rather bitterly, at the crude and trivial interruption of high matters.

"The race?" She laughed hysterically.

"Yes. 'They're off'." He mingled his laughter with hers, gently seeking to disengage his arm. "And perhaps," he said, "I, clinging to the weeds of the river's bed, shall see dimly the boats and the oars pass over me, and shall be able to gurgle a cheer for Judas."

"Don't!" she shuddered, with a woman's notion that a jest means levity. A tumult of thoughts surged in her, all confused. She only knew that he must not die—not yet! A moment ago, his death would have been beautiful. Not now! Her grip of his arm tightened. Only by breaking her wrist could he have freed himself. A moment ago, she had been in the seventh heaven . . . Men were supposed to have died for love of her. It had never been proved. There had always been something—card debts, ill-health, what not—to

account for the tragedy. No man, to the best of her recollection, had ever hinted that he was going to die for her.
Never, assuredly, had she seen the deed done. And then
came he, the first man she had loved, going to die here,
before her eyes, because she no longer loved him. But she
knew now that he must not die—not yet!

All around her was the hush that falls on Oxford when the
signal for the race has sounded. In the distance could be
heard faintly the noise of cheering—a little sing-song sound,
drawing nearer.

Ah, how could she have thought of letting him die so
soon? She gazed into his face—the face she might never
have seen again. Even now, but for that gun-shot, the waters
would have closed over him, and his soul, maybe, have
passed away. She had saved him, thank heaven! She had
him still with her.

Gently, vainly, he still sought to unclasp her fingers from
his arm.

"Not now!" she whispered. "Not yet!"

And the noise of the cheering, and of the trumpeting and
rattling, as it drew near, was an accompaniment to her joy in
having saved her lover. She would keep him with her—for a
while! Let all be done in order. She would savour the full
sweetness of his sacrifice. To-morrow—to-morrow, yes, let
him have his heart's desire of death. Not now! Not yet!

"To-morrow," she whispered, "to-morrow, if you will.
Not yet!"

The first boat came jerking past in mid-stream; and the
towing-path, with its serried throng of runners, was like a live
thing, keeping pace. As in a dream, Zuleika saw it. And the
din was in her ears. No heroine of Wagner had ever a
louder accompaniment than had ours to the surging soul
within her bosom.

And the Duke, tightly held by her, vibrated as to a
powerful electric current. He let her cling to him, and her

magnetism range through him. Ah, it was good not to have died! Fool, he had meant to drain off-hand, at one coarse draught, the delicate wine of death. He would let his lips caress the brim of the august goblet. He would dally with the aroma that was there.

"So be it!" he cried into Zuleika's ear—cried loudly, for it seemed as though all the Wagnerian orchestras of Europe, with the Straussian ones thrown in, were here to clash in unison the full volume of right music for the glory of the reprieve.

The fact was that the Judas boat had just bumped Univ., exactly opposite the Judas barge. The oarsmen in either boat sat humped, panting, some of them rocking and writhing, after their wholesome exercise. But there was not one of them whose eyes were not upcast at Zuleika. And the vocalisation and instrumentation of the dancers and stampers on the towing-path had by this time ceased to mean aught of joy in the victors or of comfort for the vanquished, and had resolved itself into a wild wordless hymn to the glory of Miss Dobson. Behind her and all around her on the roof of the barge, young Judasians were venting in like manner their hearts through their lungs. She paid no heed. It was as if she stood alone with her lover on some silent pinnacle of the world. It was as if she were a little girl with a brand-new and very expensive doll which had banished all the little other old toys from her mind.

She simply could not, in her naïve rapture, take her eyes off her companion. To the dancers and stampers of the towing-path, many of whom were now being ferried back across the river, and to the other youths on the roof of the barge, Zuleika's air of absorption must have seemed a little strange. For already the news that the Duke loved Zuleika, and that she loved him not, and would stoop to no man who loved her, had spread like wild-fire among the undergraduates. The two youths in whom the Duke had deigned to confide had not held their peace. And the effect that

Zuleika had made as she came down to the river was intensified by the knowledge that not the great paragon himself
did she deem worthy of her. The mere sight of her had
captured young Oxford. The news of her supernal haughti-
ness had riveted the chains.

"Come!" said the Duke at length, staring around him with
the eyes of one awakened from a dream. "Come! I must take
you back to Judas."

"But you won't leave me there?" pleaded Zuleika. "You
will stay to dinner? I am sure my grandfather would be
delighted."

"I am sure he would," said the Duke, as he piloted her
down the steps of the barge. "But alas, I have to dine at the
Junta to-night."

"The Junta? What is that?"

"A little dining-club. It meets every Tuesday."

"But—you don't mean you are going to refuse me for that?"

"To do so is misery. But I have no choice. I have asked a
guest."

"Then ask another: ask me!" Zuleika's notions of
Oxford life were rather hazy. It was with difficulty that the
Duke made her realise that he could not—not even if, as she
suggested, she dressed herself up as a man—invite her to the
Junta. She then fell back on the impossibility that he would
not dine with her to-night, his last night in this world. She
could not understand that admirable fidelity to social
engagements which is one of the virtues implanted in the
members of our aristocracy. Bohemian by training and by
career, she construed the Duke's refusal as either a cruel
slight to herself or an act of imbecility. The thought of being
parted from her for one moment was torture to him; but
*noblesse oblige*, and it was quite impossible for him to
break an engagement merely because a more charming
one offered itself: he would as soon have cheated at cards.

And so, as they went side by side up the avenue, in the

mellow light of the westering sun, preceded in their course, and pursued, and surrounded, by the mob of hoarse infatuate youths, Zuleika's face was as that of a little girl sulking. Vainly the Duke reasoned with her. She could *not* see the point of view.

With that sudden softening that comes to the face of an angry woman who has hit on a good argument, she turned to him and asked: "How if I hadn't saved your life just now? Much you thought about your guest when you were going to dive and die!"

"I did not forget him," answered the Duke, smiling at her casuistry. "Nor had I any scruple in disappointing him. Death cancels all engagements."

And Zuleika, worsted, resumed her sulking.

But presently, as they neared Judas, she relented. It was paltry to be cross with him who had resolved to die for her and was going to die so on the morrow. And after all, she would see him at the concert to-night. They would sit together. And all to-morrow they would be together, till the time came for parting. Hers was a naturally sunny disposition. And the evening was such a lovely one, all bathed in gold. She was ashamed of her ill-humour.

"Forgive me," she said, touching his arm. "Forgive me for being horrid." And forgiven she promptly was. "And promise you will spend all to-morrow with me." And of course he promised.

As they stood together on the steps of the Warden's front door, exalted above the level of the flushed and swaying crowd that filled the whole length and breadth of Judas Street, she implored him not to be late for the concert.

"I am never late," he smiled.

"Ah, you're so beautifully brought up!"

The door was opened.

"And—oh, you're beautiful besides!" she whispered; and waved her hand to him as she vanished into the hall.

# VIII

A FEW minutes before half-past seven, the Duke, arrayed for dinner, passed leisurely up the High. The arresting feature of his costume was a mulberry-coloured coat, with brass buttons. This, to anyone versed in Oxford lore, betokened him a member of the Junta. It is awful to think that a casual stranger might have mistaken him for a footman. It does not do to think of such things.

The tradesmen, at the doors of their shops, bowed low as he passed, rubbing their hands and smiling, hoping inwardly that they took no liberty in sharing the cool rosy air of the evening with his Grace. They noted that he wore in his shirt-front a black pearl and a pink. "Daring, but becoming," they opined.

The rooms of the Junta were over a stationer's shop, next door but one to the Mitre. They were small rooms; but as the Junta had now, besides the Duke, only two members, and as no member might introduce more than one guest, there was ample space.

The Duke had been elected in his second term. At that time there were four members; but these were all leaving Oxford at the end of the summer term, and there seemed to be in the ranks of the Bullingdon and the Loder no one quite eligible for the Junta, that holy of holies. Thus it was that the Duke inaugurated in solitude his second year of membership. From time to time, he proposed and seconded a few candidates, after "sounding" them as to whether they were willing to join. But always, when election evening—the last Tuesday of term—drew near, he began to have his doubts about these fellows. This one was "rowdy"; that one was over-dressed; another did not ride quite straight to hounds; in the pedigree of another a bar-sinister was more than suspected. Election evening was always a rather melancholy time. After dinner, when the two club servants had placed on the mahogany the time-worn Candidates' Book and the ballot-box, and had noiselessly withdrawn, the Duke clearing his throat, read aloud to himself "Mr. So-and-So, of Such-and-Such College, proposed by the Duke of Dorset, seconded by the Duke of Dorset," and, in every case, when he drew out the drawer of the ballot-box, found it was a black ball that he had dropped into the urn. Thus it was that at the end of the summer term the annual photographic "group" taken by Messrs. Hills and Saunders was a present-ment of the Duke alone.

In the course of his third year he had become less ex-clusive. Not because there seemed to be anyone really worthy of the Junta; but because the Junta, having thriven since the eighteenth century, must not die. Suppose—one never knew—he were struck by lightning, the Junta would be no more. So, not without reluctance, but unanimously, he had elected The MacQuern, of Balliol, and Sir John Marraby, of Brasenose.

To-night, as he, a doomed man, went up into the familiar rooms, he was wholly glad that he had thus relented. · As yet, he was spared the tragic knowledge that it would make no difference.*

The MacQuern and two other young men were already there.

"Mr. President," said The MacQuern, "I present Mr. Trent-Garby, of Christ Church."

"The Junta is honoured," said the Duke, bowing.

Such was the ritual of the club.

*The Junta has been reconstituted. But the apostolic line was broken, the thread was snapped; the old magic is fled.

The other young man, because his host, Sir John Marraby, was not yet on the scene, had no *locus standi*, and, though a friend of The MacQuern, and well known to the Duke, had to be ignored.

A moment later, Sir John arrived. "Mr. President," he said, "I present Lord Sayes, of Magdalen."

"The Junta is honoured," said the Duke, bowing.

Both hosts and both guests, having been prominent in the throng that vociferated around Zuleika an hour earlier, were slightly abashed in the Duke's presence. He, however, had not noticed anyone in particular, and, even if he had, that fine tradition of the club—"A member of the Junta can do no wrong; a guest of the Junta cannot err"—would have prevented him from showing his displeasure.

A Herculean figure filled the doorway.

"The Junta is honoured," said the Duke, bowing to his guest.

"Duke," said the newcomer quietly, "the honour is as much mine as that of the interesting and ancient institution which I am this night privileged to inspect."

Turning to Sir John and The MacQuern, the Duke said: "I present Mr. Abimelech V. Oover, of Trinity."

"The Junta," they replied, "is honoured."

"Gentlemen," said the Rhodes Scholar, "your good courtesy is just such as I would have anticipated from members of the ancient Junta. Like most of my countrymen, I am a man of few words. We are habituated out there to act rather than talk. Judged from the view-point of your beautiful old civilisation, I am aware my curtness must seem crude. But, gentlemen, believe me, right here——"

"Dinner is served, your Grace."

Thus interrupted, Mr. Oover, with the resourcefulness of a practised orator, brought his thanks to a quick but not abrupt conclusion. The little company passed into the front room.

Through the window, from the High, fading daylight mingled with the candle-light. The mulberry coats of the hosts, interspersed by the black ones of the guests, made a fine pattern around the oval table a-gleam with the many curious pieces of gold and silver plate that had accrued to the Junta in course of years.

The President showed much deference to his guest. He seemed to listen with close attention to the humorous anecdote with which, in the American fashion, Mr. Oover inaugurated dinner.

To all Rhodes Scholars, indeed, his courtesy was invariable. He went out of his way to cultivate them. And this he did more as a favour to Lord Milner than of his own caprice. He found these Scholars, good fellows though they were, rather oppressive. They had not—how could they have?—the undergraduate's virtue of taking Oxford as a matter of course. The Germans loved it too little, the Colonials too much. The Americans were, to a sensitive observer, the most troublesome—as being the most troubled —of the whole lot. The Duke was not one of those Englishmen who fling, or care to hear flung, cheap sneers at America. Whenever anyone in his presence said that America was not large in area, he would firmly maintain that it was. He held, too, in his enlightened way, that Americans have a perfect **right** to exist. But he did often find himself wishing Mr. Rhodes had not enabled them to exercise that right in Oxford. They were so awfully afraid of having their strenuous native characters undermined by their delight in the place. They held that the future was theirs, a glorious asset, far more glorious than the past. But a theory, as the Duke saw, is one thing, an emotion another. It is so much easier to covet what one hasn't than to revel in what one has. Also, it is so much easier to be enthusiastic about what exists than about what doesn't. The future doesn't exist. The past does. For, whereas all men can learn, the gift of prophecy has died out. A man cannot work up in his breast any real excitement about what possibly won't happen. He cannot very well help being sentimentally interested in what he knows has happened. On the other hand, he owes a duty to his country. And, if his country be America, he ought to try to feel a vivid respect for the future, and a cold contempt for the past. Also, if he be selected by his country as a specimen of the best moral, physical, and intellectual type that she can produce for the astounding of the effete foreigner, and incidentally for the purpose of raising that foreigner's tone, he must—mustn't he?—do his best to astound, to exalt. But then comes in this difficulty. Young men don't like to astound and exalt their fellows. And Americans, individually, are of all people the most anxious to please. That they talk overmuch is often taken as a sign of self-satisfaction. It is merely a mannerism. Rhetoric is a thing inbred in them. They are quite unconscious of it. It is as natural to them as breathing. And, while they talk on, they really do believe that they are a quick, businesslike people, by whom things are "put through" with an almost brutal abruptness. This notion of theirs is rather confusing to the patient English auditor.

Altogether, the American Rhodes Scholars, with their splendid native gift of oratory, and their modest desire to please, and their not less evident feeling that they ought merely to edify, and their constant delight in all that of Oxford their English brethren don't notice, and their constant fear that they are being corrupted, are a noble, rather than a comfortable, element in the social life of the University. So, at least, they seemed to the Duke.

And to-night, but that he had invited Oover to dine with him, he could have been dining with Zuleika. And this was his last dinner on earth. Such thoughts made him the less able to take pleasure in his guest. Perfect, however, the amenity of his manner.

This was the more commendable because Oover's "aura" was even more disturbing than that of the average Rhodes Scholar. To-night, besides the usual conflicts in this young man's bosom, raged a special one between his desire to behave well and his jealousy of the man who had to-day been Miss Dobson's escort. In theory he denied the Duke's right to that honour. In sentiment he admitted it. Another conflict, you see. And another. He longed to orate about the woman who had his heart; yet she was the one topic that must be shirked.

The MacQuern and Mr. Trent-Garby, Sir John Marraby and Lord Sayes, they too—though they were no orators— would fain have unpacked their hearts in words about Zuleika. They spoke of this and that, automatically, none listening to another—each man listening, wide-eyed, to his own heart's solo on the Zuleika theme, and drinking rather more champagne than was good for him. Maybe, these youths sowed in themselves, on this night, the seeds of life-long intemperance. We cannot tell. They did not live long enough for us to know.

While the six dined, a seventh, invisible to them, leaned moodily against the mantelpiece, watching them. He was not of their time. His long brown hair was knotted in a black riband behind. He wore a pale brocaded coat and lace ruffles, silken stockings, a sword. Privy to their doom, he watched them. He was loth that his Junta must die. Yes, his. Could the diners have seen him, they would have known him by his resemblance to the mezzotint portrait that hung on the wall above him. They would have risen to their feet in presence of Humphrey Greddon, founder and first president of the club.

His face was not so oval, nor were his eyes so big, nor his lips so full, nor his hands so delicate, as they appeared in the mezzotint. Yet (bating the conventions of eighteenth-century portraiture) the likeness was a good one. Humphrey

Greddon was not less well-knit and graceful than the painter had made him, and, hard though the lines of the face were, there was about him a certain air of high romance that could not be explained away by the fact that he was of a period not our own. You could understand the great love that Nellie O'Mora had borne him.

Under the mezzotint hung Hoppner's miniature of that lovely and ill-starred girl, with her soft dark eyes, and her curls all astray from beneath her little blue turban. And the Duke was telling Mr. Oover her story—how she had left her home for Humphrey Greddon when she was but sixteen, and he an undergraduate at Christ Church; and had lived for him in a cottage at Littlemore, whither he would ride, most days, to be with her; and how he tired of her, broke his oath that he would marry her, thereby broke her heart; and how she drowned herself in a mill-pond; and how Greddon was killed in Venice, two years later, duelling on the Riva Schiavoni with a Senator whose daughter he had seduced.

And he, Greddon, was not listening very attentively to the tale. He had heard it told so often in this room, and he did not understand the sentiments of the modern world. Nellie had been a monstrous pretty creature. He had adored her, and had done with her. It was right that she should always be toasted after dinner by the Junta, as in the days when first he loved her—"Here's to Nellie O'Mora, the fairest witch that ever was or will be!" He would have resented the omission of that toast. But he was sick of the pitying, melting looks that were always cast towards her miniature. Nellie had been beautiful, but, by God! she was always a dunce and a simpleton. How could he have spent his life with her? She was a fool, by God! not to marry that fool Trailby, of Merton, whom he took to see her.

Mr. Oover's moral tone, and his sense of chivalry, were of the American kind: far higher than ours, even, and far better expressed. Whereas the English guests of the Junta, when they heard the tale of Nellie O'Mora, would merely murmur: "Poor girl!" or "What a shame!" Mr. Oover said in a tone of quiet authority that compelled Greddon's ear, "Duke, I hope I am not incognisant of the laws that govern the relations of guest and host. But, Duke, I aver deliberately that the founder of this fine old club, at which you are so splendidly entertaining me to-night, was an unmitigated scoundrel. I say he was not a white man."

At the word "scoundrel", Humphrey Greddon had sprung forward, drawing his sword, and loudly, in a voice audible to himself alone, challenged the American to make good his words. Then, as this gentleman took no notice, with one clean straight thrust Greddon ran him through the heart, shouting: "Die, you damned psalm-singer and traducer! And so die all rebels against King George!"* Withdrawing the blade, he wiped it daintily on his cambric handkerchief. There was no blood. Mr. Oover, with unpunctured shirt-front, was repeating: "I say he was not a white man." And Greddon remembered himself—remembered he was only a ghost impalpable, impotent, of no account. "But I shall meet you in Hell to-morrow," he hissed in Oover's face. And there he was wrong. It is quite certain that Oover went to Heaven.

Unable to avenge himself, Greddon had looked to the Duke to act for him. When he saw that this young man did but smile at Oover and make a vague deprecatory gesture, he again, in his wrath, forgot his disabilities. Drawing himself to his full height, he took with great deliberation a pinch of snuff, and, bowing low to the Duke, said: "I am vastly obleeged to your Grace for the fine high Courage you have exhibited in the behalf of your most Admiring, most Humble Servant." Then, having brushed away a speck of snuff from his *jabot*, he turned on his heel; and only in the

*As Edward VII was at this time on the throne, it must have been to George III that Mr. Greddon was referring.

doorway, where one of the club servants, carrying a decanter in each hand, walked straight through him, did he realise that he had not spoilt the Duke's evening. With a volley of the most appalling eighteenth-century oaths, he passed back into the nether world.

To the Duke, Nellie O'Mora had never been a very vital figure. He had often repeated the legend of her. But, having never known what love was, he could not imagine her rapture or her anguish. Himself the quarry of all Mayfair's wise virgins, he had always—so far as he thought of the matter at all—suspected that Nellie's death was due to thwarted ambition. But to-night, while he told Oover about her, he could see into her soul. Nor did he pity her. She had loved. She had known the one thing worth living for— and dying for. She, as she went down to the mill-pond, had felt just that ecstasy of self-sacrifice which he himself had felt to-day and would feel to-morrow. And for a while, too— for a full year—she had known the joy of being loved, had been for Greddon "the fairest witch that ever was or will be". He could not agree with Oover's long disquisition on her sufferings. And, glancing at her well-remembered miniature, he wondered just what it was in her that had captivated Greddon. He was in that blest state when a man cannot believe the earth has been trodden by any really beautiful or desirable lady save the lady of his own heart.

The moment had come for the removal of the tablecloth. The mahogany of the Junta was laid bare—a clear dark lake, anon to reflect in its still and ruddy depths the candelabra and the fruit-cradles, the slender glasses and the stout old decanters, the forfeit-box and the snuff-box, and other paraphernalia of the dignity of dessert. Lucidly and un-waveringly inverted in the depths these good things stood; and, so soon as the wine had made its circuit, the Duke rose and with uplifted glass proposed the first of the two toasts traditional to the Junta. "Gentlemen, I give you Church and State."

The toast having been honoured by all—and by none with a richer reverence than by Oover, despite his passionate mental reservation in favour of Pittsburg-Anabaptism and the Republican Ideal—the snuff-box was handed round, and fruit was eaten.

Presently, when the wine had gone round again, the Duke rose and with uplifted glass said: "Gentlemen, I give you——" and there halted. Silent, frowning, flushed, he stood for a few moments, and then, with a deliberate gesture, tilted his glass and let fall the wine to the carpet. "No," he said, looking round the table, "I cannot give you Nellie O'Mora."

"Why not?" gasped Sir John Marraby.

"You have a right to ask that," said the Duke, still standing. "I can only say that my conscience is stronger than my sense of what is due to the customs of the club. Nellie O'Mora," he said, passing his hand over his brow, "may have been in her day the fairest witch that ever was—so fair that our founder had good reason to suppose her the fairest witch that ever would be. But his prediction was a false one. So at least it seems to me. Of course I cannot both hold this view and remain President of this club. MacQuern—Marraby—which of you is Vice-President?"

"He is," said Marraby.

"Then, MacQuern, you are hereby President, *vice* myself resigned. Take the chair and propose the toast."

"I would rather not," said The MacQuern after a pause.

"Then, Marraby, *you* must."

"Not I," said Marraby.

"Why is this?" asked the Duke, looking from one to the other.

The MacQuern, with Scotch caution, was silent. But the impulsive Marraby—Madcap Marraby, as they called him in B.N.C.—said: "It's because I won't lie!" and, leaping up, raised his glass aloft and cried: "I give you

Zuleika Dobson, the fairest witch that ever was or will be!"

Mr. Oover, Lord Sayes, Mr. Trent-Garby, sprang to their feet; The MacQuern rose to his. "Zuleika Dobson!" they cried, and drained their glasses.

Then, when they had resumed their seats, came an awkward pause. The Duke, still erect beside the chair he had vacated, looked very grave and pale. Marraby had taken an outrageous liberty. But "a member of the Junta can do no wrong," and the liberty could not be resented. The Duke felt that the blame was on himself, who had elected Marraby to the club.

Mr. Oover, too, looked grave. All the antiquarian in him deplored the sudden rupture of a fine old Oxford tradition. All the chivalrous American in him resented the slight on that fair victim of the feudal system, Miss O'Mora. And, at the same time, all the Abimelech V. in him rejoiced at having honoured by word and act the one woman in the world.

Gazing around at the flushed faces and heaving shirt-fronts of the diners, the Duke forgot Marraby's misdemeanour. What mattered far more to him was that here were five young men deeply under the spell of Zuleika. They must be saved, if possible. He knew how strong his influence was in the University. He knew also how strong was Zuleika's. He had not much hope of the issue. But his new-born sense of duty to his fellows spurred him on. "Is there," he asked with a bitter smile, "any one of you who doesn't with his whole heart love Miss Dobson?"

Nobody held up a hand.

"As I feared," said the Duke, knowing not that if a hand had been held up he would have taken it as a personal insult. No man really in love can forgive another for not sharing his ardour. His jealousy for himself when his beloved prefers another man is hardly a stronger passion than his jealousy for her when she is not preferred to all other women.

"You know her only by sight—by repute?" asked the Duke. They signified that this was so. "I wish you would introduce me to her," said Marraby.

"You are all coming to the Judas concert to-night?" the Duke asked, ignoring Marraby. "You have all secured tickets?" They nodded. "To hear me play, or to see Miss Dobson?" There was a murmur of "Both—both." "And you would all of you, like Marraby, wish to be presented to this lady?" Their eyes dilated. "That way happiness lies, think you?"

"Oh, happiness be hanged!" said Marraby.

To the Duke this seemed a profoundly sane remark—an epitome of his own sentiments. But what was right for himself was not right for all. He believed in convention as the best way for average mankind. And so, slowly, calmly, he told to his fellow-diners just what he had told a few hours earlier to those two young men in Salt Cellar. Not knowing that his words had already been spread throughout Oxford, he was rather surprised that they seemed to make no sensation. Quite flat, too, fell his appeal that the siren be shunned by all.

Mr. Oover, during his year of residence, had been sorely tried by the quaint old English custom of not making public speeches after private dinners. It was with a deep sigh of satisfaction that he now rose to his feet.

"Duke," he said in a low voice, which yet penetrated to every corner of the room, "I guess I am voicing these gentlemen when I say that your words show up your good heart, all the time. Your mentality, too, is bully, as we all predicate. One may say without exaggeration that your scholarly and social attainments are a by-word throughout the solar system, and be-yond. We rightly venerate you as our boss. Sir, we worship the ground you walk on. But we owe a duty to our own free and independent manhood. Sir, we worship the ground Miss Z. Dobson treads on. We have pegged out a claim right there. And from that location we aren't to be budged—not for bob-nuts. We asseverate we squat—where—we—squat, come—what—will. You say we have no chance to win Miss Z. Dobson. That—we—know. We aren't worthy. We lie prone. Let her walk over us. You say her heart is cold. We don't pro-fess we can take the chill off. But, Sir, we can't be diverted out of loving her —not even by you, Sir. No, Sir! We love her, and—shall, and—will, Sir, with—our—latest breath."

This peroration evoked loud applause. "I love her, and shall, and will," shouted each man. And again they honoured in wine her image. Sir John Marraby uttered a cry familiar in the hunting-field. The MacQuern contributed a few bars of a sentimental ballad in the dialect of his country. "Hurrah, hurrah!" shouted Mr. Trent-Garby. Lord Sayes hummed the latest waltz, waving his arms to its rhythm, while the wine he had just spilt on his shirt-front trickled unheeded to his waistcoat. Mr. Oover gave the Yale cheer.

The genial din was wafted down through the open window to the passers-by. The wine-merchant across the way heard it, and smiled pensively. "Youth, youth!" he murmured.

The genial din grew louder.

At any other time, the Duke would have been jarred by the disgrace to the Junta. But now, as he stood with bent head, covering his face with his hands, he thought only of the need to rid these young men, here and now, of the influence that had befallen them. To-morrow his tragic example might be too late, the mischief have sunk too deep, the agony be life-long. His good breeding forbade him to cast over a dinner-table the shadow of his death. His conscience insisted that he must. He uncovered his face, and held up one hand for silence.

"We are all of us," he said, "old enough to remember vividly the demonstrations made in the streets of London

when war was declared between us and the Transvaal
Republic. You, Mr. Oover, doubtless heard in America the
echoes of those ebullitions. The general idea was that the
war was going to be a very brief and simple affair—what was
called 'a walk-over'. To me, though I was only a small boy,
it seemed that all this delirious pride in the prospect of
crushing a trumpery foe argued a defect in our sense of
proportion. Still, I was able to understand the demon-
strators' point of view. To 'the giddy vulgar' any sort of
victory is pleasant. But defeat? If, when that war was
declared, everyone had been sure that not only should we
fail to conquer the Transvaal, but that *it* would conquer *us*—
that not only would it make good its freedom and independence, but that we should forfeit ours—how would the
cits have felt then? Would they not have pulled long faces,
spoken in whispers, wept? You must forgive me for saying
that the noise you have just made around this table was very
like to the noise made on the verge of the Boer War. And
your procedure seems to me as unaccountable as would have
seemed the antics of those mobs if England had been plainly
doomed to disaster and to vassalage. My guest here to-night,
in the course of his very eloquent and racy speech, spoke of
the need that he and you should preserve your 'free and
independent manhood.' That seemed to me an irreproach-
able ideal. But I confess I was somewhat taken aback by my
friend's scheme for realising it. He declared his intention of
lying prone and letting Miss Dobson 'walk over' him; and he
advised you to follow his example; and to this counsel you
gave evident approval. Gentlemen, suppose that on the
verge of the aforesaid war, some orator had said to the
British people: 'It is going to be a walk-over for our enemy
in the field. Mr. Kruger holds us in the hollow of his hand.
In subjection to him we shall find our long-lost freedom and
independence'—what would have been Britannia's answer?
What, on reflection, is yours to Mr. Oover? What are Mr.

Oover's own second thoughts?" The Duke paused, with a smile to his guest.

"Go right ahead, Duke," said Mr. Oover. "I'll re-ply when my turn comes."

"And not utterly demolish me, I hope," said the Duke. His was the Oxford manner. "Gentlemen," he continued, "is it possible that Britannia would have thrown her helmet in the air, shrieking: 'Slavery for ever'? You, gentlemen, seem to think slavery a pleasant and an honourable state. You have less experience of it than I. I have been enslaved to Miss Dobson since yesterday evening; you, only since this afternoon; I, at close quarters; you, at a respectful distance. Your fetters have not galled you yet. *My* wrists, *my* ankles, are excoriated. The iron has entered into my soul. I droop. I stumble. Blood flows from me. I quiver and curse. I writhe. The sun mocks me. The moon titters in my face. I can stand it no longer. I will no more of it. To-morrow I die."

The flushed faces of the diners grew gradually pale. Their eyes lost lustre. Their tongues clove to the roofs of their mouths.

At length, almost inaudibly, The MacQuern asked: "Do you mean you are going to commit suicide?"

"Yes," said the Duke, "if you choose to put it in that way. Yes. And it is only by a chance that I did not commit suicide this afternoon."

"You—don't—say," gasped Mr. Oover.

"I do indeed," said the Duke. "And I ask you all to weigh well my message."

"But—but does Miss Dobson know?" asked Sir John.

"Oh yes," was the reply. "Indeed, it was she who persuaded me not to die till to-morrow."

"But—but," faltered Lord Sayes, "I saw her saying good-bye to you in Judas Street. And—and she looked quite—as if nothing had happened."

"Nothing *had* happened," said the Duke. "And she was very much pleased to have me still with her. But she isn't so cruel as to hinder me from dying for her to-morrow. I don't think she exactly fixed the hour. It shall be just after the Eights have been rowed. An earlier death would mark in me a lack of courtesy to that contest . . . It seems strange to you that I should do this thing? Take warning by me. Muster all your will-power, and forget Miss Dobson. Tear up your tickets for the concert. Stay here and play cards. Play high. Or rather, go back to your various Colleges, and speed the news I have told you. Put all Oxford on its guard against this woman who can love no lover. Let all Oxford know that I, Dorset, who had so much reason to love life—I, the nonpareil—am going to die for the love I bear this woman. And let no man think I go unwilling. I am no lamb led to the slaughter. I am priest as well as victim. I offer myself up with a pious joy. But enough of this cold Hebraism! It is ill-attuned to my soul's mood. Self-sacrifice—bah! Regard me as a voluptuary. I am that. All my baffled ardour speeds me to the bosom of Death. She is gentle and wanton. She knows I could never have loved her for her own sake. She has no illusions about me. She knows well I come to her because not otherwise may I quench my passion."

There was a long silence. The Duke, looking around at the bent heads and drawn mouths of his auditors, saw that his words had gone home. It was Marraby who revealed how powerfully home they had gone.

"Dorset," he said huskily, "I shall die too."

The Duke flung up his hands, staring wildly.

"I stand in with that," said Mr. Oover.

"So do I!" said Lord Sayes. "And I!" said Mr. Trent-Garby. "And I!" The MacQuern.

The Duke found voice. "Are you mad?" he asked, clutching at his throat. "Are you all mad?"

"No, Duke," said Mr. Oover. "Or if we are, you have no right to be at large. You have shown us the way. We—take it."

"Just so," said The MacQuern, stolidly.

"Listen, you fools," cried the Duke. But through the open window came the vibrant stroke of some clock. He wheeled round, plucked out his watch—nine!—the concert! —his promise not to be late!—Zuleika!

All other thoughts vanished. In an instant he dodged beneath the sash of the window. From the flower-box he sprang to the road beneath. (The façade of the house is called, to this day, Dorset's Leap.) Alighting with the legerity of a cat, he swerved leftwards in the recoil, and was off, like a streak of mulberry-coloured lightning, down the High.

The other men had rushed to the window, fearing the worst. "No," cried Oover. "That's all right. Saves time!" and he raised himself on to the window-box. It splintered under his weight. He leapt heavily but well, followed by some uprooted geraniums. Squaring his shoulders, he threw back his head, and doubled down the slope.

There was a violent jostle between the remaining men. The MacQuern cannily got out of it, and rushed downstairs. He emerged at the front door just after Marraby touched ground. The Baronet's left ankle had twisted under him. His face was drawn with pain as he hopped down the High on his right foot, fingering his ticket for the concert. Next leapt Lord Sayes. And last of all leapt Mr. Trent-Garby, who, catching his foot in the ruined flower-box, fell headlong, and was, I regret to say, killed. Lord Sayes passed Sir John in a few paces. The MacQuern overtook Mr. Oover at St. Mary's and outstripped him in Radcliffe Square. The Duke came in an easy first.

Youth, youth!

# IX

ACROSS the Front Quadrangle, heedless of the great crowd to right and left, Dorset rushed. Up the stone steps to the Hall he bounded, and only on the Hall's threshold was he brought to a pause. The doorway was blocked by the backs of youths who had by hook and crook secured standing-room. The whole scene was surprisingly unlike that of the average College concert.

"Let me pass," said the Duke, rather breathlessly. "Thank you. Make way please. Thanks." And with quick-pulsing heart he made his way down the aisle to the front row. There awaited him a surprise that was like a douche of cold water full in his face. Zuleika was not there! It had never occurred to him that she herself might not be punctual.

The Warden was there, reading his programme with an air of great solemnity. "Where," asked the Duke, "is your grand-daughter?" His tone was as of a man saying: "If she is dead, don't break it gently to me."

"My grand-daughter?" said the Warden. "Ah, Duke, good evening."

"She's not ill?"

"Oh no, I think not. She said something about changing the dress she wore at dinner. She will come." And the Warden thanked his young friend for the great kindness he had shown to Zuleika. He hoped the Duke had not let her worry him with her artless prattle. "She seems to be a good, amiable girl," he added, in his detached way.

Sitting beside him, the Duke looked curiously at the venerable profile, as at a mummy's. To think that this had

once been a man! To think that his blood flowed in the
veins of Zuleika! Hitherto the Duke had seen nothing
grotesque in him—had regarded him always as a dignified
specimen of priest and scholar. Such a life as the Warden's,
year following year in ornamental seclusion from the follies
and fusses of the world, had to the Duke seemed rather
admirable and enviable. Often he himself had (for a minute
or so) meditated taking a fellowship at All Souls and spending
here in Oxford the greater part of his life. He had never been
young, and it never had occurred to him that the Warden
had been young once. To-night he saw the old man in a new
light—saw that he was mad. Here was a man who—for had
he not married and begotten a child?—must have known, in
some degree, the emotion of love. How, after that, could he
have gone on thus, year by year, rusting among his books,
asking no favour of life, waiting for death without a sign of
impatience? Why had he not killed himself long ago?
Why cumbered he the earth?

On the daïs an undergraduate was singing a song entitled
"She Loves Not Me". Such plaints are apt to leave us
unharrowed. Across the footlights of an opera-house, the
despair of some Italian tenor in red tights and a yellow wig
may be convincing enough. Not so, at a concert, the despair
of a shy British amateur in evening dress. The undergraduate on the daïs, fumbling with his sheet of music while
he predicted that only when he were "laid within the church-
yard cold and grey" would his lady begin to pity him,
seemed to the Duke rather ridiculous; but not half so
ridiculous as the Warden. This fictitious love-affair was less
nugatory than the actual humdrum for which Dr. Dobson
had sold his soul to the devil. Also, little as one might suspect
it, the warbler was perhaps expressing a genuine sentiment.
Zuleika herself, belike, was in his thoughts.

As he began the second stanza, predicting that when his
lady died too the angels of heaven would bear her straight to

him, the audience heard a loud murmur, or subdued roar, outside the Hall. And after a few bars the warbler suddenly ceased, staring straight in front of him as though he saw a vision. Automatically, all heads veered in the direction of his gaze. From the entrance, slowly along the aisle, came Zuleika, brilliant in black.

To the Duke, who had rapturously risen, she nodded and smiled as she swerved down on the chair beside him. She looked to him somehow different. He had quite forgiven her for being late; her mere presence was a perfect excuse. And the very change in her, though he could not define it, was somehow pleasing to him. He was about to question her, but she shook her head and held up to her lips a black-gloved forefinger, enjoining silence for the singer, who, with dogged British pluck, had harked back to the beginning of the second stanza. When his task was done and he shuffled down from the daïs, he received a great ovation. Zuleika, in the way peculiar to persons who are in the habit of appearing before the public, held her hands well above the level of her brow, and clapped them with a vigour demonstrative not less of her presence than of her delight.

"And now," she asked, turning to the Duke, "do you see? do you see?"

"Something, yes. But what?"

"Isn't it plain?" Lightly she touched the lobe of her left ear. "Aren't you flattered?"

He knew now what made the difference. It was that her little face was flanked by two black pearls.

"Think," said she, "how deeply I must have been brooding over you since we parted!"

"Is this really," he asked, pointing to the left ear-ring, "the pearl you wore to-day?"

"Yes. Isn't it strange? A man ought to be pleased when a woman goes quite unconsciously into mourning for him—goes just because she really does mourn him."

"I am more than pleased. I am touched. When did the change come?"

"I don't know. I only noticed it after dinner, when I saw myself in the mirror. All through dinner I had been thinking of you and of—well, of to-morrow. And this dear sensitive pink pearl had again expressed my soul. And there was I, in a yellow gown with green embroideries, gay as a jacamar, jarring hideously on myself. I covered my eyes and rushed upstairs, rang the bell and tore my things off. My maid was very cross."

Cross! The Duke was shot through with envy of one who was in a position to be unkind to Zuleika. "Happy maid!" he murmured. Zuleika replied that he was stealing her thunder: hadn't she envied the girl at his lodgings? "But *I*," she said, "wanted only to serve you in meekness. The idea of ever being pert to you didn't enter into my head. You show a side of your character as unpleasing as it was unforeseen."

"Perhaps then," said the Duke, "it is as well that I am going to die." She acknowledged his rebuke with a pretty gesture of penitence. "You may have been faultless in love," he added; "but you would not have laid down your life for me."

"Oh," she answered, "wouldn't I though? You don't know me. That is just the sort of thing I should have loved to do. I am much more romantic than you are, really. I wonder," she said, glancing at his breast, "if *your* pink pearl would have turned black? And I wonder if *you* would have taken the trouble to change that extraordinary coat you are wearing?"

In sooth, no costume could have been more beautifully Cimmerian than Zuleika's. And yet, thought the Duke, watching her as the concert proceeded, the effect of her was not lugubrious. Her darkness shone. The black satin gown she wore was a stream of shifting high-lights. Big black diamonds were around her throat and wrists, and tiny black diamonds starred the fan she wielded. In her hair gleamed a great raven's wing. And brighter, brighter than all these were her eyes. Assuredly no, there was nothing morbid about her. Would one even (wondered the Duke, for a disloyal instant) go so far as to say she was heartless? Ah no, she was merely strong. She was one who could tread the tragic plane without stumbling, and be resilient in the valley of the shadow. What she had just said was no more than the truth: she would have loved to die for him, had he not forfeited her heart. She would have asked no tears. That she had none to shed for him now, that she did but share his exhilaration, was the measure of her worthiness to have the homage of his self-slaughter.

"By the way," she whispered, "I want to ask one little favour of you. Will you, please, at the last moment to-morrow, call out my name in a loud voice, so that everyone around can hear?"

"Of course I will."

"So that no one shall ever be able to say it wasn't for me that you died, you know."

"May I use simply your Christian name?"

"Yes, I really don't see why you shouldn't—at such a moment."

"Thank you." His face glowed.

Thus did they commune, these two, radiant without and within. And behind them, throughout the Hall, the under-graduates craned their necks for a glimpse. The Duke's piano solo, which was the last item in the first half of the programme, was eagerly awaited. Already, whispered first from the lips of Oover and the others who had come on from the Junta, the news of his resolve had gone from ear to ear among the men. He, for his part, had forgotten the scene at the Junta, the baleful effect of his example. For him the Hall was a cave of solitude—no one there but Zuleika and himself. Yet almost, like the late Mr. John Bright, he heard in the air the beating of the wings of the Angel of Death.

Not awful wings; little wings that sprouted from the shoulders of a rosy and blindfold child. Love and Death—for him they were exquisitely one. And it seemed to him, when his turn came to play, that he floated, rather than walked, to the daïs.

He had not considered what he would play to-night. Nor, maybe, was he conscious now of choosing. His fingers caressed the keyboard vaguely; and anon this ivory had voice and language; and for its master, and for some of his hearers, arose a vision. And it was as though in delicate procession, very slowly, listless with weeping, certain figures passed by, hooded, and drooping forasmuch as by the loss of him whom they were following to his grave their own hold on life had been loosened. He had been so beautiful and young. Lo, he was but a burden to be carried hence, dust to be hidden out of sight. Very slowly, very wretchedly they went by. But, as they went, another feeling, faint at first, an all but imperceptible current, seemed to flow through the procession; and now one, now another of the mourners would look wanly up, with cast-back hood, as though listening; and anon all were listening on their way, first in wonder, then in rapture; for the soul of their friend was singing to them: they heard his voice, but clearer and more blithe than they had ever known it—a voice etherealised by a triumph of joy that was not yet for them to share. But presently the voice receded, its echoes dying away into the sphere whence it came. It ceased; and the mourners were left alone again with their sorrow, and passed on all unsolaced, and drooping, weeping.

Soon after the Duke had begun to play, an invisible figure came and stood by and listened: a frail man, dressed in the fashion of 1840; the shade of none other than Frédéric Chopin. Behind whom, a moment later, came a woman of somewhat masculine aspect and dominant demeanour, mounting guard over him, and, as it were, ready to catch him if he fell. He bowed his head lower and lower, he looked up with an ecstasy more and more intense, according to the procedure of his Marche Funèbre. And among the audience, too, there was a bowing and uplifting of heads, just as among the figures of the mourners evoked. Yet the head of the player himself was all the while erect, and his face glad and serene. Nobly sensitive as was his playing of the mournful passages, he smiled brilliantly through them.

And Zuleika returned his gaze with a smile not less gay. She was not sure what he was playing. But she assumed that it was for her, and that the music had some reference to his impending death. She was one of the people who say: "I don't know anything about music really, but I know what I like." And she liked this; and she beat time to it with her fan. She thought her Duke looked very handsome. She was proud of him. Strange that this time yesterday she had been wildly in love with him! Strange, too, that this time tomorrow he would be dead! She was immensely glad she had saved him this afternoon. To-morrow! There came back to her what he had told her about the omen at Tankerton, that stately home: "On the eve of the death of a Duke of Dorset, two black owls come always and perch on the battlements. They remain there through the night, hooting. At dawn they fly away, none knows whither." Perhaps, thought she, at this very moment these two birds were on the battlements.

The music ceased. In the hush that followed it, her applause rang sharp and notable. Not so Chopin's. Of him and his intense excitement none but his companion was aware. "Plus fin que Pachmann!" he reiterated, waving his arms wildly, and dancing.

"Tu auras une migraine affreuse. Rentrons, petit cœur!" said George Sand, gently but firmly.

"Laisse-moi le saluer," cried the composer, struggling in her grasp.

"Demain soir, oui. Il sera parmi nous," said the novelist,

as she hurried him away. "Moi aussi," she added to herself, "je me promets un beau plaisir en faisant la connaissance de ce jeune homme."

Zuleika was the first to rise as "ce jeune homme" came down from the daïs. Now was the interval between the two parts of the programme. There was a general creaking and scraping of pushed-back chairs as the audience rose and went forth into the night. The noise aroused from sleep the good Warden, who, having peered at his programme, complimented the Duke with old-world courtesy and went to sleep again. Zuleika, thrusting her fan under one arm, shook the player by both hands. Also, she told him that she knew nothing about music really, but that she knew what she liked. As she passed with him up the aisle, she said this again. People who say it are never tired of saying it.

Outside, the crowd was greater than ever. All the undergraduates from all the Colleges seemed now to be concentrated in the great Front Quadrangle of Judas. Even in the glow of the Japanese lanterns that hung around in honour of the concert, the faces of the lads looked a little pale. For it was known by all now that the Duke was to die. Even while the concert was in progress, the news had spread out from the Hall, through the thronged doorway, down the thronged steps, to the confines of the crowd. Nor had Oover and the other men from the Junta made any secret of their own determination. And now, as the rest saw Zuleika yet again at close quarters, and verified their remembrance of her, the half-formed desire in them to die too was hardened to a vow.

You cannot make a man by standing a sheep on its hind-legs. But by standing a flock of sheep in that position you can make a crowd of men. If man were not a gregarious animal, the world might have achieved, by this time, some real progress towards civilisation. Segregate him, and he is no fool. But let him loose among his fellows, and he is lost—

he becomes just an unit in unreason. If any one of the undergraduates had met Miss Dobson in the desert of Sahara, he would have fallen in love with her; but not one in a thousand of them would have wished to die because she did not love him. The Duke's was a peculiar case. For him to fall in love was itself a violent peripety, bound to produce a violent upheaval; and such was his pride that for his love to be unrequited would naturally enamour him of death. These other, these quite ordinary, young men were the victims less of Zuleika than of the Duke's example, and of one another. A crowd, proportionately to its size, magnifies all that in its units pertains to the emotions, and diminishes all that in them pertains to thought. It was because these undergraduates were a crowd that their passion for Zuleika was so intense; and it was because they were a crowd that they followed so blindly the lead given to them. To die for Miss Dobson was "the thing to do". The Duke was going to do it. The Junta was going to do it. It is a hateful fact, but we must face the fact, that snobbishness was one of the springs to the tragedy here chronicled.

We may set to this crowd's credit that it refrained now from following Zuleika. Not one of the ladies present was deserted by her escort. All the men recognised the Duke's right to be alone with Zuleika now. We may set also to their credit that they carefully guarded the ladies from all knowledge of what was afoot.

Side by side, the great lover and his beloved wandered away, beyond the light of the Japanese lanterns, and came to Salt Cellar.

The moon, like a gardenia in the night's button-hole—but no! why should a writer never be able to mention the moon without likening her to something else—usually something to which she bears not the faintest resemblance? . . . The moon, looking like nothing whatsoever but herself, was engaged in her old and futile endeavour to mark the hours correctly on the sun-dial at the centre of the lawn. Never, except once, late one night in the eighteenth century, when the toper who was Sub-Warden had spent an hour in trying to set his watch here, had she received the slightest encouragement. Still she wanly persisted. And this was the more absurd in her because Salt Cellar offered very good scope for those legitimate effects of hers which we one and all admire. Was it nothing to her to have cut those black shadows across the cloisters? Was it nothing to her that she so magically mingled her rays with the candlelight shed forth from Zuleika's bedroom? Nothing, that she had cleansed the lawn of all its colour, and made of it a platform of silver-grey, fit for fairies to dance on?

If Zuleika, as she paced the gravel path, had seen how transfigured—how nobly like the Tragic Muse—she was just now, she could not have gone on bothering the Duke for a keepsake of the tragedy that was to be.

She was still set on having his two studs. He was still firm in his refusal to misappropriate those heirlooms. In vain she pointed out to him that the pearls he meant, the white ones, no longer existed; that the pearls he was wearing were no more "entailed" than if he had got them yesterday. "And you actually *did* get them yesterday," she said. "And from me. And I want them back."

"You are ingenious," he admitted. "I, in my simple way, am but head of the Tanville-Tankerton family. Had you accepted my offer of marriage, you would have had the right to wear these two pearls during your life-time. I am very happy to die for you. But tamper with the property of my successor I cannot and will not. I am sorry," he added.

"Sorry!" echoed Zuleika. "Yes, and you were 'sorry' you couldn't dine with me to-night. But any little niggling scruple is more to you than I am. What old maids men are!" And viciously with her fan she struck one of the cloister pillars.

Her outburst was lost on the Duke. At her taunt about his not dining with her, he had stood still, clapping one hand to his brow. The events of the early evening swept back to him—his speech, its unforeseen and horrible reception. He saw again the preternaturally solemn face of Oover, and the flushed faces of the rest. He had thought, as he pointed down to the abyss over which he stood, these fellows would recoil, and pull themselves together. They had recoiled, and pulled themselves together, only in the manner of athletes about to spring. He was responsible for them. His own life was his to lose: others he must not squander. Besides, he had reckoned to die alone, unique; aloft and apart . . . "There is something—something I had forgotten," he said to Zuleika, "something that will be a great shock to you"; and he gave her an outline of what had passed at the Junta.

"And you are sure they really *meant* it?" she asked in a voice that trembled.

"I fear so. But they were over-excited. They will recant their folly. I shall force them to."

"They are not children. You yourself have just been calling them 'men'. Why should they obey you?"

She turned at sound of a footstep, and saw a young man approaching. He wore a coat like the Duke's, and in his hand he dangled a handkerchief. He bowed awkwardly, and, holding out the handkerchief, said to her: "I beg your pardon, but I think you dropped this. I have just picked it up."

Zuleika looked at the handkerchief, which was obviously a man's, and smilingly shook her head.

"I don't think you know The MacQuern," said the Duke, with sulky grace. "This," he said to the intruder, "is Miss Dobson.

"And is it really true," asked Zuleika, retaining The MacQuern's hand, "that you want to die for me?"

Well, the Scots are a self-seeking and a resolute, but a shy, race; swift to act, when swiftness is needed, but seldom knowing quite what to say. The MacQuern, with native reluctance to give something for nothing, had determined to have the pleasure of knowing the young lady for whom he was to lay down his life; and this purpose he had, by the simple stratagem of his own handkerchief, achieved. Nevertheless, in answer to Zuleika's question, and with the pressure of her hand to inspire him, the only word that rose to his lips was "Ay" (which may be roughly translated as "Yes").

"You will do nothing of the sort," interposed the Duke.

"There," said Zuleika, still retaining The MacQuern's hand, "you see, it is forbidden. You must not defy our dear little Duke. He is not used to it. It is not done."

"I don't know," said The MacQuern, with a stony glance at the Duke, "that he has anything to do with the matter."

"He is older and wiser than you. More a man of the world. Regard him as your tutor."

"Do *you* want me not to die for you?" asked the young man.

"Ah, *I* should not dare to impose my wishes on you," said she, dropping his hand. "Even," she added, "if I knew what my wishes were. And I don't. I know only that I think it is very, very beautiful of you to think of dying for me."

"Then that settles it," said The MacQuern.

"No, no! You must not let yourself be influenced by *me*. Besides, I am not in a mood to influence anybody. I am overwhelmed. Tell me," she said, heedless of the Duke, who stood tapping his heel on the ground, with every manifestation of disapproval and impatience, "tell me, is it true that some of the other men love me too, and—feel as you do?"

The MacQuern said cautiously that he could answer for no one but himself. "But," he allowed, "I saw a good many men whom I know, outside the Hall here, just now, and they seemed to have made up their minds."

"To die for me? To-morrow?"

"To-morrow. After the Eights, I suppose; at the same time as the Duke. It wouldn't do to leave the races undecided."

"Of *course* not. But the poor dears! It is too touching! I have done nothing, nothing to deserve it."

"Nothing whatsoever," said the Duke dryly.

"Oh *he*," said Zuleika, "thinks me an unredeemed brute; just because I don't love him. *You*, dear Mr. MacQuern—does one call you 'Mr.'? 'The' would sound so odd in the vocative. And I can't very well call you 'MacQuern'—*you* don't think me unkind, do you? I simply can't bear to think of all these young lives cut short without my having done a thing to brighten them. What can I do?—what can I do to show my gratitude?"

An idea struck her. She looked up to the lit window of her room. "Mélisande!" she called.

A figure appeared at the window. "Mademoiselle désire?"

"My tricks, Mélisande! Bring down the box, quick!" She turned excitedly to the two young men. "It is all I can do in return, you see. If I could dance for them, I would. If I could sing, I would sing to them. I do what I can. You," she said to the Duke, "must go on to the platform and announce it."

"Announce what?"

"Why, that I am going to do my tricks! All you need say is 'Ladies and gentlemen, I have the pleasure to——' What is the matter now?"

"You make me feel slightly unwell," said the Duke.

"And *you* are the most d-dis-disobliging and the unkindest and the b-beastliest person I ever met," Zuleika sobbed at him through her hands. The MacQuern glared reproaches at him. So did Mélisande, who had just appeared through the postern, holding in her arms the great casket of malachite. A painful scene; and the Duke gave in. He said he would do anything—anything. Peace was restored.

The MacQuern had relieved Mélisande of her burden, and to him was the privilege of bearing it, in procession with his adored and her quelled mentor, towards the Hall.

Zuleika babbled like a child going to a juvenile party. This was the great night, as yet, in her life. Illustrious enough already it had seemed to her, as eve of that ultimate flattery vowed her by the Duke. So fine a thing had his doom seemed to her—his doom alone—that it had sufficed to flood her pink pearl with the right hue. And now not on him alone need she ponder. Now he was but the centre of a group—a group that might grow and grow—a group that might with a little encouragement be a multitude. . . . With such hopes dimly whirling in the recesses of her soul, her beautiful red lips babbled.

# X

SOUNDS of a violin, drifting out through the open windows of the Hall, suggested that the second part of the concert had begun. All the undergraduates, however, except the few who figured in the programme, had waited outside till their mistress should re-appear. The sisters and cousins of the Judas men had been escorted back to their places and hurriedly left there.

It was a hushed, tense crowd.

"The poor darlings!" murmured Zuleika, pausing to survey them. "And oh," she exclaimed, "there won't be room for all of them in there!"

"You might give an 'overflow' performance out here afterwards," suggested the Duke, grimly.

This idea flashed on her a better. Why not give her performance here and now?—now, so eager was she for contact, as it were, with this crowd; here, by moonlight, in the pretty glow of these paper lanterns. Yes, she said, let it be here and now; and she bade the Duke make the announcement.

"What shall I say?" he asked. " 'Gentlemen, I have the pleasure to announce that Miss Zuleika Dobson, the world-renowned She-Wizard, will now oblige'? Or shall I call them 'Gents', *tout court*?"

She could afford to laugh at his ill-humour. She had his promise of obedience. She told him to say something graceful and simple.

The noise of the violin had ceased. There was not a breath of wind. The crowd in the quadrangle was as still and

as silent as the night itself. Nowhere a tremour. And it was
borne in on Zuleika that this crowd had one mind as well as
one heart—a common resolve, calm and clear, as well as a
common passion. No need for her to strengthen the spell
now. No waverers here. And thus it came true that gratitude
was the sole motive for her display.

She stood with eyes downcast and hands folded behind her,
moonlit in the glow of lanterns, modest to the point of
pathos, while the Duke gracefully and simply introduced her
to the multitude. He was, he said, empowered by the lady
who stood beside him to say that she would be pleased to
give them an exhibition of her skill in the art to which she
had devoted her life—an art which, more potently perhaps
than any other, touched in mankind the sense of mystery and
stirred the faculty of wonder; the most truly romantic of all
the arts: he referred to the art of conjuring. It was not too
much to say that by her mastery of this art, in which hitherto,
it must be confessed, women had made no very great mark,
Miss Zuleika Dobson (for such was the name of the lady who
stood beside him) had earned the esteem of the whole
civilised world. And here in Oxford, and in this College
especially, she had a peculiar claim to—might he say?—their
affectionate regard, inasmuch as she was the grand-daughter
of their venerable and venerated Warden.

As the Duke ceased, there came from his hearers a sound
like the rustling of leaves. In return for it, Zuleika performed that graceful act of subsidence to the verge of
collapse which is usually kept for the delectation of some
royal person. And indeed, in the presence of this doomed
congress, she did experience humility; for she was not
altogether without imagination. But, as she arose from her
"bob," she was her own bold self again, bright mistress of
the situation.

It was impossible for her to give her entertainment in full.
Some of her tricks (notably the Secret Aquarium, and the

Blazing Ball of Worsted) needed special preparation, and a table fitted with a "servante" or secret tray. The table for to-night's performance was an ordinary one, brought out from the porter's lodge. The MacQuern deposited on it the great casket. Zuleika, retaining him as her assistant, picked nimbly out from their places and put in array the curious appurtenances of her art—the Magic Canister, the Demon Egg-Cup, and the sundry other vessels which, lost property of young Edward Gibbs, had been by a Romanoff transmuted from wood to gold, and were now by the moon reduced temporarily to silver.

In a great dense semicircle the young men disposed themselves around her. Those who were in front squatted down on the gravel; those who were behind knelt; the rest stood. Young Oxford! Here, in this mass of boyish faces, all fused and obliterated, was the realisation of that phrase. Two or three thousands of human bodies, human souls? Yet the effect of them in the moonlight was as of one great passive monster.

So was it seen by the Duke, as he stood leaning against the wall, behind Zuleika's table. He saw it as a monster couchant and enchanted, a monster that was to die; and its death was in part his own doing. But remorse in him gave place to hostility. Zuleika had begun her performance. She was producing the Barber's Pole from her mouth. And it was to her that the Duke's heart went suddenly out in tenderness and pity. He forgot her levity and vanity—her wickedness, as he had inwardly called it. He thrilled with that intense anxiety which comes to a man when he sees his beloved offering to the public an exhibition of her skill, be it in singing, acting, dancing, or any other art. Would she acquit herself well? The lover's trepidation is painful enough when the beloved has genius—how should these clods appreciate her? and who set them in judgment over her? It must be worse when the beloved has mediocrity. And Zuleika, in conjuring, had rather less than that. Though indeed she took herself quite seriously as a conjurer, she brought to her art neither conscience nor ambition, in any true sense of those words. Since her début, she had learned nothing and forgotten nothing. The stale and narrow repertory which she had acquired from Edward Gibbs was all she had to offer; and this, and her marked lack of skill, she eked out with the self-same "patter" that had sufficed that impossible young man. It was especially her jokes that now sent shudders up the spine of her lover, and brought tears to his eyes, and kept him in a state of terror as to what she would say next. "You see," she had exclaimed lightly after the production of the Barber's Pole, "how easy it is to set up business as a hair-dresser." Over the Demon Egg-Cup she said that the egg was "as good as fresh." And her constantly reiterated catch-phrase—"Well, this is rather queer!"—was the most distressing thing of all.

The Duke blushed to think what these men thought of her. Would love were blind! These her lovers were doubtless judging her. They forgave her—confound their impudence!—because of her beauty. The banality of her performance was an added grace. It made her piteous. Damn them, they were sorry for her. Little Noaks was squatting in the front row, peering up at her through his spectacles. Noaks was as sorry for her as the rest of them. Why didn't the earth yawn and swallow them all up?

Our hero's unreasoning rage was fed by a not unreasonable jealousy. It was clear to him that Zuleika had forgotten his existence. To-day, as soon as he had killed her love, she had shown him how much less to her was his love than the crowd's. And now again it was only the crowd she cared for. He followed with his eyes her long slender figure as she threaded her way in and out of the crowd, sinuously, confidingly, producing a penny from one lad's elbow, a threepenny-bit from between another's neck and collar, half a crown from another's hair, and always repeating in that flute-like voice of hers: "Well, this is rather queer!" Hither and thither she fared, her neck and arms gleaming white from the luminous blackness of her dress, in the luminous blueness of the night. At a distance, she might have been a wraith; or a breeze made visible; a vagrom breeze, warm and delicate, and in league with death.

Yes, that is how she might have seemed to a casual observer. But to the Duke there was nothing weird about her: she was radiantly a woman; a goddess; and his first and last love. Bitter his heart was, but only against the mob she wooed, not against her for wooing it. She was cruel? All goddesses are that. She was demeaning herself? His soul welled up anew in pity, in passion.

Yonder, in the Hall, the concert ran its course, making a feeble incidental music to the dark emotions of the quadrangle. It ended somewhat before the close of Zuleika's rival show; and then the steps from the Hall were thronged by ladies, who, with a sprinkling of dons, stood in attitudes of refined displeasure and vulgar curiosity. The Warden was just awake enough to notice the sea of undergraduates. Suspecting some breach of College discipline, he retired hastily to his own quarters, for fear his dignity might be somehow compromised.

Was there ever, I wonder, an historian so pure as not to have wished just once to fob off on his readers just one bright fable for effect? I find myself sorely tempted to tell you that on Zuleika, as her entertainment drew to a close, the spirit of the higher thaumaturgy descended like a flame and found in her a worthy agent. Specious Apollyon whispers to me: "Where would be the harm? Tell your readers that she cast a seed on the ground, and that therefrom presently arose a tamarind-tree which blossomed and bore fruit and, withering, vanished. Or say she conjured from an empty basket of osier a hissing and bridling snake. Why not? Your readers would

be excited, gratified. And you would never be found out."
But the grave eyes of Clio are bent on me, her servant. Oh
pardon, madam: I did but waver for an instant. It is not too
late to tell my readers that the climax of Zuleika's entertainment was only that dismal affair, the Magic Canister.

It she took from the table, and, holding it aloft, cried:
"Now, before I say good night, I want to see if I have your
confidence. But you mustn't think this is the confidence
trick!" She handed the vessel to The MacQuern, who,
looking like an over-grown acolyte, bore it after her as she
went again among the audience. Pausing before a man in the
front row, she asked him if he would trust her with his
watch. He held it out to her. "Thank you," she said, letting
her fingers touch his for a moment before she dropped it into
the Magic Canister. From another man she borrowed a
cigarette-case, from another a neck-tie, from another a pair
of sleeve-links, from Noaks a ring—one of those iron rings
which are supposed, rightly or wrongly, to alleviate rheumatism. And when she had made an ample selection, she
began her return journey to the table.

On her way she saw in the shadow of the wall the figure of
her forgotten Duke. She saw him, the one man she had ever
loved, also the first man who had wished definitely to die for
her; and she was touched by remorse. She had said she
would remember him to her dying day; and already . . .
But had he not refused her the wherewithal to remember
him—the pearls she needed as the *clou* of her dear collection,
the great relic among relics?

"Would you trust me with your studs?" she asked him, in
a voice that could be heard throughout the quadrangle, with
a smile that was for him alone.

There was no help for it. He quickly extricated from his
shirt-front the black pearl and the pink. Her thanks had a
special emphasis.

The MacQuern placed the Magic Canister before her on

the table. She pressed the outer sheath down on it. Then she inverted it so that the contents fell into the false lid; then she opened it, looked into it, and, exclaiming: "Well, this is rather queer!" held it up so that the audience whose intelligence she was insulting might see there was nothing in it.

"Accidents," she said, "will happen in the best-regulated canisters! But I think there is just a chance that I shall be able to restore your property. Excuse me for a moment." She then shut the canister, released the false lid, made several passes over it, opened it, looked into it and said with a flourish: "Now I can clear my character!" Again she went among the crowd, attended by The MacQuern; and the loans—priceless now because she had touched them—were in due course severally restored. When she took the canister from her acolyte, only the two studs remained in it.

Not since the night of her flitting from the Gibbs' humble home had Zuleika thieved. Was she a back-slider? Would she rob the Duke, and his heir-presumptive, and Tanville-Tankertons yet unborn? Alas, yes. But what she now did was proof that she had qualms. And her way of doing it showed that for legerdemain she had after all a natural aptitude which, properly trained, might have won for her an honourable place in at least the second rank of contemporary prestidigitators. With a gesture of her disengaged hand, so swift as to be scarcely visible, she unhooked her ear-rings and "passed" them into the canister. This she did as she turned away from the crowd, on her way to the Duke. At the same moment, in a manner technically not less good, though morally deplorable, she withdrew the studs and "vanished" them into her bosom.

Was it triumph, or shame, or of both a little, that so flushed her cheeks as she stood before the man she had robbed? Or was it the excitement of giving a present to the man she had loved? Certain it is that the nakedness of her ears gave a new look to her face—a primitive look, open and sweetly wild. The Duke saw the difference, without noticing the cause. She was more adorable than ever. He blenched and swayed as in proximity to a loveliness beyond endurance. His heart cried out within him. A sudden mist came over his eyes.

In the canister that she held out to him, the two pearls rattled like dice.

"Keep them!" he whispered.

"I shall," she whispered back, almost shyly. "But these, these are for you." And she took one of his hands, and, holding it open, tilted the canister over it, and let drop into it the two ear-rings, and went quickly away.

As she re-appeared at the table, the crowd gave her a long ovation of gratitude for her performance—an ovation all the more impressive because it was solemn and subdued. She curtseyed again and again, not indeed with the timid simplicity of her first obeisance (so familiar already was she with the thought of the crowd's doom), but rather in the manner of a prima donna—chin up, eyelids down, all teeth manifest, and hands from the bosom flung ecstatically wide asunder.

You know how, at a concert, a prima donna who has just sung insists on shaking hands with the accompanist, and dragging him forward, to show how beautiful her nature is, into the applause that is for herself alone. And your heart, like mine, has gone out to the wretched victim. Even so would you have felt for The MacQuern when Zuleika, on the implied assumption that half the credit was his, grasped him by the wrist, and, continuing to curtsey, would not release him till the last echoes of the clapping had died away.

The ladies on the steps of the Hall moved down into the quadrangle, spreading their resentment like a miasma. The tragic passion of the crowd was merged in mere awkwardness. There was a general movement towards the College gate.

Zuleika was putting her tricks back into the great casket,
The MacQuern assisting her. The Scots, as I have said, are a
shy race, but a resolute and a self-seeking. This young
chieftain had not yet recovered from what his heroine had let
him in for. But he did not lose the opportunity of asking
her to lunch with him to-morrow.

"Delighted," she said, fitting the Demon Egg-Cup into
its groove. Then, looking up at him: "Are you popular?"
she asked. "Have you many friends?" He nodded. She
said he must invite them all.

This was a blow to the young man, who, at once thrifty
and infatuate, had planned a luncheon *à deux*. "I had
hoped——" he began.

"Vainly," she cut him short.

There was a pause. "Whom shall I invite, then?"

"I don't know any of them. How should I have pre-
ferences?" She remembered the Duke. She looked round
and saw him still standing in the shadow of the wall. He
came towards her. "Of course," she said hastily to her host,
"you must ask *him*."

The MacQuern complied. He turned to the Duke and told
him that Miss Dobson had very kindly promised to lunch
with him to-morrow. "And," said Zuleika, "I simply *won't*
unless you will."

The Duke looked at her. Had it not been arranged that he
and she should spend his last day together? Did it mean
nothing that she had given him her ear-rings? Quickly
drawing about him some remnants of his tattered pride, he
hid his wound, and accepted the invitation.

"It seems a shame," said Zuleika to The MacQuern, "to
ask you to bring this great heavy box all the way back again.
But——"

Those last poor rags of pride fell away now. The Duke
threw a prehensile hand on the casket, and, coldly glaring at
The MacQuern, pointed with his other hand towards the

College gate. He, and he alone, was going to see Zuleika home. It was his last night on earth, and he was not to be trifled with. Such was the message of his eyes. The Scotsman's flashed back a precisely similar message.

Men had fought for Zuleika, but never in her presence. Her eyes dilated. She had not the slightest impulse to throw herself between the two antagonists. Indeed, she stepped back, so as not to be in the way. A short sharp fight—how much better that is than bad blood! She hoped the better man would win; and (do not misjudge her) she rather hoped this man was the Duke. It occurred to her—a vague memory of some play or picture—that she ought to be holding aloft a candelabrum of lit tapers; no, that was only done indoors, and in the eighteenth century. Ought she to hold a sponge? Idle, these speculations of hers, and based on complete ignorance of the manners and customs of undergraduates. The Duke and The MacQuern would never have come to blows in the presence of a lady. Their conflict was necessarily spiritual.

And it was the Scotsman, Scots though he was, who had to yield. Cowed by something daemonic in the will-power pitted against his, he found himself retreating in the direction indicated by the Duke's forefinger.

As he disappeared into the porch, Zuleika turned to the Duke. "You were splendid," she said softly. He knew that very well. Does the stag in his hour of victory need a diploma from the hind? Holding in his hands the malachite casket that was the symbol of his triumph, the Duke smiled dictatorially at his darling. He came near to thinking of her as a chattel. Then with a pang he remembered his abject devotion to her. Abject no longer though! The victory he had just won restored his manhood, his sense of supremacy among his fellows. He loved this woman on equal terms. She was transcendent? So was he, Dorset. To-night the world had on its moonlit surface two great ornaments—Zuleika and himself. Neither of the pair could be replaced. Was one of them to be shattered? Life and love were good. He had been mad to think of dying.

No word was spoken as they went together to Salt Cellar. She expected him to talk about her conjuring tricks. Could he have been disappointed? She dared not inquire; for she had the sensitiveness, though no other quality whatsoever, of the true artist. She felt herself aggrieved. She had half a mind to ask him to give her back her ear-rings. And by the way, he hadn't yet thanked her for them! Well, she would make allowances for a condemned man. And again she remembered the omen of which he had told her. She looked at him, and then up into the sky. "This same moon," she said to herself, "sees the battlements of Tankerton. Does she see two black owls there? Does she hear them hooting?"

They were in Salt Cellar now. "Mélisande!" she called up to her window.

"Hush!" said the Duke, "I have something to say to you."

"Well, you can say it all the better without that great box in your hands. I want my maid to carry it up to my room for me." And again she called out for Mélisande, and received no answer. "I suppose she's in the housekeeper's room or somewhere. You had better put the box down inside the door. She can bring it up later."

She pushed open the postern; and the Duke, as he stepped across the threshold, thrilled with a romantic awe. Re-emerging a moment later into the moonlight, he felt that she had been right about the box: it was fatal to self-expression and he was glad he had not tried to speak on the way from the Front Quad: the soul needs gesture; and the Duke's first gesture now was to seize Zuleika's hands in his.

She was too startled to move. "Zuleika!" he whispered. She was too angry to speak, but with a sudden twist she freed her wrists and darted back.

He laughed. "You are afraid of me. You are afraid to let me kiss you, because you are afraid of loving me. This afternoon—here—I all but kissed you. I mistook you for Death. I was enamoured of Death. I was a fool. That is what *you* are, you incomparable darling: you are a fool. You are afraid of life. I am not. I love life. I am going to live for you, do you hear?"

She stood with her back to the postern. Anger in her eyes had given place to scorn. "You mean," she said, "that you go back on your promise?"

"You will release me from it."

"You mean you are afraid to die?"

"You will not be guilty of my death. You love me."

"Good night, you miserable coward." She stepped back through the postern.

"Don't, Zuleika! Miss Dobson, don't! Pull yourself together! Reflect! I implore you . . . You will re-pent . . ."

Slowly she closed the postern on him.

"You will repent. I shall wait here, under your win-dow . . ."

He heard a bolt rasped into its socket. He heard the retreat of a light tread on the paven hall.

And he hadn't even kissed her! That was his first thought. He ground his heel in the gravel.

And he had hurt her wrists! This was Zuleika's first thought, as she came into her bedroom. Yes, there were two red marks where he had held her. No man had ever dared to lay hands on her. With a sense of contamination, she proceeded to wash her hands thoroughly with soap and water. From time to time such words as "cad" and "beast" came through her teeth.

She dried her hands and flung herself into a chair, arose and went pacing the room. So this was the end of her great night! What had she done to deserve it? How had he dared?

There was a sound as of rain against the window. She was glad. The night needed cleansing.

He had told her she was afraid of life. Life!—to have herself caressed by *him*; humbly to devote herself to being humbly doted on; to be the slave of a slave; to swim in a private pond of treacle—ugh! If the thought weren't so cloying and degrading, it would be laughable.

For a moment her hands hovered over those two golden and gemmed volumes encasing Bradshaw and the A.B.C. Guide. To leave Oxford by an early train, leave him to drown unthanked, unlooked-at. . . . But this could not be done without slighting all those hundreds of other men . . . And besides . . .

Again that sound on the window-pane. This time it startled her. There seemed to be no rain. Could it have been—little bits of gravel? She darted noiselessly to the window, pushed it open, and looked down. She saw the upturned face of the Duke. She stepped back, trembling with fury, staring around her. Inspiration came.

She thrust her head out again. "Are you there?" she whispered.

"Yes, yes. I knew you would come."

"Wait a moment, wait!"

The water-jug stood where she had left it, on the floor by the wash-stand. It was almost full, rather heavy. She bore it steadily to the window, and looked out.

"Come a little nearer!" she whispered.

The upturned and moonlit face obeyed her. She saw its lips forming the word "Zuleika." She took careful aim.

Full on the face crashed the cascade of moonlit water, shooting out on all sides like the petals of some great silver anemone.

She laughed shrilly as she leapt back, letting the empty jug roll over on the carpet. Then she stood tense crouching, her hands to her mouth, her eyes askance, as much as to say: "Now I've done it!" She listened hard, holding her breath. In the stillness of the night was a faint sound of dripping water, and presently of footsteps going away. Then stillness unbroken.

## XI

I SAID that I was Clio's servant. And I felt, when I said it, that you looked at me dubiously, and murmured among yourselves.

Not that you doubted I was somewhat connected with Clio's household. The lady after whom I have named this book is alive, and well known to some of you personally, to all of you by repute. Nor had you finished my first page before you guessed my theme to be that episode in her life which caused so great a sensation among the newspaper-reading public a few years ago. (It all seems but yesterday, does it not? They are still vivid to us, those headlines. We have hardly yet ceased to be edified by the morals pointed in those leading articles.) And yet very soon you found me behaving just like any novelist—reporting the exact words that passed between the protagonists at private interviews—aye, and the exact thoughts and emotions that were in their breasts. Little wonder that you wondered! Let me make things clear to you.

I have my mistress's leave to do this. At first (for reasons which you will presently understand) she demurred. But I pointed out to her that I had been placed in a false position, and that until this were rectified neither she nor I could reap the credit due to us.

Know, then, that for a long time Clio had been thoroughly discontented. She was happy enough, she says, when first she left the home of Pierus, her father, to become a Muse. On those humble beginnings she looks back with affection. She kept only one servant, Herodotus. The romantic element in him appealed to her. He died, and she had about her a large staff of able and faithful servants, whose way of doing their work irritated and depressed her. To them, apparently, life consisted of nothing but politics and military operations—things to which she, being a woman, was somewhat indifferent. She was jealous of Melpomene. It seemed to her that her own servants worked from without at a mass of dry details which might as well be forgotten. Melpomene's worked on material that was eternally interesting— the souls of men and women; and not from without, either; but rather casting themselves into those souls and showing to us the essence of them. She was particularly struck by a remark of Aristotle's, that tragedy was *more philosophic* than history, inasmuch as it concerned itself with what might be, while history was concerned with merely what had been. This summed up for her what she had often felt, but could not have exactly formulated. She saw that the department over which she presided was at best an inferior one. She saw that just what she had liked—and rightly liked—in poor dear Herodotus was just what prevented him from being a good historian. It was wrong to mix up facts and fancies. But why should her present servants deal with only one little special set of the variegated facts of life? It was not in her power to interfere. The Nine, by the terms of the charter that Zeús had granted to them, were bound to leave their servants an absolutely free hand. But Clio could at least refrain from reading the works which, by a legal fiction, she was supposed to inspire. Once or twice in the course of a century, she would glance into this or that new history book, only to lay it down with a shrug of her shoulders. Some of the mediæval chronicles she rather liked. But when, one day, Pallas asked her what she thought of *The Decline and Fall of the Roman Empire* her only answer was ὅστις τοῖα ἔχει ἐν ἡδονῇ ἔχει ἐν ἡδονῇ τοῖα (For people who like that kind of thing, that is the kind of thing they like.) This she did let slip. Generally, throughout all the centuries, she kept up a pretence of thinking history the greatest of all the arts. She always held her head high among her Sisters. It was only on the sly that she was an omnivorous reader of dramatic and lyric poetry. She watched with keen interest the earliest developments of the prose romance in southern Europe; and after the publication of "Clarissa Harlowe" she spent practically all her time in reading novels. It was not until the spring of the year 1863 that an entirely new element forced itself into her peaceful life. Zeus fell in love with her.

To us, for whom so quickly "time doth transfix the flourish set on youth", there is something strange, even a trifle ludicrous, in the thought that Zeus, after all these years, is still at the beck and call of his passions. And it seems anyhow lamentable that he has not yet gained self-confidence enough to appear in his own person to the lady of his choice, and is still at pains to transform himself into whatever object he deems likeliest to please her. To Clio, suddenly from Olympus, he flashed down in the semblance of Kinglake's *Invasion of the Crimea* (four vols., large 8vo, half-calf). She saw through his disguise immediately, and, with great courage and independence, bade him begone. Rebuffed, he was not deflected. Indeed it would seem that Clio's high spirit did but sharpen his desire. Hardly a day passed but he appeared in what he hoped would be the irresistible form—a recently discovered fragment of Polybius, an advance copy of the forthcoming issue of *The Historical Review*, the notebook of Professor Carl Vörtschlaffen . . . One day, all-prying Hermes told him of Clio's secret addiction to novel-reading. Thenceforth, year in, year out, it was in the form of fiction that Zeus wooed her. The sole result was that she grew sick of the sight of novels, and found a perverse pleasure in reading history. These dry details of what had actually happened were a relief, she told herself, from all that make-believe.

One Sunday afternoon—the day before that very Monday on which this narrative opens—it occurred to her how fine a thing history might be if the historian had the novelist's privileges. Suppose he could be present at every scene which he was going to describe, a presence invisible and inevitable, and equipped with power to see into the breasts of all the persons whose actions he set himself to watch . . .

While the Muse was thus musing, Zeus (disguised as Mrs. Annie S. Swan's latest work) paid his usual visit. She let her eyes rest on him. Hither and thither she divided her swift mind, and addressed him in winged words: "Zeus, father of gods and men, cloud-compeller, what wouldst thou of me? But first will I say what I would of thee"; and she besought him to extend to the writers of history such privileges as are granted to novelists. His whole manner had changed. He listened to her with the massive gravity of a ruler who never yet has allowed private influence to obscure his judgment. He was silent for some time after her appeal. Then, in a voice of thunder, which made quake the slopes of Parnassus, he gave his answer. He admitted the disabilities under which historians laboured. But the novelists—were they not equally handicapped? They had to treat of persons who never existed, events which never were. Only by the privilege of being in the thick of those events, and in the very bowels of those persons, could they hope to hold the reader's attention. If similar privileges were granted to the historian, the demand for novels would cease forthwith, and many thousands of hard-working, deserving men and women would be thrown out of employment. In fact, Clio had asked him an impossible favour. But he might—he said he conceivably might—be induced to let her have her way just once. In that event, all she would have to do was to keep her eye on the world's surface, and then, so soon as she had reason to think that somewhere was impending something of great import, to choose an historian. On him, straightway,

Zeus would confer invisibility, inevitability, and psychic penetration, with a flawless memory thrown in.

On the following afternoon, Clio's roving eye saw Zuleika stepping from the Paddington platform into the Oxford train. A few moments later I found myself suddenly on Parnassus. In hurried words Clio told me how I came there, and what I had to do. She said she had selected me because she knew me to be honest, sober, and capable, and no stranger to Oxford. Another moment, and I was at the throne of Zeus. With a majesty of gesture which I shall never forget, he stretched his hand over me, and I was indued with the promised gifts. And then, lo! I was on the platform of Oxford station. The train was not due for another hour. But the time passed pleasantly enough.

It was fun to float all unseen, to float all unhampered by any corporeal nonsense, up and down the platform. It was fun to watch the inmost thoughts of the stationmaster, of the porters, of the young person at the buffet. But of course I did not let the holiday mood master me. I realised the seriousness of my mission. I must concentrate myself on the matter in hand: Miss Dobson's visit. What was going to happen? Prescience was no part of my outfit. From what I knew about Miss Dobson, I deduced that she would be a great success. That was all. Had I had the instinct that was given to those Emperors in stone, and even to the dog Corker, I should have begged Clio to send in my stead some man of stronger nerve. She had charged me to be calmly vigilant, scrupulously fair. I could have been neither, had I from the outset foreseen all. Only because the immediate future was broken to me by degrees, first as a set of possibilities, then as a set of probabilities that yet might not come off, was I able to fulfil the trust imposed on me. Even so, it was hard. I had always accepted the doctrine that to understand all is to forgive all. Thanks to Zeus, I understood all about Miss Dobson, and yet there were moments when she repelled me—

moments when I wished to see her neither from without nor from within. So soon as the Duke of Dorset met her on the Monday night, I felt I was in duty bound to keep him under constant surveillance. Yet were there moments when I was so sorry for him that I deemed myself a brute for shadowing him.

Ever since I can remember, I have been beset by a recurring doubt as to whether I be or be not quite a gentleman. I have never attempted to define that term: I have but feverishly wondered whether in its usual acceptation (whatever that is) it be strictly applicable to myself. Many people hold that the qualities connoted by it are primarily moral—a kind heart, honourable conduct, and so forth. On Clio's mission, I found honour and kindness tugging me in precisely opposite directions. In so far as honour tugged the harder, was I the more or the less gentlemanly? But the test is not a fair one. Curiosity tugged on the side of honour. This goes to prove me a cad? Oh, set against it the fact that I did at one point betray Clio's trust. When Miss Dobson had done the deed recorded at the close of the foregoing chapter, I gave the Duke of Dorset an hour's grace.

I could have done no less. In the lives of most of us is some one thing that we would not after the lapse of how many years soever confess to our most understanding friend; the thing that does not bear thinking of; the one thing to be forgotten; the unforgettable thing. Not the commission of some great crime: this can be atoned for by great penances; and the very enormity of it has a dark grandeur. Maybe, some little deadly act of meanness, some hole-and-corner treachery? But what a man has once willed to do, his will helps him to forget. The unforgettable thing in his life is usually not a thing he has done or left undone, but a thing done to him— some insolence or cruelty for which he could not, or did not, avenge himself. This it is that often comes back to him, years after, in his dreams, and thrusts itself suddenly into his waking thoughts, so that he clenches his hands, and shakes his head, and hums a tune loudly—anything to beat it off. In the very hour when first befell him that odious humiliation, would you have spied on him? I gave the Duke of Dorset an hour's grace.

What were his thoughts in that interval, what words, if any, he uttered to the night, never will be known. For this, Clio has abused me in language less befitting a Muse than a fish-wife. I do not care. I would rather be chidden by Clio than by my own sense of delicacy, any day.

## XII

NOT less averse than from dogging the Duke was I from remaining another instant in the presence of Miss Dobson. There seemed to be no possible excuse for her. This time she had gone too far. She was outrageous. As soon as the Duke had had time to get clear away, I floated out into the night.

I may have consciously reasoned that the best way to forget the present was in the revival of memories. Or I may have been driven by a mere homing instinct. Anyhow, it was in the direction of my old College that I went. Midnight was tolling as I floated in through the shut grim gate at which I had so often stood knocking for admission.

The man who now occupied my room had sported his oak—my oak. I read the name on the visiting-card attached thereto—E. J. Craddock—and went in.

E. J. Craddock, interloper, was sitting at my table, with elbows squared and head on one side, in the act of literary composition. The oars and caps on my walls betokened him a rowing-man. Indeed, I recognised his somewhat heavy face as that of the man whom, from the Judas barge this afternoon, I had seen rowing "stroke" in my College Eight.

He ought, therefore, to have been in bed and asleep two hours ago. And the offence of his vigil was aggravated by a large tumbler that stood in front of him, containing whisky and soda. From this he took a deep draught. Then he read over what he had written. I did not care to peer over his shoulder at MS. which, though written in my room, was not intended for my eyes. But the writer's brain was open to me; and he had written: "I, the undersigned Edward Joseph Craddock, do hereby leave and bequeath all my personal and other property to Zuleika Dobson, spinster. This is my last will and testament."

He gnawed his pen, and presently altered the "hereby leave" to "hereby and herewith leave". Fool!

I thereby and therewith left him. As I emerged through the floor of the room above—through the very carpet that had so often been steeped in wine, and encrusted with smithereens of glass, in the brave old days of a well-remembered occupant—I found two men, both of them evidently reading-men. One of them was pacing round the room. "Do you know," he was saying, "what she reminded me of, all the time? Those words—aren't they in the Song of Solomon?—'fair as the moon, clear as the sun, and . . . and . . .'"

"'Terrible as an army with banners,'" supplied his host—rather testily, for he was writing a letter. It began "My dear Father. By the time you receive this I shall have taken a step which . . ."

Clearly it was vain to seek distraction in my old College. I floated out into the untenanted meadows. Over them was the usual coverlet of white vapour, trailed from the Isis right up to Merton Wall. The scent of these meadows' moisture is the scent of Oxford. Even in hottest noon, one feels that the sun has not dried *them*. Always there is moisture drifting across them, drifting into the Colleges. It, one suspects, must have had much to do with the evocation of what is called the Oxford spirit—that gentlest spirit, so lingering and searching, so dear to them who as youths were brought into ken of it, so exasperating to them who were not. Yes, certainly, it is this mild, miasmal air, not less than the grey beauty and gravity of the buildings, that has helped Oxford to produce, and foster eternally, her peculiar race of artist-scholars, scholar-artists. The undergraduate, in his brief periods of residence, is too buoyant to be mastered by the spirit of the place. He does but salute it, and catch the manner. It is on him who stays to spend his maturity here that the spirit will in its fulness gradually descend. The

buildings and their traditions keep astir in his mind whatsoever is gracious; the climate, enfolding and enfeebling him,
lulling him, keeps him careless of the sharp, harsh, exigent
realities of the outer world. Careless? Not utterly. These
realities may be seen by him. He may study them, be amused
or touched by them. But they cannot fire him. Oxford is too
damp for that. The "movements" made there have been no
more than protests against the mobility of others. They have
been without the dynamic quality implied in their name.
They have been no more than the sighs of men gazing at
what other men had left behind them; faint, impossible
appeals to the god of retrogression, uttered for their own sake
and ritual, rather than with any intent that they should be
heard. Oxford, that lotus-land, saps the will-power, the
power of action. But, in doing so, it clarifies the mind, makes
larger the vision, gives, above all, that playful and caressing
suavity of manner which comes of a conviction that nothing
matters, except ideas, and that not even ideas are worth
dying for, inasmuch as the ghosts of them slain seem worthy
of yet more piously elaborate homage than can be given to
them in their hey-day. If the Colleges could be transferred
to the dry and bracing top of some hill, doubtless they would
be more evidently useful to the nation. But let us be glad
there is no engineer or enchanter to compass that task.
*Egomet*, I would liefer have the rest of England subside into
the sea than have Oxford set on a salubrious level. For there
is nothing in England to be matched with what lurks in the
vapours of these meadows, and in the shadows of these
spires—that mysterious, inenubilable spirit, spirit of Oxford.
Oxford! The very sight of the word printed, or sound of it
spoken, is fraught for me with most actual magic.

And on that moonlit night, when I floated among the
vapours of these meadows, myself less than a vapour,
I knew and loved Oxford as never before, as never since.
Yonder, in the Colleges, was the fume and fret of tragedy

—Love as Death's decoy, and Youth following her. What then? Not Oxford was menaced. Come what might, not a stone of Oxford's walls would be loosened, not a wreath of her vapours be undone, nor lost a breath of her sacred spirit.

I floated up into the higher drier air, that I might, for once, see the total body of that spirit.

There lay Oxford far beneath me, like a map in grey and black and silver. All that I had known only as great single things I saw now outspread in apposition, and tiny; tiny symbols, as it were, of themselves, greatly symbolising their oneness. There they lay, these multitudinous and disparate quadrangles, all their rivalries merged in the making of a great catholic pattern. And the roofs of the buildings around them seemed level with their lawns. No higher the roofs of the very towers. Up from their tiny segment of the earth's spinning surface they stood negligible beneath infinity. And new, too, quite new, in eternity; transient upstarts. I saw Oxford as a place that had no more past and no more future than a mining-camp. I smiled down. O hoary and unassailable mushroom! . . . But if a man carry his sense of proportion far enough, lo! he is back at the point from which he started. He knows that eternity, as conceived by him, is but an instant in eternity, and infinity but a speck in infinity. How should they belittle the things near to him? . . . Oxford was venerable and magical, after all, and enduring. Aye, and not because she would endure was it the less lamentable that the young lives within her walls were like to be taken. My equanimity was gone; and a tear fell on Oxford.

And then, as though Oxford herself were speaking up to me, the air vibrated with a sweet noise of music. It was the hour of one; the end of the Duke's hour of grace. Through the silvery tangle of sounds from other clocks I floated quickly down to the Broad.

# XIII

I HAD on the way a horrible apprehension. What if the Duke, in his agony, had taken the one means to forgetfulness? His room, I could see, was lit up; but a man does not necessarily choose to die in the dark. I hovered, afraid, over the dome of the Sheldonian. I saw that the window of the room above the Duke's was also lit up. And there was no reason at all to doubt the survival of Noaks. Perhaps the sight of him would hearten me.

I was wrong. The sight of Noaks in his room was as dismal a thing as could be. With his chin sunk on his breast, he sat there, on a rickety chair, staring up at the mantelpiece. This he had decked out as a sort of shrine. In the centre, aloft on an inverted tin that had contained Abernethy biscuits, stood a blue plush frame, with an inner rim of brass, several sizes too big for the picture-postcard installed in it. Zuleika's image gazed forth with a smile that was obviously not intended for the humble worshipper at this execrable shrine. On either side of her stood a small vase, one holding some geraniums, the other some mignonette. And just beneath her was placed that iron ring which, rightly or wrongly, Noaks supposed to alleviate rheumatism—that same iron ring which, by her touch to-night, had been charged for him with a yet deeper magic, insomuch that he dared no longer wear it, and had set it before her as an oblation.

Yet, for all his humility, he was possessed by a spirit of egoism that repelled me. While he sat peering over his spectacles at the beauteous image, he said again and again to himself, in a hollow voice: "I am so young to die." Every time he said this, two large, pear-shaped tears emerged from behind his spectacles, and found their way to his waistcoat. It did not seem to strike him that quite half of the under-graduates who contemplated death—and contemplated it in a fearless, wholesome, manly fashion—were his juniors. It seemed to seem to him that his own death, even though all those other far brighter and more promising lives than his were to be sacrificed, was a thing to bother about. Well, if he did not want to die, why could he not have, at least, the courage of his cowardice? The world would not cease to revolve because Noaks still clung to its surface. For me the whole tragedy was cheapened by his participation in it. I was fain to leave him. His squint, his short legs dangling towards the floor, his tea-sodden waistcoat, and his refrain: "I am so young to die," were beyond measure exasperating. Yet I hesitated to pass into the room beneath, for fear of what I might see there.

How long I might have paltered, had no sound come from that room, I know not. But a sound came, sharp and sudden in the night, instantly reassuring. I swept down into the presence of the Duke.

He stood with his head flung back and his arms folded, gorgeous in a dressing-gown of crimson brocade. In animation of pride and pomp, he looked less like a mortal man than like a figure from some great biblical group by Paul Veronese.

And this was he whom I had presumed to pity! And this was he whom I had half expected to find dead.

His face, usually pale, was now red; and his hair, which no eye had ever yet seen disordered, stood up in a glistening shock. These two changes in him intensified the effect of vitality. One of them, however, vanished as I watched it. The Duke's face resumed its pallor. I realised then that he had but blushed; and I realised, simultaneously, that what had called that blush to his cheek was what had also been the signal to me that he was alive. His blush had been a pendant to his sneeze. And his sneeze had been a pendant to that outrage which he had been striving to forget. He had caught cold.

He had caught cold. In the hour of his soul's bitter need, his body had been suborned against him. Base! Had he not stripped his body of its wet vesture? Had he not vigorously dried his hair, and robed himself in crimson, and struck in solitude such attitudes as were most congruous with his high spirit and high rank? He had set himself to crush remembrance of that by which through his body his soul had been assailed. And well had he known that in this conflict a giant demon was his antagonist. But that his own body would play traitor—no, this he had not foreseen. This was too base a thing to be foreseen.

He stood quite still, a figure orgulous and splendent. And it seemed as though the hot night, too, stood still, to watch him, in awe, through the open lattices of his window, breathlessly. But to me, equipped to see beneath the surface, he was piteous, piteous in ratio to the pretension of his aspect. Had he crouched down and sobbed, I should have been as much relieved as he. But he stood seignorial and aquiline.

Painless, by comparison with this conflict in him, seemed the conflict that had raged in him yesternight. Then, it had been his dandihood against his passion for Zuleika. What mattered the issue? Whichever won, the victory were sweet. And of this he had all the while been subconscious, gallantly though he fought for his pride of dandihood. To-night in the battle between pride and memory, he knew from the outset that pride's was but a forlorn hope, and that memory would be barbarous in her triumph. Not winning to oblivion, he must hate with a fathomless hatred. Of all the emotions, hatred is the most excruciating. Of all the objects of hatred, a woman once loved is the most hateful. Of all deaths, the bitterest that can befall a man is that he lay down his life to flatter the woman he deems vilest of her sex.

Such was the death that the Duke of Dorset saw confronting him. Most men, when they are at war with the past, have the future as ally. Looking steadfastly forward, they can forget. The Duke's future was openly in league with his past. For him, prospect was memory. All that there was for him of future was the death to which his honour was pledged. To envisage that was to . . . no, he would *not* envisage it! With a passionate effort he hypnotised himself to think of nothing at all. His brain, into which, by the power Zeus gave me, I was gazing, became a perfect vacuum, insulated by the will. It was the kind of experiment which scientists call "beautiful". And yes, beautiful it was.

But not in the eyes of Nature. She abhors a vacuum. Seeing the enormous odds against which the Duke was fighting, she might well have stood aside. But she has no sense of sport whatsoever. She stepped in.

At first I did not realise what was happening. I saw the Duke's eyes contract, and the muscles of his mouth drawn down, and, at the same time, a tense upward movement of his whole body. Then, suddenly, the strain undone: a downward dart of the head, a loud percussion. Thrice the Duke sneezed, with a sound that was as the bursting of the dams of body and soul together; then sneezed again.

Now was his will broken. He capitulated. In rushed shame and horror and hatred, pell-mell, to ravage him.

What care now, what use, for deportment? He walked coweringly round and round his room, with frantic gestures, with head bowed. He shuffled and slunk. His dressing-gown had the look of a gabardine.

Shame and horror and hatred went slashing and hewing throughout the fallen citadel. At length, exhausted, he flung himself down on the window-seat and leaned out into the night, panting. The air was full of thunder. He clutched at his throat. From the depths of the black caverns beneath their brows the eyes of the unsleeping Emperors watched him.

He had gone through much in the day that was past. He had loved and lost. He had striven to recapture, and had failed. In a strange resolve he had found serenity and joy. He had been at the point of death, and had been saved. He had seen that his beloved was worthless, and he had not cared. He had fought for her, and conquered; and had pled with her, and—all these memories were loathsome by reason of that final thing which had all the while lain in wait for him.

He looked back and saw himself as he had been at a score of crucial moments in the day—always in the shadow of that final thing. He saw himself as he had been on the playing-fields of Eton; aye! and in the arms of his nurse, to and fro on the terrace of Tankerton—always in the shadow of that final thing, always piteous and ludicrous, doomed. Thank heaven the future was unknowable? It wasn't, now. To-morrow—to-day—he must die for that accursed fiend of a woman—the woman with the hyena laugh.

What to do meanwhile? Impossible to sleep. He felt in his body the strain of his quick sequence of spiritual adventures. He was dog-tired. But his brain was furiously out of hand: no stopping it. And the night was stifling. And all the while, in the dead silence, as though his soul had ears, there was a sound. It was a very faint, unearthly sound, and seemed to come from nowhere, yet to have a meaning. He feared he was rather over-wrought.

He must express himself. That would soothe him. Ever since childhood he had had, from time to time, the impulse to set down in writing his thoughts or his moods. In such exercises he had found for his self-consciousness the vent which natures less reserved than his find in casual talk with

Tom, Dick, and Harry, with Jane, Susan, and Liz. Aloof from either of these triads, he had in his first term at Eton taken to himself as confidant, and retained ever since, a great quarto volume, bound in red morocco and stamped with his coronet and cypher. It was herein, year by year, that his soul spread itself.

He wrote mostly in English prose; but other modes were not infrequent. Whenever he was abroad, it was his courteous habit to write in the language of the country where he was residing—French, when he was in his house on the Champs Elysées; Italian, when he was in his villa at Baiae; and so on. When he was in his own country he felt himself free to deviate sometimes from the vernacular into whatever language were aptest to his frame of mind. In his sterner moods he gravitated to Latin, and wrought the noble iron of that language to effects that were, if anything, a trifle over-impressive. He found for his highest flights of contemplation a handy vehicle in Sanscrit. In hours of mere joy it was Greek poetry that flowed likeliest from his pen; and he had a special fondness for the metre of Alcaeus.

And now, too, in his darkest hour, it was Greek that surged in him—iambics of thunderous wrath such as those which are volleyed by Prometheus. But as he sat down to his writing-table, and unlocked the dear old album, and dipped his pen in the ink, a great calm fell on him. The iambics in him began to breathe such sweetness as is on the lips of Alcestis going to her doom. But, just as he set pen to paper, his hand faltered, and he sprang up, victim of another and yet more violent fit of sneezing.

Disbuskined, dangerous. The spirit of Juvenal woke in him. He would flay. He would make Woman (as he called Zuleika) writhe. Latin hexameters, of course. An epistle to his heir presumptive . . . "Vae tibi," he began.

"Vae tibi, vae miscro, nisi circumspexeris artes Femineas,

nam nulla salus quin femina possit Tradere, nulla fides
quin"——

"Quin," he repeated. In writing soliloquies, his trouble
was to curb inspiration. The thought that he was addressing
his heir-presumptive—now heir-only-too-apparent—gave
him pause. Nor, he reflected, was he addressing this brute
only, but a huge posthumous audience. These hexameters
would be sure to appear in the "authorised" biography. "A
melancholy interest attaches to the following lines, written, it
would seem, on the very eve of" . . . He winced. Was it
really possible, and no dream, that he was to die to-morrow—
to-day?

Even you, unassuming reader, go about with a vague
notion that in your case, somehow, the ultimate demand of
nature will be waived. The Duke, until he conceived his
sudden desire to die, had deemed himself certainly exempt.
And now, as he sat staring at his window, he saw in the
paling of the night the presage of the dawn of his own last
day. Sometimes (orphaned though he was in early childhood) he had even found it hard to believe there was no
exemption for those to whom he stood in any personal
relation. He remembered how, soon after he went to Eton,
he had received almost with incredulity the news of the death
of his god-father, Lord Stackley, an octogenarian. . . . He
took from the table his album, knowing that on one of the
earliest pages was inscribed his boyish sense of that bereavement. Yes, here the passage was, written in a large round
hand:

"Death knocks, as we know, at the door of the cottage and
of the castle. He stalks up the front-garden and the steep
steps of the semi-detached villa, and plies the ornamental
knocker so imperiously that the panels of imitation stained
glass quiver in the thin front-door. Even the family that

occupies the topmost story of a building without a lift is on his ghastly visiting-list. He rattles his fleshless knuckles against the door of the gypsy's caravan. Into the savage's tent, wigwam, or wattled hut, he darts unbidden. Even on the hermit in the cave he forces his obnoxious presence. His is an universal beat, and he walks it with a grin. But be sure it is at the sombre portal of the nobleman that he knocks with the greatest gusto. It is there, where haply his visit will be commemorated with a hatchment; it is then, when the muffled thunder of the Dead March in 'Saul' will soon be rolling in cathedrals; it is then, it is there, that the pride of his unquestioned power comes grimliest home to him. Is there no withstanding him? Why should he be admitted always with awe, a cravenly-honoured guest? When next he calls, let the butler send him about his business, or tell him to step round to the servants' entrance. If it be made plain to him that his visits are an impertinence, he will soon be disemboldened. Once the aristocracy make a stand against him, there need be no more trouble about the exorbitant Duties named after him. And for the hereditary system—that system which both offends the common sense of the Radical, and wounds the Tory by its implied admission that noblemen are mortal—a seemly substitute will have been found."

Artless and crude in expression, very boyish, it seemed now to its author. Yet, in its simple wistfulness, it had quality: it rang true. The Duke wondered whether, with all that he had since mastered in the great art of English prose, he had not lost something, too.

"Is there no withstanding him?" To think that the boy who uttered that cry, and gave back so brave an answer, was within nine years to go seek death of his own accord! How the gods must be laughing! Yes, the exquisite point of the joke, for them, was that he *chose* to die. But—and, as the

thought flashed through him, he started like a man shot—
what if he chose not to? Stay, surely there was some reason
why he *must* die. Else, why throughout the night had he
taken his doom for granted? . . . Honour: yes, he had
pledged himself. Better death than dishonour. Was it,
though? was it? Ah, he, who had come so near to death, saw
dishonour as a tiny trifle. Where was the sting of it? Not he
would be ridiculous to-morrow—to-day. Everyone would
acclaim his splendid act of moral courage. She, she, the
hyena woman, would be the fool. No one would have
thought of dying for her, had he not set the example. Every
one would follow his new example. Yes, he would save
Oxford yet. That was his duty. Duty and darling vengeance!
And life—life!

It was full dawn now. Gone was that faint, monotonous
sound which had punctuated in his soul the horrors of his
vigil. But, in reminder of those hours, his lamp was still
burning. He extinguished it; and the going-out of that
tarnished light made perfect his sense of release.

He threw wide his arms in welcome of the great adorable
day, and of all the great adorable days that were to be his.

He leaned out from his window, drinking the dawn in.
The gods had made merry over him, had they? And the cry
of the hyena had made night hideous. Well, it was his turn
now. He would laugh last and loudest.

And already, for what was to be, he laughed outright into
the morning; insomuch that the birds in the trees of Trinity,
and still more the Emperors over the way, marvelled greatly.

## XIV

THEY had awaited thousands and innumerable thousands of daybreaks in the Broad, these Emperors, counting the long slow hours till the night were over. It is in the night especially that their fallen greatness haunts them. Day brings some distraction. They are not incurious of the lives around them—these little lives that succeed one another so quickly. To them, in their immemorial old age, youth is a constant wonder. And so is death, which to them comes not. Youth or death—which, they had often asked themselves, was the goodlier? But it was ill that these two things should be mated. It was ill-come, this day of days.

Long after the Duke was in bed and asleep, his peal of laughter echoed in the ears of the Emperors. Why had he laughed?

And they said to themselves: "We are very old men, and broken, and in a land not our own. There are things that we do not understand."

Brief was the freshness of the dawn. From all points of the compass, dark grey clouds mounted into the sky. There, taking their places as though in accordance to a strategic plan laid down for them, they ponderously massed themselves, and presently, as at a given signal, drew nearer to earth, and halted, an irresistible great army, awaiting orders.

Somewhere under cover of them the sun went his way, transmitting a sulphurous heat. The very birds in the trees of Trinity were oppressed and did not twitter. The very leaves did not whisper.

Out through the railings, and across the road, prowled a skimpy and dingy cat, trying to look like a tiger.

It was all very sinister and dismal.

The hours passed. The Broad put forth, one by one, its signs of waking.

Soon after eight o'clock, as usual, the front door of the Duke's lodgings was opened from within. The Emperors watched for the faint cloud of dust that presently emerged, and for her whom it preceded. To them, this first outcoming of the landlady's daughter was a moment of daily interest. Katie!—they had known her as a toddling child; and later as a little girl scampering off to school, all legs and pinafore and streaming golden hair. And now she was sixteen years old. Her hair, tied back at the nape of her neck, would very soon be "up". Her big blue eyes were as they had always been; but she had long passed out of pinafores into aprons, had taken on a sedateness befitting her years and her duties, and was anxious to be regarded rather as an aunt than as a sister by her brother Clarence, aged twelve. The Emperors had always predicted that she would be pretty. And very pretty she was.

As she came slowly out, with eyes downcast to her broom, sweeping the dust so seriously over the doorstep and then across the pavement, and anon when she reappeared with pail and scrubbing-brush, and abased herself before the doorstep, and wrought so vehemently there, what filled her little soul was not the dignity of manual labour. The duties that Zuleika had envied her were dear to her exactly as they would have been, yesterday morning, to Zuleika. The Emperors had often noticed that during vacations their little favourite's treatment of the doorstep was languid and perfunctory. They knew well her secret, and always (for who can be long in England without becoming sentimental?) they cherished the hope of a romantic union between her and "a certain young gentleman," as they archly called the Duke. His continued indifference to her they took almost as an affront to themselves. Where in all England was a prettier,

sweeter girl than their Katie? The sudden irruption of
Zuleika into Oxford was especially grievious to them because
they could no longer hope against hope that Katie would be
led by the Duke to the altar, and thence into the highest
social circles, and live happily ever after.

Lucky it was for Katie, however, that they had no power
to fill her head with their foolish notions. It was well for her
to have never doubted she loved in vain. She had soon
grown used to her lot. Not until yesterday had there been
any bitterness. Jealousy surged in Katie at the very moment
when she beheld Zuleika on the threshold. A glance at the
Duke's face when she showed the visitor up was enough to
acquaint her with the state of his heart. And she did not, for
confirming her intuition, need the two or three opportunities
she took of listening at the keyhole. What in the course of
those informal audiences did surprise her—so much indeed
that she could hardly believe her ear—was that it was
possible for a woman not to love the Duke. Her jealousy of
"that Miss Dobson" was for a while swallowed up in her pity
for him. What she had borne so cheerfully for herself she
could not bear for her hero. She wished she had not
happened to listen.

And this morning, while she knelt swaying and spreading
over "his" doorstep, her blue eyes added certain tears to be
scrubbed away in the general moisture of the stone. Rising,
she dried her hands in her apron, and dried her eyes with her
hands. Lest her mother should see that she had been crying,
she loitered outside the door. Suddenly, her roving glance
changed to a stare of acute hostility. She knew well that the
person wandering towards her was—no, not "that Miss
Dobson", as she had for the fraction of an instant supposed,
but the next worst thing.

It has been said that Mélisande indoors was an evidently
French maid. Out of doors she was not less evidently
Zuleika's. Not that she aped her mistress. The resemblance

had come by force of propinquity and devotion. Nature had
laid no basis for it. Not one point of form or colour had the
two women in common. It has been said that Zuleika was
not strictly beautiful. Mélisande, like most Frenchwomen,
was strictly plain. But in expression and port, in her whole
*tournure*, she had become, as every good maid does, her
mistress's replica. The poise of her head, the boldness of her
regard and brilliance of her smile, the leisurely and swinging
way in which she walked, with a hand on the hip—all these
things of hers were Zuleika's too. She was no conqueror.
None but the man to whom she was betrothed—a waiter at
the Café Tourtel, named Pelléas—had ever paid court to her;
nor was she covetous of other hearts. Yet she looked
victorious, and insatiable of victories, and "terrible as an
army with banners."

In the hand that was not on her hip she carried a letter.
And on her shoulders she had to bear the full burden of the
hatred that Zuleika had inspired in Katie. But this she did
not know. She came glancing boldly, leisurely, at the
numbers on the front doors.

Katie stepped back on to the doorstep, lest the inferiority
of her stature should mar the effect of her disdain.

"Good day. Is it here that Duke D'Orsay lives?" asked
Mélisande, as nearly accurate as a Gaul may be in such
matters.

"The Duke of Dorset," said Katie with a cold and
insular emphasis, "lives here." And "You," she tried to
convey with her eyes, "you, for all your smart black silk, are
a hireling. I am Miss Batch. I happen to have a hobby for
housework. I have not been crying."

"Then please mount this to him at once," said Mélisande,
holding out the letter. "It is from Miss Dobson's part.
Very express. I wait response."

"You are very ugly," Katie signalled with her eyes. "I
am very pretty. I have the Oxfordshire complexion. And I

play the piano." With her lips she said merely: "His Grace is not called before nine o'clock."

"But to-day you go wake him now—quick—is it not?"

"Quite out of the question," said Katie. "If you care to leave that letter here, I will see that it is placed on his Grace's breakfast-table, with the morning's post." "For the rest," added her eyes, "Down with France!"

"I find you droll, but droll, my little one!" cried Mélisande.

Katie stepped back and shut the door in her face. "Like a little Empress," the Emperors commented.

The Frenchwoman threw up her hands and apostrophised heaven. To this day she believes that all the *bonnes* of Oxford are mad, but mad, and of a madness.

She stared at the door, at the pail and scrubbing-brush that had been shut out with her, at the letter in her hand. She decided that she had better drop the letter into the slit in the door and make report to Miss Dobson.

As the envelope fell through the slit to the door-mat, Katie made at Mélisande a grimace which, had not the panels been opaque, would have astonished the Emperors. Resuming her dignity, she picked the thing up, and, at arm's length, examined it. It was inscribed in pencil. Katie's lips curled at sight of the large, audacious handwriting. But it is probable that whatever kind of handwriting Zuleika might have had would have been just the kind that Katie would have expected.

Fingering the envelope, she wondered what the wretched woman had to say. It occurred to her that the kettle was simmering on the hob in the kitchen, and that she might easily steam open the envelope and master its contents. However, her doing this would have in no way affected the course of the tragedy. And so the gods (being to-day in a strictly artistic mood) prompted her to mind her own business.

Laying the Duke's table for breakfast, she made as usual a neat rectangular pile of the letters that had come for him by post. Zuleika's letter she threw down askew. That luxury she allowed herself.

And he, when he saw the letter, allowed himself the luxury of leaving it unopened awhile. Whatever its purport, he knew it could but minister to his happy malice. A few hours ago, with what shame and dread it would have stricken him! Now it was a dainty to be dallied with.

His eyes rested on the black tin boxes that contained his robes of the Garter. Hateful had been the sight of them in the watches of the night, when he thought he had worn those robes for the last time. But now——!

He opened Zuleika's letter. It did not disappoint him.

"DEAR DUKE,—*Do, do* forgive me. I am beyond words ashamed of the silly tomboyish thing I did last night. Of course it was no worse than that, but an awful fear haunts me that you *may* have thought I acted in anger at the idea of your breaking your promise to me. Well, it is quite true I had been hurt and angry when you hinted at doing that, but the moment I left you I saw that you had been only in fun, and I enjoyed the joke against myself, though I thought it was rather too bad of you. And then, as a sort of revenge, but almost before I knew what I was doing, I played that *idiotic* practical joke on you. I have been *miserable* ever since. *Do* come round as early as possible and tell me I am forgiven. But before you tell me that, please lecture me till I cry— though indeed I have been crying half through the night. And then if you want to be *very* horrid you may tease me for being so slow to see a joke. And then you might take me to see some of the Colleges and things before we go on to lunch at The MacQuern's? Forgive pencil and scrawl. Am sitting up in bed to write.—Your sincere friend, "Z. D.

"P.S.—Please burn this."

At that final injunction, the Duke abandoned himself to

his mirth. "Please burn this." Poor dear young woman, how modest she was in the glare of her diplomacy! Why there was nothing, not one phrase, to compromise her in the eyes of a coroner's jury! . . . Seriously, she had good reason to be proud of her letter. For the purpose in view it couldn't have been better done. That was what made it so touchingly absurd. He put himself in her position. He pictured himself as her, "sitting up in bed", pencil in hand, to explain away, to soothe, to clinch and bind . . . Yes, if he had happened to be some other man—one whom her insult might have angered without giving love its death-blow, and one who could be frightened out of not keeping his word—this letter would have been capital.

He helped himself to some more marmalade, and poured out another cup of coffee. Nothing is more thrilling, thought he, than to be treated as a cully by the person you hold in the hollow of your hand.

But within this great irony lay (to be glided over) another irony. He knew well in what mood Zuleika had done what she had done to him last night; yet he preferred to accept her explanation of it.

Officially, then, he acquitted her of anything worse than tomboyishness. But this verdict for his own convenience implied no mercy to the culprit. The sole point for him was how to administer her punishment the most poignantly. Just how should he word his letter?

He rose from his chair, and "Dear Miss Dobson—no, *My* dear Miss Dobson," he murmured, pacing the room, "I am so very sorry I cannot come to see you: I have to attend two lectures this morning. By contrast with this weariness, it will be the more delightful to meet you at The MacQuern's. I want to see as much as I can of you to-day, because to-night there is the Bump Supper, and to-morrow morning, alas! I must motor to Windsor for this wretched Investiture. Meanwhile, how can you ask to be forgiven when there is nothing whatever to forgive? It seems to me that mine, not yours, is the form of humour that needs explanation. My proposal to die for you was made in as playful a spirit as my proposal to marry you. And it is really for me to ask forgiveness of you. One thing especially," he murmured, fingering in his waistcoat-pocket the ear-rings she had given him, "pricks my conscience. I do feel that I ought not to have let you give me these two pearls—at any rate, not the one which went into premature mourning for me. As I have no means of deciding which of the two this one is, I enclose them both, with the hope that the pretty difference between them will in time re-appear" . . . Or words to that effect. . . . Stay! why not add to the joy of contriving that effect the greater joy of watching it? Why send Zuleika a letter? He would obey her summons. He would speed to her side. He snatched up a hat.

In this haste, however, he detected a certain lack of dignity. He steadied himself, and went slowly to the mirror. There he adjusted his hat with care, and regarded himself very seriously, very sternly, from various angles, like a man invited to paint his own portrait for the Uffizi. He must be worthy of himself. It was well that Zuleika should be chastened. Great was her sin. Out of life and death she had fashioned toys for her vanity. But his joy must be in vindication of what was noble, not in making suffer what was vile. Yesterday he had been her puppet, her Jumping-Jack; to-day it was as avenging angel that he would appear before her. The gods had mocked him who was now their minister. Their minister? Their master, as being once more master of himself. It was they who had plotted his undoing. Because they loved him they were fain that he should die young. The Dobson woman was but their agent, their cat's-paw. By her they had all but got him. Not quite! And now, to teach them, through her, a lesson they would not soon forget, he would go forth.

Shaking with laughter, the gods leaned over the thunder-clouds to watch him.

He went forth.

On the well-whitened doorstep he was confronted by a small boy in uniform bearing a telegram.

"Duke of Dorset?" asked the small boy.

Opening the envelope, the Duke saw that the message, with which was a prepaid form for reply, had been handed in at the Tankerton post-office. It ran thus:

> *Deeply regret inform your grace last night two black owls came and perched on battlements remained there through night hooting at dawn flew away none knows whither awaiting instructions*
>
> > *Jellings*

The Duke's face, though it grew white, moved not one muscle.

Somewhat shamed now, the gods ceased from laughing.

The Duke looked from the telegram to the boy. "Have you a pencil?" he asked.

"Yes, my Lord," said the boy, producing a stump of pencil.

Holding the prepaid form against the door, the Duke wrote:

> *Jellings      Tankerton Hall*
> > *Prepare vault for funeral Monday*
> > > *Dorset*

His handwriting was as firmly and minutely beautiful as ever. Only in that he forgot there was nothing to pay did he belie his calm. "Here," he said to the boy, "is a shilling; and you may keep the change."

"Thank you, my Lord," said the boy, and went his way, as happy as a postman.

## XV

HUMPHREY GREDDON, in the Duke's place, would have taken a pinch of snuff. But he could not have made that gesture with a finer air than the Duke gave to its modern equivalent. In the art of taking and lighting a cigarette, there was one man who had no rival in Europe. This time he outdid even himself.

"Ah," you say, "but 'pluck' is one thing, endurance another. A man who doesn't reel on receipt of his death-warrant may yet break down when he has had time to think it over. How did the Duke acquit himself when he came to the end of his cigarette? And by the way, how was it that after he had read the telegram you didn't give him again an hour's grace?"

In a way, you have a perfect right to ask both those questions. But their very pertinence shows that you think I might omit things that matter. Please don't interrupt me again.

Though the news that he must die was a yet sharper douche, as you have suggested, than the douche inflicted by Zuleika, it did at least leave unscathed the Duke's pride. The gods can make a man ridiculous through a woman, but they cannot make him ridiculous when they deal him a blow direct. The very greatness of their power makes them, in that respect, impotent. They had decreed that the Duke should die, and they had told him so. There was nothing to demean him in that. True, he had just measured himself against them. But there was no shame in being gravelled. The peripety was according to the best rules of tragic art. The whole thing was in the grand manner.

Thus I felt that there were no indelicacy, this time, in watching him. Just as "pluck" comes of breeding, so is endurance especially an attribute of the artist. Because he can stand outside himself, and (if there be nothing ignoble in them) take a pleasure in his own sufferings, the artist has a huge advantage over you and me. The Duke, so soon as Zuleika's spell was broken, had become himself again—a highly self-conscious artist in life. And now, standing pensive on the doorstep, he was almost enviable in his great affliction.

Through the wreaths of smoke which, as they came from his lips, hung in the sultry air as they would have hung in a closed room, he gazed up at the steadfast thunder-clouds. How nobly they had been massed for him! One of them, a particularly large and dark one, might with advantage, he thought, have been placed a little further to the left. He made a gesture to that effect. Instantly the cloud rolled into position. The gods were painfully anxious, now, to humour him in trifles. His behaviour in the great emergency had so impressed them at a distance that they rather dreaded meeting him anon at close quarters. They rather wished they had not uncaged, last night, the two black owls. Too late. What they had done they had done.

That faint monotonous sound in the stillness of the night— the Duke remembered it now. What he had thought to be only his fancy had been his death-knell, wafted to him along uncharted waves of ether, from the battlements of Tankerton. It had ceased at daybreak. He wondered now that he had not guessed its meaning. And he was glad that he had not. He was thankful for the peace that had been granted to him, the joyous arrogance in which he had gone to bed and got up for breakfast. He valued these mercies the more for the great tragic irony that came of them. Aye, and he was inclined to blame the gods for not having kept him still longer in the dark and so made the irony still more awful. Why had they not caused the telegram to be delayed in transmission? They ought to have let him go and riddle Zuleika with his scorn and his indifference. They ought to have let him hurl through her his defiance of them. Art aside, they need not have grudged him that excursion.

He could not, he told himself, face Zuleika now. As artist, he saw that there was irony enough left over to make the meeting a fine one. As theologian, he did not hold her responsible for his destiny. But as a man, after what she had done to him last night, and before what he had to do for her to-day, he would not go out of his way to meet her. Of course, he would not actually avoid her. To seem to run away from her were beneath his dignity. But, if he did meet her, what in heaven's name should he say to her? He remembered his promise to lunch with The MacQuern, and shuddered. She would be there. Death, as he had said, cancelled all engagements. A very simple way out of the difficulty would be to go straight to the river. No, that would be like running away. It couldn't be done.

Hardly had he rejected the notion when he had a glimpse of a female figure coming quickly round the corner—a glimpse that sent him walking quickly away, across the road, towards Turl Street, blushing violently. Had she seen him? he asked himself. And had she seen that he saw her? He heard her running after him. He did not look round, he quickened his pace. She was gaining on him. Involuntarily, he ran—ran like a hare, and, at the corner of Turl Street, rose like a trout, saw the pavement rise at him, and fell, with a bang, prone.

Let it be said at once that in this matter the gods were absolutely blameless. It is true they had decreed that a piece of orange-peel should be thrown down this morning at the corner of Turl Street. But the Master of Balliol, not the Duke, was the person they had destined to slip on it. You must not imagine that they think out and appoint everything that is to befall us, down to the smallest detail. Generally, they just draw a sort of broad outline, and leave us to fill it in according to our taste. Thus, in the matters of which this book is record, it was they who made the Warden invite his grand-daughter to Oxford, and invite the Duke to meet her on the evening of her arrival. And it was they who prompted the Duke to die for her on the following (Tuesday) afternoon. They had intended that he should execute his resolve after, or before, the boat-race of that evening. But an oversight upset this plan. They had forgotten on Monday night to uncage the two black owls; and so it was necessary that the Duke's death should be postponed. They accordingly prompted Zuleika to save him. For the rest, they let the tragedy run its own course—merely putting in a felicitous touch here and there, or vetoing a superfluity, such as that Katie should open Zuleika's letter. It was no part of their scheme that the Duke should mistake Mélisande for her mistress, or that he should run away from her, and they were genuinely sorry when he, instead of the Master of Balliol, came to grief over the orange-peel.

Them, however, the Duke cursed as he fell; them again as he raised himself on one elbow, giddy and sore; and when he found that the woman bending over him was not she whom he dreaded, but her innocent maid, it was against them that he almost foamed at the mouth.

"Monsieur le Duc has done himself harm—no?" panted Mélisande. "Here is a letter from Miss Dobson's part. She say to me: 'Give it him with your own hand.'"

The Duke received the letter and, sitting upright, tore it to shreds, thus confirming a suspicion which Mélisande had conceived at the moment when he took to his heels, that all English noblemen are mad, but mad, and of a madness.

"Nom de Dieu," she cried, wringing her hands, "what shall I tell to Mademoiselle?"

"Tell her——" the Duke choked back a phrase of which

the memory would have shamed his last hours. "Tell her," he substituted, "that you have seen Marius sitting among the ruins of Carthage," and limped quickly away down the Turl.

Both his hands had been abraded by the fall. He tended them angrily with his handkerchief. Mr. Druce, the chemist, had anon the privilege of bathing and plastering them, also of balming and binding the right knee and the left shin. "Might have been a very nasty accident, your Grace," he said. "It was," said the Duke. Mr. Druce concurred.

Nevertheless, Mr. Druce's remark sank deep. The Duke thought it quite likely that the gods had intended the accident to be fatal, and that only by his own skill and lightness in falling had he escaped the ignominy of dying in full flight from a lady's-maid. He had not, you see, lost all sense of free-will. While Mr. Druce put the finishing touches to his shin, "I am utterly purposed," he said to himself, "that for this death of mine I will choose my own manner and my own—well, not 'time' exactly, but whatever moment within my brief span of life shall seem aptest to me. *Unberufen*," he added, lightly tapping Mr. Druce's counter.

The sight of some bottles of Cold Mixture on that hospitable board reminded him of a painful fact. In the clash of the morning's excitements, he had hardly felt the gross ailment that was on him. He became fully conscious of it now, and there leapt in him a hideous doubt: had he escaped a violent death only to succumb to "natural causes"? He had never hitherto had anything the matter with him, and thus he belonged to the worst, the most apprehensive, class of patients. He knew that a cold, were it neglected, might turn malignant; and he had a vision of himself gripped suddenly in the street by internal agonies—a sympathetic crowd, an ambulance, his darkened bedroom; local doctor making hopelessly wrong diagnosis; eminent specialists served up hot by special train, commending local doctor's treatment, but shaking their heads and refusing to say more

than: "He has youth on his side"; a slight rally at sunset; the
end. All this flashed through his mind. He quailed. There
was not a moment to lose. He frankly confessed to Mr.
Druce that he had a cold.

Mr. Druce, trying to insinuate by his manner that this fact
had not been obvious, suggested the Mixture—a teaspoonful
every two hours. "Give me some now, please, at once," said
the Duke.

He felt magically better for the draught. He handled the
little glass lovingly, and eyed the bottle. "Why not two
teaspoonfuls every hour?" he suggested with an eagerness
almost dipsomaniacal. But Mr. Druce was respectfully firm
against that. The Duke yielded. He fancied, indeed, that the
gods had meant him to die of an overdose.

Still, he had a craving for more. Few though his hours
were, he hoped the next two would pass quickly. And,
though he knew Mr. Druce could be trusted to send the
bottle round to his rooms immediately, he preferred to carry
it away with him. He slipped it into the breast-pocket of his
coat, almost heedless of the slight extrusion it made there.

Just as he was about to cross the High again, on his way
home, a butcher's cart dashed down the slope, recklessly
driven. He stepped well back on the pavement, and smiled a
sardonic smile. He looked to right and to left, carefully
gauging the traffic. Some time elapsed before he deemed
the road clear enough for transit.

Safely across, he encountered a figure that seemed to loom
up out of the dim past. Oover! Was it but yesternight that
Oover dined with him? With the sensation of a man groping
among archives, he began to apologise to the Rhodes
Scholar for having left him so abruptly at the Junta. Then,
presto!—as though those musty archives were changed to a
crisp morning paper agog with terrific headlines—he remembered the awful resolve of Oover, and of all young
Oxford.

"Of course," he asked, with a lightness that hardly hid his dread of the answer, "you have dismissed the notion you were toying with when I left you?"

Oover's face, like his nature, was as sensitive as it was massive, and it instantly expressed his pain at the doubt cast on his high seriousness. "Duke," he asked, "d'you take me for a skunk?"

"Without pretending to be quite sure what a skunk is," said the Duke, "I take you to be all that it isn't. And the high esteem in which I hold you is the measure for me of the loss that your death would be to America and to Oxford."

Oover blushed. "Duke," he said, "that's a bully testimonial. But don't worry. America can turn out millions just like me, and Oxford can have as many of them as she can hold. On the other hand, how many of *you* can be turned out, as per sample, in England? Yet you choose to destroy yourself. You avail yourself of the Unwritten Law. And you're right, Sir. Love transcends all."

"But does it? What if I told you I had changed my mind?"

"Then, Duke," said Oover, slowly, "I should believe that all those yarns I used to hear about the British aristocracy were true, after all. I should aver that you were not a white man. Leading us on like that, and then—— Say, Duke! Are you going to die to-day, or not?"

"As a matter of fact, I am, but——"

"Shake!"

"But——"

Oover wrung the Duke's hand, and was passing on. "Stay!" he was adjured.

"Sorry, unable. It's just turning eleven o'clock, and I've a lecture. While life lasts, I'm bound to respect Rhodes' intentions." The conscientious Scholar hurried away.

The Duke wandered down the High, taking counsel with himself. He was ashamed of having so utterly forgotten the mischief he had wrought at large. At dawn he had vowed to undo it. Undo it he must. But the task was not a simple one now. If he could say: "Behold, I take back my word. I spurn Miss Dobson, and embrace life," it was possible that his example would suffice. But now that he could only say: "Behold, I spurn Miss Dobson, and will not die for her, but I am going to commit suicide, all the same," it was clear that his words could carry very little force. Also, he saw with pain that they placed him in a somewhat ludicrous position. His end, as designed yesterday, had a large and simple grandeur. So had his recantation of it. But this new compromise between the two things had a fumbled, a feeble, an ignoble look. It seemed to combine all the disadvantages of both courses. It stained his honour without prolonging his life. Surely, this was a high price to pay for snubbing Zuleika. . . . Yes, he must revert without more ado to his first scheme. He must die in the manner that he had blazoned forth. And he must do it with a good grace, none knowing he was not glad; else the action lost all dignity. True, this was no way to be a saviour. But only by not dying at all could he have set a really potent example. . . . He remembered the look that had come into Oover's eyes just now at the notion of his unfaith. Perhaps he would have been the mock, not the saviour of Oxford. Better dishonour than death, maybe. But, since die he must, he must die not belittling or tarnishing the name of Tanville-Tankerton.

Within these bounds, however, he must put forth his full might to avert the general catastrophe—and to punish Zuleika nearly well enough, after all, by intercepting that vast nosegay from her outstretched hands and her distended nostrils. There was no time to be lost, then. But he wondered, as he paced the grand curve between St. Mary's and Magdalen Bridge, just how was he to begin?

Down the flight of steps from Queen's came lounging an average undergraduate.

"Mr. Smith," said the Duke, "a word with you."

"But my name is not Smith," said the young man.

"Generically it is," replied the Duke. "You are Smith to all intents and purposes. That, indeed, is why I address you. In making your acquaintance, I make a thousand acquaintances. You are a short cut to knowledge. Tell me, do you seriously think of drowning yourself this afternoon?"

"Rather," said the undergraduate.

"A meiosis in common use, equivalent to 'Yes, assuredly,'" murmured the Duke. "And why," he then asked, "do you mean to do this?"

"Why? How can you ask? Why are *you* going to do it?"

"The Socratic manner is not a game at which two can play. Please answer my question, to the best of your ability."

"Well, because I can't live without her. Because I want to prove my love for her. Because——"

"One reason at a time please," said the Duke, holding up his hand. "You can't live without her? Then I am to assume that you look forward to dying?"

"Rather."

"You are truly happy in that prospect?"

"Yes. Rather."

"Now, suppose I showed you two pieces of equally fine amber—a big one and a little one. Which of these would you rather possess?"

"The big one, I suppose."

"And this because it is better to have more than to have less of a good thing?"

"Just so."

"Do you consider happiness a good thing or a bad one?"

"A good one."

"So that a man would rather have more than less of happiness?"

"Undoubtedly."

"Then does it not seem to you that you would do well to postpone your suicide indefinitely?"

"But I have just said I can't live without her."

"You have still more recently declared yourself truly happy."

"Yes, but——"

"Now, be careful, Mr. Smith. Remember, this is a matter of life and death. Try to do yourself justice. I have asked you——"

But the undergraduate was walking away, not without a certain dignity.

The Duke felt that he had not handled his man skilfully. He remembered that even Socrates, for all the popular charm of his mock-modesty and his true geniality, had ceased after a while to be tolerable. Without such a manner to grace his method, Socrates would have had a very brief time indeed. The Duke recoiled from what he took to be another pitfall. He almost smelt hemlock.

A party of four undergraduates abreast was approaching. How should he address them? His choice wavered between the evangelic wistfulness of "Are you saved?" and the breeziness of the recruiting sergeant's "Come, you're fine upstanding young fellows. "Isn't it a pity," etc. Meanwhile, the quartet had passed by.

Two other undergraduates approached. The Duke asked them simply as a personal favour to himself not to throw away their lives. They said they were very sorry, but in this particular matter they must please themselves. In vain he pled. They admitted that but for his example they would never have thought of dying. They wished they could show him their gratitude in any way but the one which would rob them of it.

The Duke drifted further down the High, bespeaking every undergraduate he met, leaving untried no argument, no inducement. For one man whose name he happened to know, he invented an urgent personal message from Miss Dobson imploring him not to die on her account. On another man he offered to settle by hasty codicil a sum of money sufficient to yield an annual income of two thousand pounds—three thousand—any sum within reason. With another he offered to walk, arm in arm, to Carfax and back again. All to no avail.

He found himself in the precincts of Magdalen, preaching from the little open-air pulpit there an impassioned sermon on the sacredness of human life, and referring to Zuleika in terms which John Knox would have hesitated to utter. As he piled up the invective, he noticed an ominous restiveness in the congregation—murmurs, clenching of hands, dark looks. He saw the pulpit as yet another trap laid for him by the gods. He had walked straight into it: another moment, and he might be dragged down, overwhelmed by numbers, torn limb from limb. All that was in him of quelling power he put hastily into his eyes, and manœuvred his tongue to gentler discourse, deprecating his right to judge "this lady", and merely pointing the marvel, the awful though noble folly, of his resolve. He ended on a note of quiet pathos. "To-night I shall be among the shades. There be not you, my brothers."

Good though the sermon was in style and sentiment, the flaw in its reasoning was too patent for any converts to be made. As he walked out of the quadrangle, the Duke felt the hopelessness of his cause. Still he battled bravely for it up the High, waylaying, cajoling, commanding, offering vast bribes. He carried his crusade into the Loder, and thence into Vincent's, and out into the street again, eager, untiring, unavailing: everywhere he found his precept checkmated by his example.

The sight of The MacQuern coming out top-speed from the Market, with a large but inexpensive bunch of flowers, reminded him of the luncheon that was to be. Never to throw over an engagement was for him, as we have seen, a point of honour. But this particular engagement—hateful, when he accepted it, by reason of his love—was now impossible for the reason which had made him take so ignominiously to his heels this morning. He curtly told the Scot not to expect him.

"Is *she* not coming?" gasped the Scot, with quick suspicion.

"Oh," said the Duke, turning on his heel, "she doesn't know that I shan't be there. You may count on her." This he took to be the very truth, and he was glad to have made of it a thrust at the man who had so uncouthly asserted himself last night. He could not help smiling, though, at this little resentment erect after the cataclysm that had swept away all else. Then he smiled to think how uneasy Zuleika would be at his absence. What agonies of suspense she must have had all this morning! He imagined her silent at the luncheon, with a vacant gaze at the door, eating nothing at all. And he became aware that he was rather hungry. He had done all he could to save young Oxford. Now for some sandwiches! He went into the Junta.

As he rang the dining-room bell, his eyes rested on the miniature of Nellie O'Mora. And the eyes of Nellie O'Mora seemed to meet his in reproach. Just as she may have gazed at Greddon when he cast her off, so now did she gaze at him who a few hours ago had refused to honour her memory.

Yes, and many other eyes than hers rebuked him. It was around the walls of this room that hung those presentments of the Junta as focused, year after year, in a certain corner of Tom Quad, by Messrs. Hills and Saunders. All around, the members of the little hierarchy, a hierarchy ever changing in all but youth and a certain sternness of aspect that comes at the moment of being immortalised, were gazing forth now with a sternness beyond their wont. Not one of them but had in his day handed on loyally the praise of Nellie O'Mora, in the form their Founder had ordained. And the Duke's revolt last night had so incensed them that they would, if they could, have come down from their frames and walked straight out of the club, in chronological order—first, the men of the 'sixties, almost as near in time to Greddon as to the Duke, all so gloriously be-whiskered and cravated, but how faded now, alas, by exposure; and last of all in the procession and angrier perhaps than any of them, the Duke himself—the Duke of a year ago, President and sole Member.

But, as he gazed into the eyes of Nellie O'Mora now, Dorset needed not for penitence the reproaches of his past self or of his fore-runners. "Sweet girl," he murmured, "forgive me. I was mad. I was under the sway of a deplorable infatuation. It is past. See," he murmured with a delicacy of feeling that justified the untruth, "I am come here for the express purpose of undoing my impiety." And, turning to the club-waiter who at this moment answered the bell, he said: "Bring me a glass of port, please, Barrett." Of sandwiches he said nothing.

At the word "See" he had stretched one hand towards Nellie; the other he had laid on his heart, where it seemed to encounter some sort of hard obstruction. This he vaguely fingered, wondering what it might be, while he gave his order to Barrett. With a sudden cry he dipped his hand into his breast-pocket and drew forth the bottle he had borne away from Mr. Druce's. He snatched out his watch: one o'clock!—fifteen minutes overdue. Wildly, he called the waiter back. "A tea-spoon, quick! No port. A wine-glass and a tea-spoon. And—for I don't mind telling you, Barrett, that your mission is of an urgency beyond conjecture—take lightning for your model. Go!"

Agitation mastered him. He tried vainly to feel his pulse, well knowing that if he found it he could deduce nothing from its action. He saw himself haggard in the looking-glass. Would Barrett never come? "Every two hours"—the directions were explicit. Had he delivered himself into the gods' hands? The eyes of Nellie O'Mora were on him compassionately; and all the eyes of his forerunners were on him in austere scorn: "See," they seemed to be saying, "the chastisement of last night's blasphemy." Violently, insistently, he rang the bell.

In rushed Barrett at last. From the tea-spoon into the wine-glass the Duke poured the draught of salvation, and then, raising it aloft, he looked around at his forerunners and in a firm voice cried: "Gentlemen, I give you Nellie O'Mora, the fairest witch that ever was or will be." He drained his glass, heaved the deep sigh of a double satisfaction, dismissed with a glance the wondering Barrett, and sat down.

He was glad to be able to face Nellie with a clear conscience. Her eyes were not less sad now, but it seemed to him that their sadness came of a knowledge that she would never see him again. She seemed to be saying to him: "Had you lived in my day, it is you that I would have loved, not Greddon." And he made silent answer. "Had you lived in my day, I should have been Dobson-proof." He realised, however, that to Zuleika he owed the tenderness he now felt for Miss O'Mora. It was Zuleika that had cured him of his aseity. She it was that had made his heart a warm and negotiable thing. Yes, and that was the final cruelty. To love and be loved—this, he had come to know, was all that mattered. Yesterday, to love and die had seemed felicity enough. Now he knew that the secret, the open secret, of happiness was in mutual love—a state that needed not the fillip of death. And he had to die without having ever lived. Admiration, homage, fear, he had sown broadcast. The one woman who had loved him had turned to stone because he loved her. Death would lose much of its sting for him if there were somewhere in the world just one woman, however lowly, whose heart would be broken by his dying. What a pity Nellie O'Mora was not really extant!

Suddenly he recalled certain words lightly spoken yesterday by Zuleika. She had told him he was loved by the girl who waited on him—the daughter of his landlady. Was this so? He had seen no sign of it, had received no token of it.

But, after all, how should he have seen a sign of anything in one whom he had never consciously visualised? That she had never thrust herself on his notice might mean merely that she had been well brought-up. What likelier than that the daughter of Mrs. Batch, that worthy soul, had been well brought-up?

Here, at any rate, was the chance of a new element in his life, or rather in his death. Here, possibly, was a maiden to mourn him. He would lunch in his rooms.

With a farewell look at Nellie's miniature, he took the medicine-bottle from the table, and went quickly out. The heavens had grown steadily darker and darker, the air more sulphurous and baleful. And the High had a strangely woebegone look, being all forsaken by youth, in this hour of luncheon. Even so would its look be all to-morrow, thought the Duke, and for many morrows. Well, he had done what he could. He was free now to brighten a little his own last hours. He hastened on, eager to see the landlady's daughter. He wondered what she was like, and whether she really loved him.

As he threw open the door of his sitting-room, he was aware of a rustle, a rush, a cry. In another instant, he was aware of Zuleika Dobson at his feet, at his knees, clasping him to her, sobbing, laughing, sobbing.

# XVI

FOR what happened a few moments later you must not blame him. Some measure of force was the only way out of an impossible situation. It was in vain that he commanded the young lady to let go: she did but cling the closer. It was in vain that he tried to disentangle himself of her by standing first on one foot, then on the other, and veering sharply on his heel: she did but sway as though hinged to him. He had no choice but to grasp her by the wrists, cast her aside, and step clear of her into the room.

Her hat, gauzily basking with a pair of long white gloves on one of his arm-chairs, proclaimed that she had come to stay.

Nor did she rise. Propped on one elbow with heaving bosom and parted lips, she seemed to be trying to realise what had been done to her. Through her undried tears her eyes shone up to him.

He asked: "To what am I indebted for this visit?"

"Ah, say that again!" she murmured. "Your voice is music."

He repeated his question.

"Music!" she said dreamily; and such is the force of habit that "I don't," she added, "know anything about music, really. But I know what I like."

"Had you not better get up from the floor?" he said. "The door is open, and anyone who passed might see you."

Softly she stroked the carpet with the palms of her hands. "Happy carpet!" she crooned. "Aye, happy the very women that wove the threads that are trod by the feet of my beloved master. But hark! he bids his slave rise and stand before him!"

Just after she had risen, a figure appeared in the doorway.

"I beg pardon, your Grace; Mother wants to know, will you be lunching in?"

"Yes," said the Duke. "I will ring when I am ready." And it dawned on him that this girl, who perhaps loved him, was, according to all known standards, extraordinarily pretty.

"Will——" she hesitated, "will Miss Dobson be——"

"No," he said. "I shall be alone." And there was in the girl's parting half-glance at Zuleika that which told him he was truly loved, and made him the more impatient of his offensive and accursed visitor.

"You want to be rid of me?" asked Zuleika, when the girl was gone.

"I have no wish to be rude; but—since you force me to say it—yes."

"Then take me," she cried, throwing back her arms, "and throw me out of the window."

He smiled coldly.

"You think I don't mean it? You think I would struggle? Try me." She let herself droop sideways, in an attitude limp and portable. "Try me," she repeated.

"All this is very well conceived, no doubt," said he, "and well executed. But it happens to be otiose."

"What do you mean?"

"I mean you may set your mind at rest. I am not going to back out of my promise."

Zuleika flushed. "You are cruel. I would give the world and all not to have written you that hateful letter. Forget it, forget it, for pity's sake!"

The Duke looked searchingly at her. "You mean that you now wish to release me from my promise?"

"Release you? As if you were ever bound! Don't torture me!"

He wondered what deep game she was playing. Very real, though, her anguish seemed; and, if real it was, then—he stared, he gasped—there could be but one explanation. He put it to her. "You love me?"

"With all my soul."

His heart leapt. If she spoke truth, then indeed vengeance was his! But: "What proof have I?" he asked her.

"Proof? Have men absolutely *no* intuition? If you need proof, produce it. Where are my ear-rings?"

"Your ear-rings? Why?"

Impatiently she pointed to two white pearls that fastened the front of her blouse. "These are your studs. It was from them I had the great first hint this morning."

"Black and pink, were they not, when you took them?"

"Of course. And then I forgot that I had them. When I undressed, they must have rolled on to the carpet. Mélisande found them this morning when she was making the room ready for me to dress. That was just after she came back from bringing you my first letter. I was bewildered. I doubted. Might not the pearls have gone back to their natural state simply through being yours no more? That is why I wrote again to you, my own darling—a frantic little questioning letter. When I heard how you had torn it up, I knew, I knew that the pearls had not mocked me. I tele-scoped my toilet and came rushing round to you. How many hours have I been waiting for you?"

The Duke had drawn her ear-rings from his waistcoat pocket, and was contemplating them in the palm of his hand. Blanched, both of them, yes. He laid them on the table. "Take them," he said.

"No," she shuddered. "I could never forget that once they were both black." She flung them into the fender. "Oh John," she cried, turning to him and falling again to her knees, "I do so want to forget what I have been. I want to atone. You think you can drive me out of your life. You cannot, darling—since you won't kill me. Always I shall follow you on my knees, thus."

He looked down at her over his folded arms. "I am not going to back out of my promise," he repeated.

She stopped her ears.

With a stern joy he unfolded his arms, took some papers from his breast-pocket, and, selecting one of them, handed it to her. It was the telegram sent by his steward.

She read it. With a stern joy he watched her reading it.

Wild-eyed, she looked up from it to him, tried to speak, and swerved down senseless.

He had not foreseen this. "Help!" he vaguely cried—was she not a fellow-creature?—and rushed blindly out to his bedroom, whence he returned, a moment later, with the water-jug. He dipped his hand, and sprinkled the upturned face (Dew-drops on a white rose? But some other, sharper analogy hovered to him). He dipped and sprinkled. The water-beads broke, mingled—rivulets now. He dipped and flung, then caught the horrible analogy and rebounded.

It was at this moment that Zuleika opened her eyes. "Where am I?" She weakly raised herself on one elbow; and the suspension of the Duke's hatred would have been repealed simultaneously with that of her consciousness, had it not already been repealed by the analogy. She put a hand to her face, then looked at the wet palm wonderingly, looked at the Duke, saw the water-jug beside him. She, too, it seemed, had caught the analogy; for with a wan smile she said: "We are quits now, John, aren't we?"

Her poor little jest drew to the Duke's face no answering smile, did but make hotter the blush there. The wave of her returning memory swept on—swept up to her with a roar the instant past. "Oh," she cried, staggering to her feet, "the owls, the owls!"

Vengeance was his, and, "Yes, there," he said, "is the ineluctable hard fact you wake to. The owls have hooted.

The gods have spoken. This day your wish is to be fulfilled."

"The owls have hooted. The gods have spoken. This day —oh, it must not be, John! Heaven have mercy on me!"

"The unerring owls have hooted. The dispiteous and humorous gods have spoken. Miss Dobson, it has to be. And let me remind you," he added, with a glance at his watch, "that you ought not to keep The MacQuern waiting for luncheon."

"That is unworthy of you," she said. There was in her eyes a look that made the words sound as if they had been spoken by a dumb animal.

"You have sent him an excuse?"

"No, I have forgotten him."

"That is unworthy of you. After all, he is going to die for you, like the rest of us. I am but one of a number, you know. Use your sense of proportion."

"If I do that," she said after a pause, "you may not be pleased by the issue. I may find that whereas yesterday I was great in my sinfulness, and to-day am great in my love, you, in your hate of me, are small. I may find that what I had taken to be a great indifference is nothing but a very small hate. . . . Ah, I have wounded you? Forgive me, a weak woman, talking at random in her wretchedness. Oh John, John, if I thought you small, my love would but take on the crown of pity. Don't forbid me to call you John. I looked you up in Debrett while I was waiting for you. That seemed to bring you nearer to me. So many other names you have, too. I remember you told me them all yesterday, here in this room—not twenty-four hours ago. Hours? Years!" She laughed hysterically. "John, don't you see why I won't stop talking? It's because I dare not think."

"Yonder in Balliol," he suavely said, "you will find the matter of my death easier to forget than here." He took her hat and gloves from the arm-chair, and held them carefully out to her; but she did not take them.

"I give you three minutes," he told her. "Two minutes, that is, in which to make yourself tidy before the mirror. A third in which to say good-bye and be outside the front door."

"If I refuse?"

"You will not."

"If I do?"

"I shall send for a policeman."

She looked well at him. "Yes," she slowly said, "I think you would do that."

She took her things from him, and laid them by the mirror. With a high hand she quelled the excesses of her hair—some of the curls still agleam with water—and knowingly poised and pinned her hat. Then, after a few swift touches and passes at neck and waist, she took her gloves and, wheeling round to him: "There!" she said, "I have been quick."

"Admirably," he allowed.

"Quick in more than meets the eye, John. Spiritually quick. You saw me putting on my hat; you did not see love taking on the crown of pity, and me bonneting her with it, tripping her up and trampling the life out of her. Oh, a most cold-blooded business, John! Had to be done, though. No other way out. So I just used my sense of proportion, as you rashly bade me, and then hardened my heart at sight of you as you are. One of a number? Yes, and a quite unlovable unit. So I am all right again. And now, where is Balliol? Far from here?"

"No," he answered, choking a little, as might a card-player who, having been dealt a splendid hand, and having played it with flawless skill, has yet—damn it!—lost the odd trick. "Balliol is quite near. At the end of this street in fact. I can show it to you from the front door."

Yes, he had controlled himself. But this, he furiously felt, did not make him look the less a fool. What ought he to have *said?* He prayed, as he followed the victorious young woman downstairs, that *l'esprit de l'escalier* might befall him. Alas, it did not.

"By the way," she said, when he had shown her where Balliol lay, "have you told anybody that you aren't dying just for me?"

"No," he answered, "I have preferred not to."

"Then officially, as it were, and in the eyes of the world, you die for me? Then all's well that ends well. Shall we say good-bye here? I shall be on the Judas Barge; but I suppose there will be a crush, as yesterday?"

"Sure to be. There always is on the last night of the Eights, you know. Good-bye."

"Good-bye, little John—small John," she cried across her shoulder, having the last word.

# XVII

He might not have grudged her the last word, had she properly needed it. Its utter superfluity—the perfection of her victory without it—was what galled him. Yes, she had outflanked him, taken him unawares, and he had fired not one shot. *Esprit de l'escalier*—it was as he went upstairs that he saw how he might yet have snatched from her, if not the victory, the palm. Of course he ought to have laughed aloud —"Capital, capital! You really do deserve to fool me. But ah, yours is a love that can't be dissembled. Never was man by maiden loved more ardently than I by you, my poor girl, at this moment."

And stay!—what if she really *had* been but pretending to have killed her love? He paused on the threshold of his room. The sudden doubt made his lost chance the more sickening. Yet was the doubt dear to him . . . What likelier, after all, than that she had been pretending? She had already twitted him with his lack of intuition. He had not seen that she loved him when she certainly did love him. He had needed the pearls' demonstration of that.—The pearls! *They* would betray her. He darted to the fender, and one of them he espied there instantly—white? A rather flushed white, certainly. For the other he had to peer down. There it lay, not very distinct on the hearth's black-leading.

He turned away. He blamed himself for not dismissing from his mind the hussy he had dismissed from his room. Oh for an ounce of civet and a few poppies! The water-jug stood as a reminder of the hateful visit and of . . . He took it hastily away into his bedroom. There he washed his hands. The fact that he had touched Zuleika gave to this ablution a symbolism that made it the more refreshing.

Civet, poppies? Was there not, at his call, a sweeter perfume, a stronger anodyne? He rang the bell, almost caressingly.

His heart beat at sound of the clinking and rattling of the tray borne up the stairs. She was coming, the girl who loved him, the girl whose heart would be broken when he died. Yet, when the tray appeared in the doorway, and she behind it, the tray took precedence of her in his soul not less than in his sight. Twice, after an arduous morning, had his luncheon been postponed, and the coming of it now made intolerable the pangs of his hunger.

Also, while the girl laid the table-cloth, it occurred to him how flimsy, after all, was the evidence that she loved him. Suppose she did nothing of the kind! At the Junta, he had foreseen no difficulty in asking her. Now he found himself a prey to embarrassment. He wondered why. He had not failed in flow of gracious words to Nellie O'Mora. Well, a miniature by Hoppner was one thing, a landlady's live daughter was another. At any rate, he must prime himself with food. He wished Mrs. Batch had sent up something more calorific than cold salmon. He asked her daughter what was to follow.

"There's a pigeon-pie, your Grace."

"Cold? Then please ask your mother to heat it in the oven—quickly. Anything after that?"

"A custard pudding, your Grace."

"Cold? Let this, too, be heated. And bring up a bottle of champagne, please; and—and a bottle of port."

His was a head that had always hitherto defied the grape. But he thought that to-day, by all he had gone through, by all the shocks he had suffered, and the strains he had steeled himself to bear, as well as by the actual malady that gripped him, he might perchance have been sapped enough to experience by reaction that cordial glow of which he had now and again seen symptoms in his fellows.

Nor was he altogether disappointed of this hope. As the meal progressed, and the last of the champagne sparkled in his glass, certain things said to him by Zuleika—certain implied criticisms that had rankled, yes—lost their power to discommode him. He was able to smile at the impertinences of an angry woman, the tantrums of a tenth-rate conjurer told to go away. He felt he had perhaps acted harshly. With all her faults, she had adored him. Yes, he had been arbitrary. There seemed to be a strain of brutality in his nature. Poor Zuleika! He was glad for her that she had contrived to master her infatuation . . . Enough for him that he was loved by this exquisite meek girl who had served him at the feast. Anon, when he summoned her to clear the things away, he would bid her tell him the tale of her lowly passion. He poured a second glass of port, sipped it, quaffed it, poured a third. The grey gloom of the weather did but, as he eyed the bottle, heighten his sense of the rich sunshine so long ago imprisoned by the vintner and now released to make glad his soul. Even so to be released was the love pent for him in the heart of this sweet girl. Would that he loved her in return! . . . Why not?

> "Prius insolentem
> Serva Briseis niveo colore
> Movit Achillem."

Nor were it gracious to invite an avowal of love and offer none in return. Yet, yet, expansive though his mood was, he could not pretend to himself that he was about to feel in this girl's presence anything but gratitude. He might pretend to her? Deception were a very poor return indeed for all her kindness. Besides, it might turn her head. Some small token of his gratitude—some trinket by which to remember him—was all that he could allow himself to offer . . . What trinket? Would she like to have one of his scarf-pins? Absurd to give a girl a scarf-pin. Studs? Still more abs—— Ah! he had it, he literally and most providentially had it, there, in the fender: a pair of ear-rings!

He plucked the pink pearl and the black from where they lay, and rang the bell.

His sense of dramatic propriety needed that the girl should, before he addressed her, perform her task of clearing the table. If she had it to perform after telling her love, and after receiving his gift and his farewell, the bathos would be distressing for them both.

But, while he watched her at her task, he did wish she would be a little quicker. For the glow in him seemed to be cooling momently. He wished he had had more than three glasses from the crusted bottle which she was putting away into the chiffonier. Down, doubt! Down, sense of disparity! The moment was at hand. Would he let it slip? Now she was folding up the table-cloth, now she was going.

"Stay!" he uttered. "I have something to say to you." The girl turned to him.

He forced his eyes to meet hers. "I understand," he said in a constrained voice, "that you regard me with sentiments of something more than esteem.—Is this so?"

The girl had stepped quickly back, and her face was scarlet.

"Nay," he said, having to go through with it now, "there is no cause for embarrassment. And I am sure you will acquit me of wanton curiosity. Is it a fact that you—love me?"

She tried to speak, could not. But she nodded her head.

The Duke, much relieved, came nearer to her. "What is your name?" he asked gently.

"Katie," she was able to gasp.

"Well, Katie, how long have you loved me?"

"Ever since," she faltered, "ever since you came to engage the rooms."

"You are not, of course, given to idolising any tenant of your mother's?"

"No."

"May I boast myself the first possessor of your heart?"

"Yes." She had become very pale now, and was trembling painfully.

"And may I assume that your love for me has been entirely disinterested? . . . You do not catch my meaning? I will put my question in another way. In loving me, you never supposed me likely to return your love?"

The girl looked up at him quickly, but at once her eyelids fluttered down again.

"Come, come!" said the Duke. "My question is a plain one. Did you ever for an instant suppose, Katie, that I might come to love you?"

"No," she said in a whisper; "I never dared to hope that."

"Precisely," said he. "You never imagined that you had anything to gain by your affection. You were not contriving a trap for me. You were upheld by no hope of becoming a young Duchess, with more frocks than you could wear and more dross than you could scatter. I am glad. I am touched. You are the first woman that has loved me in that way. Or rather," he muttered, "the first but one. And she . . . Answer me," he said, standing over the girl, and speaking with a great intensity. "If I were to tell you that I loved you, would you cease to love me?"

"Oh, your Grace!" cried the girl. "Why no! I never dared——"

"Enough!" he said. "The catechism is ended. I have something which I should like to give you. Are your ears pierced?"

"Yes, your Grace."

"Then, Katie, honour me by accepting this present." So saying, he placed in the girl's hand the black pearl and the pink. The sight of them banished for a moment all other emotions in their recipient. She forgot herself. "Lor!" she said.

"I hope you will wear them always for my sake," said the Duke.

She had expressed herself in the monosyllable. No words came to her lips, but to her eyes many tears, through which the pearls were invisible. They whirled in her bewildered brain as a token that she was loved—loved by *him*, though but yesterday he had loved another. It was all so sudden, so beautiful. You might have knocked her down (she says so to this day) with a feather. Seeing her agitation, the Duke pointed to a chair, bade her be seated.

Her mind was cleared by the new posture. Suspicion crept into it, followed by alarm. She looked at the ear-rings, then up at the Duke.

"No," said he, misinterpreting the question in her eyes, "they are real pearls."

"It isn't that," she quavered, "it is—it is——"

"That they were given to me by Miss Dobson?"

"Oh, they were, were they? Then"—Katie rose, throwing the pearls on the floor—"I'll have nothing to do with them. I hate her."

"So do I," said the Duke, in a burst of confidence. "No, I don't," he added hastily. "Please forget that I said that."

It occurred to Katie that Miss Dobson would be ill-pleased that the pearls should pass to her. She picked them up.

"Only—only——" again her doubts beset her and she looked from the pearls to the Duke.

"Speak on," he said.

"Oh you aren't playing with me, are you? You don't mean me harm, do you? I have been well brought-up. I have been warned against things. And it seems so strange, what you have said to me. You are a Duke, and I—I am only——"

"It is the privilege of nobility to condescend."

"Yes, yes," she cried. "I see. Oh, I was wicked to doubt you. And love levels all, doesn't it? love and the Board school. Our stations are far apart, but I've been educated far above mine. I've learnt more than most real ladies have. I passed the Seventh Standard when I was only just fourteen. I was considered one of the sharpest girls in the school. And I've gone on learning since then," she continued eagerly. "I utilise all my spare moments. I've read twenty-seven of the Hundred Best Books. I collect ferns. I play the piano, whenever . . ." She broke off, for she remembered that her music was always interrupted by the ringing of the Duke's bell and a polite request that it should cease.

"I am glad to hear of these accomplishments. They do you great credit, I am sure. But—well, I do not quite see why you enumerate them just now."

"It isn't that I am vain," she pleaded. "I only mentioned them because . . . oh, don't you see? If I'm not ignorant, I shan't disgrace you. People won't be so able to say you've been and thrown yourself away."

"Thrown myself away? What do you mean?"

"Oh, they'll make all sorts of objections, I know. They'll all be against me, and——"

"For heaven's sake, explain yourself."

"Your aunt, she looked a very proud lady—very high and hard. I thought so when she came here last term. But you're of age. You're your own master. Oh, I trust you; you'll stand by me. If you love me really you won't listen to them."

"Love you? I? Are you mad?"

Each stared at the other, utterly bewildered.

The girl was the first to break the silence. Her voice came in a whisper. "You've not been playing a joke on me! You meant what you said, didn't you?"

"What have I said?"

"You said you loved me."

"You must be dreaming."

"I'm not. Here are the ear-rings you gave me." She pinched them as material proof. "You said you loved me just before you gave me them. You know you did. And if I thought you'd been laughing at me all the time—I'd—I'd"—a sob choked her voice—"I'd throw them in your face!"

"You must not speak to me in that manner," said the Duke coldly. "And let me warn you that this attempt to trap me and intimidate me——"

The girl had flung the ear-rings at his face. She had missed her mark. But this did not extenuate the outrageous gesture. He pointed to the door. "Go!" he said.

"Don't try that on!" she laughed. "I shan't go—not unless you drag me out. And if you do that, I'll raise the house. I'll have in the neighbours. I'll tell them all what you've done, and——" But defiance melted in the hot shame of humiliation. "Oh, you coward!" she gasped. "You coward!" She caught her apron to her face and, swaying against the wall, sobbed piteously.

Unaccustomed to love affairs, the Duke could not sail lightly over a flood of woman's tears. He was filled with pity for the poor quivering figure against the wall. How should he soothe her? Mechanically he picked up the two pearls from the carpet, and crossed to her side. He touched her on the shoulder. She shuddered away from him.

"Don't," he said gently. "Don't cry. I can't bear it. I have been stupid and thoughtless. What did you say your name was? 'Katie', to be sure. Well, Katie, I want to beg your pardon. I expressed myself badly. I was unhappy and lonely, and I saw in you a means of comfort. I snatched at you, Katie, as at a straw. And then, I suppose, I must have said something which made you think I loved you. I almost wish I did. I don't wonder you threw the ear-rings at me. I—I almost wish they had hit me. . . . You see, I have

quite forgiven you. Now do you forgive me. You will not
refuse now to wear the ear-rings. I gave them to you as a
keepsake. Wear them always in memory of me. For you will
never see me again."

The girl had ceased from crying, and her anger had spent
itself in sobs. She was gazing at him woebegone but
composed.

"Where are you going?"

"You must not ask that," said he. "Enough that my wings
are spread."

"Are you going because of *me*?"

"Not in the least. Indeed, your devotion is one of the
things which make bitter my departure. And yet—I am glad
you love me."

"Don't go," she faltered. He came nearer to her, and this
time she did not shrink from him. "Don't you find the
rooms comfortable?" she asked, gazing up at him. "Have
you ever had any complaint to make about the attendance?"

"No," said the Duke, "the attendance has always been
quite satisfactory. I have never felt that so keenly as I do
to-day."

"Then why are you leaving? Why are you breaking my
heart?"

"Suffice it that I cannot do otherwise. Henceforth you
will see me no more. But I doubt not that in the cultivation
of my memory you will find some sort of lugubrious satisfaction. See! here are the ear-rings. If you like, I will put
them in with my own hands."

She held up her face sideways. Into the lobe of her left
ear he insinuated the hook of the black pearl. On the cheek
upturned to him there were still traces of tears; the eyelashes
were still spangled. For all her blondeness, they were quite
dark, these glistening eyelashes. He had an impulse, which
he put from him. "Now the other ear," he said. The girl
turned her head. Soon the pink pearl was in its place. Yet

the girl did not move. She seemed to be waiting. Nor did the Duke himself seem to be quite satisfied. He let his fingers dally with the pearl. Anon, with a sigh, he withdrew them. The girl looked up. Their eyes met. He looked away from her. He turned away from her. "You may kiss my hand," he murmured, extending it towards her. After a pause, the warm pressure of her lips was laid on it. He sighed, but did not look round. Another pause, a longer pause, and then the clatter and clink of the outgoing tray.

# XVIII

HER actual offspring does not suffice a very motherly
woman. Such a woman was Mrs. Batch. Had she been blest
with a dozen children, she must yet have regarded herself as
also a mother to whatever two young gentlemen were lodging
under her roof. Childless but for Katie and Clarence, she
had for her successive pairs of tenants a truly vast fund of
maternal feeling to draw on. Nor were the drafts made in
secret. To every young gentleman, from the outset, she
proclaimed the relation in which she would stand to him.
Moreover, always she needed a strong filial sense in return:
this was only fair.

Because the Duke was an orphan, even more than because
he was a Duke, her heart had with a special rush gone out to
him when he and Mr. Noaks became her tenants. But,
perhaps because he had never known a mother, he was
evidently quite incapable of conceiving either Mrs. Batch as
his mother or himself as her son. Indeed, there was that in
his manner, in his look, which made her falter, for once, in
exposition of her theory—made her postpone the matter to
some more favourable time. That time never came, somehow. Still, her solicitude for him, her pride in him, her
sense that he was a great credit to her, rather waxed than
waned. He was more to her (such are the vagaries of the
maternal instinct) than Katie or Mr. Noaks: he was as much
as Clarence.

It was, therefore, a deeply agitated woman who now came
heaving up into the Duke's presence. His Grace was
"giving notice"? She was sure she begged his pardon for

coming up so sudden. But the news was that sudden. Hadn't her girl made a mistake, maybe? Girls were so vague-like nowadays. She was sure it was most kind of him to give those handsome ear-rings. But the thought of him going off so unexpected—middle of term, too—with never a why or a but! Well!

In some such welter of homely phrase (how foreign to these classic pages!) did Mrs. Batch utter her pain. The Duke answered her tersely but kindly. He apologised for going so abruptly, and said he would be very happy to write for her future use a testimonial to the excellence of her rooms and of her cooking; and with it he would give her a cheque not only for the full term's rent, and for his board since the beginning of term, but also for such board as he would have been likely to have in the term's remainder. He asked her to present her accounts forthwith.

He occupied the few minutes of her absence by writing the testimonial. It had shaped itself in his mind as a short ode in Doric Greek. But, for the benefit of Mrs. Batch, he chose to do a rough equivalent in English.

### TO AN UNDERGRADUATE NEEDING ROOMS IN OXFORD
#### (*A Sonnet in Oxfordshire Dialect*)

Zeek w'ere thee will in t'Univürsity,
Lad, thee'll not vind nör bread nör bed that matches
Them as thee'll vind, roight züre, at Mrs. Batch's . . .

I do not quote the poem *in extenso*, because, frankly, I think it was one of his least happily inspired works. His was not a Muse that could with a good grace doff the grand manner. Also, his command of the Oxfordshire dialect seems to me based less on study than on conjecture. In fact, I do not place the poem higher than among the curiosities of literature. It has extrinsic value, however, as illustrating the

Duke's thoughtfulness for others in the last hours of his life. And to Mrs. Batch the MS., framed and glazed in her hall, is an asset beyond price (witness her recent refusal of Mr. Pierpont Morgan's sensational bid for it).

This MS. she received together with the Duke's cheque. The presentation was made some twenty minutes after she had laid her accounts before him.

Lavish in giving large sums of his own accord, he was apt to be circumspect in the matter of small payments. Such is ever the way of opulent men. Nor do I see that we have a right to sneer at them for it. We cannot deny that their existence is a temptation to us. It is in our fallen nature to want to get something out of them; and, as we think in small sums (heaven knows), it is of small sums that they are careful. Absurd to suppose they really care about halfpence. It must, therefore, be about us that they care; and we ought to be grateful to them for the pains they are at to keep us guiltless. I do not suggest that Mrs. Batch had at any point overcharged the Duke; but how was he to know that she had not done so, except by checking the items, as was his wont? The reductions that he made, here and there, did not in all amount to three-and-sixpence. I do not say they were just. But I do say that his motive for making them, and his satisfaction at having made them, were rather beautiful than otherwise.

Having struck an average of Mrs. Batch's weekly charges, and a similar average of his own reductions, he had a basis on which to reckon his board for the rest of the term. This amount he added to Mrs. Batch's amended total, *plus* the full term's rent, and accordingly drew a cheque on the local bank where he had an account. Mrs. Batch said she would bring up a stamped receipt directly; but this the Duke waived, saying that the cashed cheque itself would be a sufficient receipt. Accordingly, he reduced by one penny the amount written on the cheque. Remembering to initial the correction, he remembered also, with a melancholy smile, that to-morrow the cheque would not be negotiable. Handing it, and the sonnet, to Mrs. Batch, he bade her cash it before the bank closed. "And," he said, with a glance at his watch, "you have no time to lose. It is a quarter to four." Only two hours and a quarter before the final races! How quickly the sands were running out!

Mrs. Batch paused on the threshold, wanted to know if she could "help with the packing". The Duke replied that he was taking nothing with him: his various things would be sent for, packed, and removed, within a few days. No, he did not want her to order a cab. He was going to walk. And: "Good-bye, Mrs. Batch," he said. "For legal reasons with which I won't burden you, you really must cash that cheque at once."

He sat down in solitude; and there crept over him a mood of deep depression. . . . Almost two hours and a quarter before the final races! What on earth should he do in the meantime? He seemed to have done all that there was for him to do. His executors would do the rest. He had no farewell letters to write. He had no friends with whom he was on terms of valediction. There was nothing at all for him to do. He stared blankly out of the window, at the greyness and blackness of the sky. What a day! What a climate! Why did any sane person live in England? He felt positively suicidal.

His dully vagrant eye lighted on the bottle of Cold Mixture. He ought to have dosed himself a full hour ago. Well, he didn't care.

Had Zuleika noticed the bottle? he idly wondered. Probably not. She would have made some sprightly reference to it before she went.

Since there was nothing to do but sit and think, he wished he could recapture that mood in which at luncheon he had been able to see Zuleika as an object for pity. Never, till to-day, had he seen things otherwise than they were. Nor had he ever needed to. Never, till last night, had there been in his life anything he needed to forget. That woman! As if it really mattered what she thought of him. He despised himself for wishing to forget she despised him. But the wish was the measure of the need. He eyed the chiffonier. Should he again solicit the grape?

Reluctantly he uncorked the crusted bottle, and filled a glass. Was he come to this? He sighed and sipped, quaffed and sighed. The spell of the old stored sunshine seemed not to work, this time. He could not cease from plucking at the net of ignominies in which his soul lay enmeshed. Would that he had died yesterday, escaping how much!

Not for an instant did he flinch from the mere fact of dying to-day. Since he was not immortal, as he had supposed, it were as well he should die now as fifty years hence. Better, indeed. To die "untimely", as men called it, was the timeliest of all deaths for one who had carved his youth to greatness. What perfection could he, Dorset, achieve beyond what was already his? Future years could but stale, if not actually mar, that perfection. Yes, it was lucky to perish leaving much to the imagination of posterity. Dear posterity was of a sentimental, not a realistic, habit. She always imagined the dead young hero prancing gloriously up to the Psalmist's limit a young hero still; and it was the sense of her vast loss that kept his memory green. Byron!—he would be all forgotten to-day if he had lived to be a florid old gentleman with iron-grey whiskers, writing very long, very able letters to *The Times* about the Repeal of the Corn Laws. Yes, Byron would have been that. It was indicated in him. He would have been an old gentleman exacerbated by Queen Victoria's invincible prejudice against him, her brusque refusal to "entertain" Lord John Russell's timid nomination of him for a post in the Government. . . . Shelley would have been a poet to the last. But how dull, how very dull, would have been the poetry of his middle age!—a great unreadable mass interposed between him and us. . . . Did Byron, mused the Duke, know what was to be at Missolonghi? Did he know that he was to die in service of the Greeks whom he despised? Byron might not have minded that. But what if the Greeks had told him, in so many words, that they despised *him?* How would he have felt then? Would he have been content with his potations of barley-water? . . . The Duke replenished his glass, hoping the spell might work yet. . . . Perhaps, had Byron not been a dandy—but ah, had he not been in his soul a dandy there would have been no Byron worth mentioning. And it was because he guarded not his dandyism against this and that irrelevant passion, sexual or political, that he cut so annoyingly incomplete a figure. He was absurd in his politics, vulgar in his loves. Only in himself, at the times when he stood haughtily aloof, was he impressive. Nature, fashioning him, had fashioned also a pedestal for him to stand and brood on, to pose and sing on. Off that pedestal he was lost . . . "The idol has come sliding down from its pedestal"—the Duke remembered these words spoken yesterday by Zuleika. Yes, at the moment when he slid down, he, too, was lost. For him, master-dandy, the common arena was no place. What had he to do with love? He was an utter fool at it. Byron had at least had some fun out of it. What fun had *he* had? Last night, he had forgotten to kiss Zuleika when he held her by the wrists. To-day it had been as much as he could do to let poor little Katie kiss his hand. Better be vulgar with Byron than a noodle with Dorset! he bitterly reflected. . . . Still, noodledom was nearer than vulgarity to dandyism. It was a less flagrant lapse. And he had over Byron this further advantage: his noodledom was not a matter of common knowledge; whereas Byron's vulgarity had ever needed to be in the glare of the footlights of Europe. The world would say of him that he

# ZULEIKA DOBSON

laid down his life for a woman. Deplorable somersault? But
nothing evident save this in his whole life was faulty . . .
The one other thing that might be carped at—the partisan
speech he made in the Lords—had exquisitely justified itself
by its result. For it was as a Knight of the Garter that he had
set the perfect seal on his dandyism. Yes, he reflected, it was
on the day when first he donned the most grandiose of all
costumes, and wore it grandlier than ever yet in history had
it been worn, than ever would it be worn hereafter, flaunting
the robes with a grace unparalleled and inimitable, and
lending, as it were, to the very insignia a glory beyond their
own, that he once and for all fulfilled himself, doer of that
which he had been sent into the world to do.

And there floated into his mind a desire, vague at first,
soon definite, imperious, irresistible, to see himself once
more, before he died, indued in the fulness of his glory and
his might.

Nothing hindered. There was yet a whole hour before he
need start for the river. His eyes dilated, somewhat as might
those of a child about to "dress up" for a charade; and
already, in his impatience, he had undone his neck-tie.

One after another, he unlocked and threw open the black
tin boxes, snatching out greedily their great good splendours
of crimson and white and royal blue and gold. You wonder
he was not appalled by the task of essaying unaided a toilet so
extensive and so intricate? You wondered even when you
heard that he was wont at Oxford to make without help his
toilet of every day. Well, the true dandy is always capable of
such high independence. He is craftsman as well as artist.
And, though any unaided Knight but he with whom we are
here concerned would belike have doddered hopeless in that
labyrinth of hooks and buckles which underlies the visible
glory of a Knight "arraied full and proper," Dorset threaded
his way featly and without pause. He had mastered his first
excitement. In his swiftness was no haste. His procedure

195

had the ease and inevitability of a natural phenomenon, and was most like to the coming of a rainbow.

Crimson-doubleted, blue-ribanded, white-trunk-hosed, he stooped to understrap his left knee with that strap of velvet round which sparkles the proud gay motto of the Order. He affixed to his breast the octoradiant star, so much larger and more lustrous than any actual star in heaven. Round his neck he slung that long dædal chain wherefrom St. George, slaying the Dragon, dangles. He bowed his shoulders to assume that vast mantle of blue velvet, so voluminous, so enveloping, that, despite the Cross of St. George blazing on it, and the shoulder-knots like two great white tropical flowers planted on it, we seem to know from it in what manner of mantle Elijah prophesied. Across his breast he knotted this mantle's two cords of gleaming bullion, one tassel a due trifle higher than its fellow. All these things being done, he moved away from the mirror, and drew on a pair of white kid gloves. Both of these being buttoned, he plucked up certain folds of his mantle into the hollow of his left arm, and with his right hand gave to his left hand that ostrich-plumed and heron-plumed hat of black velvet in which a Knight of the Garter is entitled to take his walks abroad. Then, with head erect, and measured tread, he returned to the mirror.

You are thinking, I know, of Mr. Sargent's famous portrait of him. Forget it. Tankerton Hall is open to the public on Wednesdays. Go there, and in the dining-hall stand to study well Sir Thomas Lawrence's portrait of the eleventh Duke. Imagine a man some twenty years younger than he whom you there behold, but having some such features and some such bearing, and clad in just such robes. Sublimate the dignity of that bearing and of those features, and you will then have seen the fourteenth Duke somewhat as he stood reflected in the mirror of his room. Resist your impulse to pass on to the painting which hangs next but two to Lawrence's. It deserves, I know, all that you said about it when (at the very time of the events in this chronicle) it was hanging in Burlington House. Marvellous, I grant you, are those passes of the swirling brush by which the velvet of the mantle is rendered—passes so light and seemingly so fortuitous, yet, seen at the right distance, so absolute in their power to create an illusion of the actual velvet. Sheen of white satin and silk, glint of gold, glitter of diamonds—never were such things caught by surer hand obedient to more voracious eye. Yes, all the splendid surface of everything is there. Yet must you not look. The soul is not there. An expensive, very new costume is there, but no evocation of the high antique things it stands for; whereas by the Duke it was just these things that were evoked to make an aura round him, a warm symbolic glow sharpening the outlines of his own particular magnificence. Reflecting him, the mirror reflected, in due subordination, the history of England. There is nothing of that on Mr. Sargent's canvas. Obtruded instead is the astounding slickness of Mr. Sargent's technique: not the sitter, but the painter, is master here. Nay, though I hate to say it, there is in the portrayal of the Duke's attitude and expression a hint of something like mockery—unintentional, I am sure, but to a sensitive eye discernible. And—but it is clumsy of me to be reminding you of the very picture I would have you forget.

Long stood the Duke gazing, immobile. One thing alone ruffled his deep inward calm. This was the thought that he must presently put off from him all his splendour, and be his normal self.

The shadow passed from his brow. He would go forth as he was. He would be true to the motto he wore, and true to himself. A dandy he had lived. In the full pomp and radiance of his dandyism he would die.

His soul rose from calm to triumph. A smile lit his face, and he held his head higher than ever. He had brought nothing into this world and could take nothing out of it? Well, what he loved best he could carry with him to the very end; and in death they would not be divided.

The smile was still on his face as he passed out from his room. Down the stairs he passed, and "Oh," every stair creaked faintly, "I ought to have been marble!"

And it did indeed seem that Mrs. Batch and Katie, who had hurried out into the hall, were turned to some kind of stone at sight of the descending apparition. A moment ago, Mrs. Batch had been hoping she might yet at the last speak motherly words. A hopeless mute now! A moment ago, Katie's eyelids had been red with much weeping. Even from them the colour suddenly ebbed now. Death-white her face was between the black pearl and the pink. "And this is the man of whom I dared once for an instant hope that he loved me!"—it was thus that the Duke, quite correctly, interpreted her gaze.

To her and to her mother he gave an inclusive bow as he swept slowly by. Stone was the matron, and stone the maid.

Stone, too, the Emperors over the way; and the more poignantly thereby was the Duke a sight to anguish them, being the very incarnation of what themselves had erst been, or tried to be. But in this bitterness they did not forget their sorrow at his doom. They were in a mood to forgive him the one fault they had ever found in him—his indifference to their Katie. And now—*o mirum mirorum*—even this one fault was wiped out.

For, stung by memory of a gibe lately cast at him by himself, the Duke had paused and, impulsively looking back into the hall, had beckoned Katie to him; and she had come (she knew not how) to him; and there, standing on the door-step whose whiteness was the symbol of her love, he—very lightly, it is true, and on the upmost confines of the brow, but quite perceptibly—had kissed her.

# XIX

AND now he had passed under the little arch between the eighth and the ninth Emperor, rounded the Sheldonian, and been lost to sight of Katie, whom, as he was equally glad and sorry he had kissed her, he was able to dismiss from his mind.

In the quadrangle of the Old Schools he glanced round at the familiar labels, blue and gold, over the iron-studded doors—Schola Theologiæ et Antiquæ Philosophiæ; Museum Arundelianum; Schola Musicæ. And Bibliotheca Bodleiana —he paused there, to feel for the last time the vague thrill he had always felt at sight of the small and devious portal that had lured to itself, and would always lure, so many scholars from the ends of the earth, scholars famous and scholars obscure, scholars polyglot and of the most diverse bents, but none of them not stirred in heart somewhat on the found threshold of the treasure-house. "How deep, how perfect, the effect made here by refusal to make any effect whatsoever!" thought the Duke. Perhaps, after all . . . but no: one could lay down no general rule. He flung his mantle a little wider from his breast, and passed into Radcliffe Square.

Another farewell look he gave to the old vast horse-chestnut that is called Bishop Heber's tree. Certainly, no: there was no general rule. With its towering and bulging masses of verdure tricked out all over in their annual finery of catkins, Bishop Heber's tree stood for the very type of ingenuous ostentation. And who should dare cavil? who not be gladdened? Yet awful, more than gladdening, was the effect that the tree made to-day. Strangely pale was the verdure against the black sky; and the multitudinous catkins had a look almost ghostly. The Duke remembered the legend that every one of these fair white spires of blossom is the spirit of some dead man who, having loved Oxford much and well, is suffered thus to revisit her, for a brief while, year by year. And it pleased him to doubt not that on one of the topmost branches, next spring, his own spirit would be.

"Oh, look!" cried a young lady emerging with her brother and her aunt through the gate of Brasenose.

"For heaven's sake, Jessie, try to behave yourself," hissed her brother. "Aunt Mabel, for heaven's sake don't stare." He compelled the pair to walk on with him. "Jessie, if you look round over your shoulder . . . No, it is *not* the Vice-Chancellor. It's Dorset, of Judas—the Duke of Dorset . . . Why on earth shouldn't he? . . . No, it isn't odd in the least . . . No, I'm *not* losing my temper. Only, don't call me your dear boy . . . No, we will *not* walk slowly so as to let him pass us . . . Jessie, if you look round . . ."

Poor fellow! However fond an undergraduate be of his womenfolk, at Oxford they keep him in a painful state of tension: at any moment they may somehow disgrace him. And if throughout the long day he shall have had the added strain of guarding them from the knowledge that he is about to commit suicide, a certain measure of irritability must be condoned.

Poor Jessie and Aunt Mabel! They were destined to remember that Harold had been "very peculiar" all day. They had arrived in the morning, happy and eager despite the menace of the sky, and—well, they were destined to reproach themselves for having felt that Harold was "really rather impossible". Oh, if he had only confided in them! They could have reasoned with him, saved him—surely they could have saved him! When he told them that the "First Division" of the races was always very dull, and that they had much better let him go to it alone—when he told them that it was always very rowdy, and that ladies were not supposed to be there—oh, why had they not guessed and clung to him, and kept him away from the river?

Well, here they were, walking on Harold's either side, blind to fate, and only longing to look back at the gorgeous personage behind them. Aunt Mabel had inwardly calculated that the velvet of the mantle alone could not have cost less than four guineas a yard. One good look back, and she would be able to calculate how many yards there were . . . She followed the example of Lot's wife; and Jessie followed hers.

"Very well," said Harold. "That settles it. I go alone." And he was gone like an arrow, across the High, down Oriel Street.

The two women stood staring ruefully at each other.

"Pardon me," said the Duke, with a sweep of his plumed hat. "I observe you are stranded; and, if I read your thoughts aright, you are impugning the courtesy of that young runagate. Neither of you, I am very sure, is as one of those ladies who in Imperial Rome took a saucy pleasure in the spectacle of death. Neither of you can have been warned by your escort that you were on the way to see him die, of his own accord, in company with many hundreds of other lads, myself included. Therefore, regard his flight from you as an act not of unkindness, but of tardy compunction. The hint you have had from him let me turn into a counsel. Go back, both of you, to the place whence you came."

"Thank you *so* much," said Aunt Mabel, with what she took to be great presence of mind. "*Most* kind of you. We'll do *just* what you tell us. Come, Jessie dear," and she hurried her niece away with her.

Something in her manner of fixing him with her eye had made the Duke suspect what was in her mind. Well, she would find out her mistake soon enough, poor woman. He desired, however, that her mistake should be made by no one else. He would give no more warnings.

Tragic it was for him, in Merton Street, to see among the crowd converging to the meadows so many women, young and old, all imprescient, troubled by nothing but the thunder that was in the air, that was on the brows of their escorts. He knew not whether it was for their escorts or for them that he felt the greater pity; and an added load for his heart was the sense of his partial responsibility for what impended. But his lips were sealed now. Why should he not enjoy the effect he was creating?

It was with a measured tread, as yesterday with Zuleika, that he entered the avenue of elms. The throng streamed past from behind him, parting wide, and marvelling as it streamed. Under the pall of this evil evening his splendour was the more inspiring. And, just as yesterday no man had questioned his right to be with Zuleika, so to-day there was none to deem him caparisoned too much. All the men felt at a glance that he, coming to meet death thus, did no more than the right homage to Zuleika—aye, and that he made them all partakers in his own glory, casting his great mantle over all commorients. Reverence forbade them to do more than glance. But the women with them were impelled by wonder to stare hard, uttering sharp little cries that mingled with the cawing of the rooks overhead. Thus did scores of men find themselves shamed like our friend Harold. But this, you say, was no more than a just return for their behaviour yesterday, when, in this very avenue, so many women were almost crushed to death by them in their insensate eagerness to see Miss Dobson.

To-day by scores of women it was calculated not only that the velvet of the Duke's mantle could not have cost less than four guineas a yard, but also that there must be quite twenty-five yards of it. Some of the fair mathematicians had, in the course of the past fortnight, visited the Royal Academy and seen there Mr. Sargent's portrait of the wearer, so that their estimate now was but the endorsement of an estimate already made. Yet their impression of the Duke was above all a spiritual one. The nobility of his face and bearing was what most thrilled them as they went by; and those of them who had heard the rumour that he was in love with that frightfully flashy-looking creature, Zuleika Dobson, were more than ever sure there wasn't a word of truth in it.

As he neared the end of the avenue, the Duke was conscious of a thinning in the procession on either side of him and anon he was aware that not one undergraduate was therein. And he knew at once—did not need to look back to know—why this was. *She* was coming.

Yes, she had come into the avenue, her magnetism speeding before her, insomuch that all along the way the men immediately ahead of her looked round, beheld her, stood aside for her. With her walked The MacQuern, and a little bodyguard of other blest acquaintances; and behind her swayed the dense mass of the disorganised procession. And now the last rank between her and the Duke was broken, and at the revealed vision of him she faltered midway in some raillery she was addressing to The MacQuern. Her eyes were fixed, her lips were parted, her tread had become stealthy. With a brusque gesture of dismissal to the men beside her, she darted forward, and lightly overtook the Duke just as he was turning towards the barges.

"May I?" she whispered, smiling round into his face.

His shoulder-knots just perceptibly rose.

"There isn't a policeman in sight, John. You're at my mercy. No, no; I'm at yours. Tolerate me. You really do look quite wonderful. There, I won't be so impertinent as to praise you. Only let me be with you. Will you?"

The shoulder-knots repeated their answer.

"You needn't listen to me; needn't look at me—unless you care to use my eyes as mirrors. Only let me be seen with you. That's what I want. Not that your society isn't a boon in itself, John. Oh, I've been so bored since I left you. The

MacQuern is too, too dull, and so are his friends. Oh, that meal with them in Balliol! As soon as I grew used to the thought that they were going to die for me, I simply couldn't stand them. Poor boys! it was as much as I could do not to tell them I wished them dead already. Indeed, when they brought me down for the first races, I did suggest that they might as well die now as later. Only they looked very solemn and said it couldn't possibly be done till after the final races. And oh, the tea with them! What have *you* been doing all the afternoon? Oh John, after *them*, I could almost love you again. Why can't one fall in love with a man's clothes? To think that all those splendid things you have on are going to be spoilt—all for me. Nominally for me, that is. It is very wonderful, John. I do appreciate it, really and truly, though I know you think I don't. John, if it weren't mere spite you feel for me—but it's no good talking about that. Come, let us be as cheerful as we may be. Is this the Judas house-boat?"

"The Judas barge," said the Duke, irritated by a mistake which but yesterday had rather charmed him.

As he followed his companion across the plank, there came dully from the hills the first low growl of the pent storm. The sound struck for him a strange contrast with the prattle he had perforce been listening to.

"Thunder," said Zuleika over her shoulder.

"Evidently," he answered.

Halfway up the stairs to the roof, she looked round. "Aren't you coming?" she asked.

He shook his head, and pointed to the raft in front of the barge. She quickly descended.

"Forgive me," he said, "my gesture was not a summons. The raft is for men."

"What do you want to do on it?"

"To wait there till the races are over."

"But—what do you mean? Aren't you coming up on to the roof at all? Yesterday——"

"Oh, I see," said the Duke, unable to repress a smile. "But to-day I am not dressed for a flying-leap."

Zuleika put a finger to her lips. "Don't talk so loud. Those women up there will hear you. No one must ever know I knew what was going to happen. What evidence should I have that I tried to prevent it? Only my own unsupported word—and the world is always against a woman. So do be careful. I've thought it all out. The whole thing must be *sprung* on me. Don't look so horribly cynical. . . . What was I saying? Oh yes; well, it doesn't really matter. I had it fixed in my mind that you—but no, of course, in that mantle you couldn't. But why not come up on the roof with me meanwhile, and then afterwards make some excuse and——" The rest of her whisper was lost in another growl of thunder.

"I would rather make my excuses forthwith," said the Duke. "And, as the races must be almost due now, I advise you to go straight up and secure a place against the railing."

"It will look very odd, my going all alone into a crowd of people whom I don't know. I'm an unmarried girl. I do think you might——"

"Good-bye," said the Duke.

Again Zuleika raised a warning finger.

"Good-bye, John," she whispered. "See, I am still wearing your studs. Good-bye. Don't forget to call my name in a loud voice. You promised."

"Yes."

"And," she added, after a pause, "remember this. I have loved but twice in my life; and none but you have I loved. This, too: if you hadn't forced me to kill my love, I would have died with you. And you know it is true."

"Yes." It was true enough.

Courteously he watched her up the stairs.

As she reached the roof, she cried down to him from the

throng: "Then you will wait down there to take me home afterwards?"

He bowed silently.

The raft was even more crowded than yesterday, but way was made for him by Judasians past and present. He took his place in the centre of the front row.

At his feet flowed the fateful river. From the various barges the last punt-loads had been ferried across to the towing-path, and the last of the men who were to follow the boats in their course had vanished towards the starting-point. There remained, however, a fringe of lesser enthusiasts. Their figures stood outlined sharply in that strange dark clearness which immediately precedes a storm.

The thunder rumbled around the hills, and now and again there was a faint glare on the horizon.

Would Judas bump Magdalen? Opinion on the raft seemed to be divided. But the sanguine spirits were in a majority.

"If I were making a book on the event," said a middle-aged clergyman, with that air of breezy emancipation which is so distressing to the laity, "I'd bet two to one we bump."

"You demean your cloth, sir," the Duke would have said, "without cheating its disabilities," had not his mouth been stopped by a loud and prolonged thunder-clap.

In the hush thereafter, came the puny sound of a gunshot. The boats were starting. Would Judas bump Magdalen? Would Judas be head of the river?

Strange, thought the Duke, that for him, standing as he did on the peak of dandyism, on the brink of eternity, this trivial question of boats could have importance. And yet, and yet, for this it was that his heart was beating. A few minutes hence, an end to victors and vanquished alike; and yet . . .

A sudden white vertical streak slid down the sky. Then there was a consonance to split the drums of the world's

ears, followed by a horrific rattling as of actual artillery—
tens of thousands of gun-carriages simultaneously at the
gallop, colliding, crashing, heeling over in the blackness.

Then, and yet more awful, silence; the little earth cowering
voiceless under the heavens' menace. And, audible in the
hush now, a faint sound; the sound of the runners on the
towing-path cheering the crews forward, forward.

And there was another faint sound that came to the Duke's
ears. It he understood when, a moment later, he saw the
surface of the river alive with infinitesimal fountains.

Rain!

His very mantle was aspersed. In another minute he
would stand sodden, inglorious, a mock. He didn't hesitate.

"Zuleika!" he cried in a loud voice. Then he took a deep
breath, and, burying his face in his mantle, plunged.

Full on the river lay the mantle outspread. Then it, too,
went under. A great roll of water marked the spot. The
plumed hat floated.

There was a confusion of shouts from the raft, of screams
from the roof. Many youths—all the youths there—cried
"Zuleika!" and leapt emulously headlong into the water.
"Brave fellows!" shouted the elder men, supposing rescue-
work. The rain pelted, the thunder pealed. Here and there
was a glimpse of a young head above water—for an instant
only.

Shouts and screams now from the infected barges on either
side. A score of fresh plunges. "Splendid fellows!"

Meanwhile, what of the Duke? I am glad to say that he
was alive and (but for the cold he had caught last night) well.
Indeed, his mind had never worked more clearly than in this
swift dim underworld. His mantle, the cords of it having
come untied, had drifted off him, leaving his arms free. With
breath, well-pent, he steadily swam, scarcely less amused
than annoyed that the gods had, after all, dictated the exact
time at which he should seek death.

I am loth to interrupt my narrative at this rather exciting moment—a moment when the quick, tense style, exemplified in the last paragraph but one, is so very desirable. But in justice to the gods I must pause to put in a word of excuse for them. They had imagined that it was in mere irony that the Duke had said he could not die till after the bumping-races; and not until it seemed that he stood ready to make an end of himself had the signal been given by Zeus for the rain to fall. One is taught to refrain from irony, because mankind does tend to take it literally. In the hearing of the gods, who hear all, it is conversely unsafe to make a simple and direct statement. So what is one to do? The dilemma needs a whole volume to itself.

But to return to the Duke. He had now been under water for a full minute, swimming down stream; and he calculated that he had yet another full minute of consciousness. Already the whole of his past life had vividly presented itself to him— myriads of tiny incidents, long forgotten, now standing out sharply in their due sequence. He had mastered this conspectus in a flash of time, and was already tired of it. How smooth and yielding were the weeds against his face! He wondered if Mrs. Batch had been in time to cash the cheque. If not, of course, his executors would pay the amount, but there would be delays, long delays, Mrs. Batch in meshes of red tape. Red tape for her, green weeds for him—he smiled at this poor conceit, classifying it as a fair sample of merman's wit. He swam on through the quiet cool darkness, less quickly now. Not many more strokes now, he told himself; a few, only a few; then sleep. How was he come here? Some woman had sent him. Ever so many years ago, some woman. He forgave her. There was nothing to forgive her. It was the gods who had sent him—too soon, too soon. He let his arms rise in the water, and he floated up. There was air in that over-world, and something he needed to know there before he came down again to sleep.

He gasped the air into his lungs, and he remembered what it was that he needed to know.

Had he risen in mid-stream, the keel of the Magdalen boat might have killed him. The oars of Magdalen did all but graze his face. The eyes of the Magdalen cox met his. The cords of the Magdalen rudder slipped from the hands that held them; whereupon the Magdalen man who rowed "bow" missed his stroke.

An instant later, just where the line of barges begins, Judas had bumped Magdalen.

A crash of thunder deadened the din of the stamping and dancing crowd on the towing-path. The rain was a deluge making land and water as one.

And the conquered crew, and the conquering, both now had seen the face of the Duke. A white smiling face, anon it was gone. Dorset was gone down to his last sleep.

Victory and defeat alike forgotten, the crews staggered erect and flung themselves into the river, the slender boats capsizing and spinning futile around in a melley of oars.

From the towing-path—no more din there now, but great single cries of "Zuleika!"—leapt figures innumerable through rain to river. The arrested boats of the other crews drifted zigzag hither and thither. The dropped oars rocked and clashed, sank and rebounded, as the men plunged across them into the swirling stream.

And over all this confusion and concussion of men and man-made things crashed the vaster discords of the heavens; and the waters of the heavens fell ever denser and denser, as though to the aid of waters that could not in themselves envelop so many hundreds of struggling human forms.

All along the soaked towing-path lay strewn the horns, the rattles, the motor-hooters, that the youths had flung aside before they leapt. Here and there among these relics stood dazed elder men, staring through the storm. There was one of them—a grey-beard—who stripped off his blazer, plunged, grabbed at some live man, grappled him, was dragged under. He came up again further along stream, swam choking to the bank, clung to the grasses. He whimpered as he sought foot-hold in the slime. It was ill to be down in that abominable sink of death.

Abominable, yes, to them who discerned there death only; but sacramental and sweet enough to the men who were dying there for love. Any face that rose was smiling.

The thunder receded; the rain was less vehement; the boats and the oars had drifted against the banks. And always the patient river bore its awful burden towards Iffley.

As on the towing-path, so on the youth-bereft rafts of the barges, yonder, stood many stupefied elders, staring at the river, staring back from the river into one another's faces.

Dispeopled now were the roofs of the barges. Under the first drops of the rain most of the women had come huddling down for shelter inside; panic had presently driven down the rest. Yet on one roof one woman still was. A strange, drenched figure, she stood bright-eyed in the dimness; alone, as it was well she should be in her great hour; draining the lees of such homage as had come to no woman in history recorded.

## XX

ARTISTICALLY, there is a good deal to be said for that old Greek friend of ours, the Messenger; and I dare say you blame me for having, as it were, made you an eye-witness of the death of the undergraduates, when I might so easily have brought someone in to tell you about it after it was all over. . . . Someone? Whom? Are you not begging the question? I admit there were, that evening in Oxford, many people who, when they went home from the river, gave vivid reports of what they had seen. But among them was none who had seen more than a small portion of the whole affair. Certainly, I might have pieced together a dozen of the various accounts, and put them all into the mouth of one person. But credibility is not enough for Clio's servant. I aim at truth. And so, as I by my Zeus-given incorporeity was the one person who had a good view of the scene at large, you must pardon me for having withheld the veil of indirect narration.

"Too late," you will say if I offer you a Messenger now. But it was not thus that Mrs. Batch and Katie greeted Clarence when, lamentably soaked with rain, that Messenger appeared on the threshold of the kitchen. Katie was laying the table-cloth for seven o'clock supper. Neither she nor her mother was clairvoyante. Neither of them knew what had been happening. But, as Clarence had not come home since afternoon-school, they had assumed that he was at the river; and they now assumed from the look of him that something very unusual had been happening there. As to what this was, they were not quickly enlightened. Our old Greek friend, after a run of twenty miles, would always reel off a round hundred of graphic verses unimpeachable in scansion. Clarence was of degenerate mould. He collapsed on to a chair, and sat there gasping; and his recovery was rather delayed than hastened by his mother, who, in her solicitude, patted him vigorously between the shoulders.

"Let him alone, mother, do," cried Katie, wringing her hands.

"The Duke, he's drowned himself," presently gasped the Messenger.

Blank verse, yes, so far as it went; but delivered without the slightest regard for rhythm, and composed in stark defiance of those laws which should regulate the breaking of bad news.

Mrs. Batch herself did not faint, but she was too much overwhelmed to notice that her daughter had done so.

"No! Mercy on us! Speak, boy, can't you?"

"The river," gasped Clarence. "Threw himself in. On purpose. I was on the towing-path. Saw him do it."

Mrs. Batch gave a low moan.

"Katie's fainted," added the Messenger, not without a touch of personal pride.

"Saw him do it," Mrs. Batch repeated dully. "Katie," she said, in the same voice, "get up this instant." But Katie did not hear her.

The mother was loth to have been outdone in sensibility by the daughter, and it was with some temper that she hastened to make the necessary ministrations.

"Where am I?" asked Katie, at length, echoing the words used in this very house, at a similar juncture, on this very day, by another lover of the Duke.

"Ah, you may well ask that," said Mrs. Batch, with more force than reason. "A mother's support indeed! Well! And as for you," she cried, turning on Clarence, "sending her off like that with your——" She was face to face again with the tragic news. Katie, remembering it simultaneously, uttered a loud sob. Mrs. Batch capped this with a much louder one. Clarence stood before the fire, slowly revolving on one heel. His clothes steamed briskly.

"It isn't true," said Katie. She rose and came uncertainly towards her brother, half threatening, half imploring.

"All right," said he, strong in his advantage. "Then I shan't tell either of you anything more."

Mrs. Batch through her tears called Katie a bad girl, and Clarence a bad boy.

"Where did you get *them?*" asked Clarence, pointing to the ear-rings worn by his sister.

"*He* gave me them," said Katie. Clarence curbed the brotherly intention of telling her she looked "a sight" in them.

She stood staring into vacancy. "He didn't love *her*," she murmured. "That was all over. I'll vow he didn't love *her*."

"Who d'you mean by her?" asked Clarence.

"That Miss Dobson that's been here."

"What's her other name?"

"Zuleika," Katie enunciated with bitterest abhorrence.

"Well, then, he jolly well did love her. That's the name he called out just before he threw himself in. 'Zuleika!'—like that," added the boy, with a most infelicitous attempt to reproduce the Duke's manner.

Katie had shut her eyes, and clenched her hands.

"He hated her. He told me so," she said.

"I was always a mother to him," sobbed Mrs. Batch, rocking to and fro on a chair in a corner. "Why didn't he come to me in his trouble?"

"He kissed me," said Katie, as in a trance. "No other man shall ever do that."

"He did?" exclaimed Clarence. "And you let him?"

"You wretched little whipper-snapper!" flashed Katie.

"Oh, I am, am I?" shouted Clarence, squaring up to his

sister. "Say that again, will you?"

There is no doubt that Katie would have said it again, had not her mother closed the scene with a prolonged wail of censure.

"You ought to be thinking of *me*, you wicked girl," said Mrs. Batch. Katie went across, and laid a gentle hand on her mother's shoulder. This, however, did but evoke a fresh flood of tears. Mrs. Batch had a keen sense of the deportment owed to tragedy. Katie, by bickering with Clarence, had thrown away the advantage she had gained by fainting. Mrs. Batch was not going to let her retrieve it by shining as a consoler. I hasten to add that this resolve was only subconscious in the good woman. Her grief was perfectly sincere. And it was not the less so because with it was mingled a certain joy in the greatness of the calamity. She came of good sound peasant stock. Abiding in her was the spirit of those old songs and ballads in which daisies and daffodillies and lovers' vows and smiles are so strangely inwoven with tombs and ghosts, with murders and all manner of grim things. She had not had education enough to spoil her nerve. She was able to take the rough with the smooth. She was able to take all life for her province, and death too.

The Duke was dead. This was the stupendous outline she had grasped: now let it be filled in. She had been stricken: now let her be racked. Soon after her daughter had moved away, Mrs. Batch dried her eyes, and bade Clarence tell just what had happened. She did not flinch. Modern Katie did.

Such had ever been the Duke's magic in the household that Clarence had at first forgotten to mention that anyone else was dead. Of this omission he was glad. It promised him a new lease of importance. Meanwhile, he described in greater detail the Duke's plunge. Mrs. Batch's mind, while she listened, ran ahead, dog-like, into the immediate future, ranging around: "the family" would all be here to-morrow, the Duke's own room must be "put straight" to-night, "I was always a mother to him, my Lady, in a manner of speaking" . . .

Katie's mind harked back to the immediate past—to the tone of that voice, to that hand which she had kissed, to the touch of those lips on her brow, to the door-step she had made so white for him, day by day . . .

The sound of the rain had long ceased. There was the noise of a gathering wind.

"Then in went a lot of others," Clarence was saying. "And they all shouted out 'Zuleika!' just like he did. Then a lot more went in. First I thought it was some sort of fun. Not it!" And he told how, by inquiries further down the river, he had learned the extent of the disaster. "Hundreds and hundreds of them—*all* of them," he summed up. "And all for the love of *her*," he added, as with a sulky salute to Romance.

Mrs. Batch had risen from her chair, the better to cope with such magnitude. She stood with wide-spread arms, silent, gaping. She seemed, by sheer force of sympathy, to be expanding to the dimensions of a crowd.

Intensive Katie recked little of all these other deaths. "I only know," she said, "that he hated her."

"Hundreds and hundreds—*all*," intoned Mrs. Batch, then gave a sudden start, as having remembered something. Mr. Noaks! He, too! She staggered to the door, leaving her actual offspring to their own devices, and went heavily up the stairs, her mind scampering again before her. . . . If he was safe and sound, dear young gentleman, heaven be praised! and she would break the awful news to him, very gradually. If not, there was another "family" to be solaced; "I'm a mother myself, Mrs. Noaks" . . .

The sitting-room door was closed. Twice did Mrs. Batch tap on the panel, receiving no answer. She went in, gazed around in the dimness, sighed deeply, and struck a match.

Conspicuous on the table lay a piece of paper. She bent to examine it. A piece of lined paper, torn from an exercise book, it was neatly inscribed with the words *What is Life without Love?* The final word and the note of interrogation were somewhat blurred, as by a tear. The match had burnt itself out. The landlady lit another, and read the legend a second time, that she might take in the full pathos of it. Then she sat down in the arm-chair. For some minutes she wept there. Then, having no more tears, she went out on tiptoe, closing the door very quietly.

As she descended the last flight of stairs, her daughter had just shut the front door, and was coming along the hall.

"Poor Mr. Noaks—he's gone," said the mother.

"Has he?" said Katie listlessly.

"Yes he has, you heartless girl. What's that you've got in your hand? Why, if it isn't the black-leading! And what have you been doing with that?"

"Let me alone, mother, do," said poor Katie. She had done her lowly task. She had expressed her mourning, as best she could, there where she had been wont to express her love.

## XXI

AND Zuleika? She had done a wise thing, and was where it was best that she should be.

Her face lay upturned on the water's surface, and round it were the masses of her dark hair, half floating, half submerged. Her eyes were closed, and her lips were parted. Not Ophelia in the brook could have seemed more at peace.

> "Like a creature native and indued
> Unto that element,"

tranquil Zuleika lay.

Gently, to and fro her tresses drifted on the water, or under the water went ever ravelling and unravelling. Nothing else of her stirred.

What to her now the loves that she had inspired and played on? the lives lost for her? Little thought had she now of them. Aloof she lay.

Steadily rising from the water was a thick vapour that turned to dew on the window-pane. The air was heavy with scent of violets. These are the flowers of mourning; but their scent here and now signified nothing; for Eau de Violettes was the bath-essence that Zuleika always had.

The bathroom was not of the white-gleaming kind to which she was accustomed. The walls were papered, not tiled, and the bath itself was of japanned tin, framed in mahogany. These things, on the evening of her arrival at the Warden's, had rather distressed her. But she was the better able to bear them because of that well-remembered past when a bathroom was in itself a luxury pined for—days when a not-large and not-full can of not-hot water, slammed down at her bedroom door by a governess-resenting housemaid, was as much as the gods allowed her. And there was, to dulcify for her the bath of this evening, the yet sharper contrast with the plight she had just come home in, sopped, shivering, clung to by her clothes. Because this bath was not a mere luxury, but a necessary precaution, a sure means of salvation from chill, she did the more gratefully bask in it, till Mélisande came back to her, laden with warmed towels.

A few minutes before eight o'clock she was fully ready to go down to dinner, with even more than the usual glow of health, and hungry beyond her wont.

Yet, as she went down, her heart somewhat misgave her. Indeed, by force of the wide experience she had had as a governess, she never did feel quite at her ease when she was staying in a private house: the fear of not giving satisfaction haunted her; she was always on her guard; the shadow of dismissal absurdly hovered. And to-night she could not tell herself, as she usually did, not to be so silly. If her grandfather knew already the motive by which those young men had been actuated, dinner with him might be a rather strained affair. He might tell her, in so many words, that he wished he had not invited her to Oxford.

Through the open door of the drawing-room she saw him, standing majestic, draped in a voluminous black gown. Her instinct was to run away; but this she conquered. She went straight in, remembering not to smile.

"Ah, ah," said the Warden, shaking a forefinger at her with old-world playfulness. "And what have you to say for yourself?"

Relieved, she was also a trifle shocked. Was it possible that he, a responsible old man, could take things so lightly?

"Oh, grand-papa," she answered, hanging her head, "what *can* I say? It is—it is too, too dreadful."

"There, there, my dear. I was but jesting. If you have had an agreeable time, you are forgiven for playing truant. Where have you been all day?"

She saw that she had misjudged him. "I have just come from the river," she said gravely.

"Yes? And did the College make its fourth bump to-night?"

"I—I don't know, grand-papa. There was so much happening. It—I will tell you all about it at dinner."

"Ah, but to-night," he said, indicating his gown, "I cannot be with you. The bump-supper, you know. I have to preside in Hall."

Zuleika had forgotten there was to be a bump-supper, and, though she was not very sure what a bump-supper was, she felt it would be a mockery to-night.

"But grand-papa——" she began.

"My dear, I cannot dissociate myself from the life of the College. And, alas," he said, looking at the clock, "I must leave you now. As soon as you have finished dinner, you might, if you would care to, come and peep down at us from the gallery. There is apt to be some measure of noise and racket, but all of it good-humoured and—boys will be boys—pardonable. Will you come?"

"Perhaps, grand-papa," she said awkwardly.

Left alone, she hardly knew whether to laugh or cry. In a moment, the butler came to her rescue, telling her that dinner was served.

As the figure of the Warden emerged from Salt Cellar into the Front Quadrangle, a hush fell on the group of gowned Fellows outside the Hall. Most of them had only just been told the news, and (such is the force of routine in an University) were still sceptical of it. And in face of these doubts the three or four dons who had been down at the river were now half ready to believe that there must, after all, be some mistake, and that in this world of illusions they had to-night been specially tricked. To rebut this theory, there was the notable absence of undergraduates. Or was this an illusion, too? Men of thought, agile on the plane of ideas, devils of fellows among books, they groped feebly in this matter of actual life and death. The sight of their Warden heartened them. After all, he was the responsible person. He was father of the flock that had strayed, and grandfather of the beautiful Miss Zuleika.

Like her, they remembered not to smile in greeting him.

"Good evening, gentlemen," he said. "The storm seems to have passed."

There was a murmur of: "Yes, Warden."

"And how did our boat acquit itself?"

There was a shuffling pause. Everyone looked at the Sub-Warden: it was manifestly for him to break the news, or to report the hallucination. He was nudged forward—a large man, with a large beard at which he plucked nervously.

"Well, really, Warden," he said, "we—we hardly know,"* and he ended with what can only be described as a giggle. He fell low in the esteem of his fellows.

Thinking of that past Sub-Warden whose fame was linked with the sun-dial, the Warden eyed this one keenly.

"Well, gentlemen," he presently said, "our young men seem to be already at table. Shall we follow their example?" And he led the way up the steps.

Already at table? The dons' dubiety toyed with this hypothesis. But the aspect of the Hall's interior was hard to explain away. Here were the three long tables, stretching white towards the daïs, and laden with the usual crockery and cutlery, and with pots of flowers in honour of the occasion. And here, ranged along either wall, was the usual array of scouts, motionless, with napkins across their arms. But that was all.

*Those of my readers who are interested in athletic sports will remember the long controversy that raged as to whether Judas had actually bumped Magdalen; and they will not need to be reminded that it was mainly through the evidence of Mr. T. E. A. Cook, who had been on the towing-path at the time, that the O.U.B.C. decided the point in Judas's favour, and fixed the order of the boats for the following year accordingly.

It became clear to the Warden that some organised prank or protest was afoot. Dignity required that he should take no heed whatsoever. Looking neither to the right nor to the left, stately he approached the daïs, his Fellows to heel.

In Judas, as in other Colleges, grace before meat is read by the Senior Scholar. The Judas grace (composed, they say, by Christopher Whitrid himself) is noted for its length and for the excellence of its Latinity. Who was to read it to-night? The Warden, having searched his mind vainly for a precedent, was driven to create one.

"The Junior Fellow," he said, "will read grace."

Blushing to the roots of his hair, and with crab-like gait, Mr. Pedby, the Junior Fellow, went and unhooked from the wall that little shield of wood on which the words of the grace are carven. Mr. Pedby was—Mr. Pedby is—a mathematician. His treatise on the Higher Theory of Short Division by Decimals had already won for him an European reputation. Judas was—Judas is—proud of Pedby. Nor is it denied that in undertaking the duty thrust on him he quickly controlled his nerves and read the Latin out in ringing accents. Better for him had he not done so. The false quantities he made were so excruciating and so many that, while the very scouts exchanged glances, the dons at the high table lost all command of their features, and made horrible noises in the effort to contain themselves. The very Warden dared not look from his plate.

In every breast around the high table, behind every shirtfront or black silk waistcoat, glowed the recognition of a new birth. Suddenly, unheralded, a thing of highest destiny had fallen into their academic midst. The stock of Common Room talk had to-night been re-inforced and enriched for all time. Summers and winters would come and go, old faces would vanish, giving place to new, but the story of Pedby's grace would be told always. Here was a tradition that generations of dons yet unborn would cherish and chuckle over. Something akin to awe mingled itself with the subsiding merriment. And the dons, having finished their soup, sipped in silence the dry brown sherry.

Those who sat opposite to the Warden, with their backs to the void, were oblivious of the matter that had so recently teased them. They were conscious only of an agreeable hush, in which they peered down the vistas of the future, watching the tradition of Pedby's grace as it rolled brighter and ever brighter down to eternity.

The pop of a champagne cork startled them to remembrance that this was a bump-supper, and a bump-supper of a peculiar kind. The turbot that came after the sole, the champagne that succeeded the sherry, helped to quicken in these men of thought the power to grapple with a reality. The aforesaid three or four who had been down at the river recovered their lost belief in the evidence of their eyes and ears. In the rest was a spirit of receptivity which, as the meal went on, mounted to conviction. The Sub-Warden made a second and more determined attempt to enlighten the Warden; but the Warden's eye met his with a suspicion so cruelly pointed that he again floundered and gave in.

All adown those empty other tables gleamed the undisturbed cutlery, and the flowers in the pots innocently bloomed. And all adown either wall, unneeded but undisbanded, the scouts remained. Some of the elder ones stood with closed eyes and heads sunk forward, now and again jerking themselves erect, and blinking around, wondering, remembering.

And for a while this scene was looked down on by a not disinterested stranger. For a while, her chin propped on her hands, Zuleika leaned over the rail of the gallery, just as she had lately leaned over the barge's rail, staring down and along. But there was no spark of triumph now in her eyes: only a deep melancholy; and in her mouth a taste as of dust and ashes. She thought of last night, and of all the buoyant

life that this Hall had held. Of the Duke she thought, and
of the whole vivid and eager throng of his fellows in love.
Her will, their will, had been done. But there rose to her lips
the old, old question that withers victory—"To what end?"
Her eyes ranged along the tables, and an appalling sense of
loneliness swept over her. She turned away, wrapping the
folds of her cloak closer across her breast. Not in this
College only, but through and through Oxford, there was no
heart that beat for her—no, not one, she told herself, with
that instinct for self-torture which comes to souls in torment.
She was utterly alone to-night in the midst of a vast indifference. She! She! Was it possible? Were the gods so
merciless? Ah no, surely . . .

Down at the high table the feast drew to its close, and very
different was the mood of the feasters from that of the young
woman whose glance had for a moment rested on their un-
romantic heads. Generations of undergraduates had said that
Oxford would be all very well but for the dons. Do you
suppose that the dons had had no answering sentiment?
Youth is a very good thing to possess, no doubt; but it is a
tiresome setting for maturity. Youth all around prancing,
vociferating, mocking; callow and alien youth, having to be
looked after and studied and taught, as though nothing but it
mattered, term after term—and now, all of a sudden, in mid-
term, peace, ataraxy, a profound and leisured stillness. No
lectures to deliver to-morrow; no "essays" to hear and
criticise; time for the unvexed pursuit of pure learning . . .

As the Fellows passed out on their way to Common
Room, there to tackle with a fresh appetite Pedby's grace,
they paused, as was their wont, on the steps of the Hall,
looking up at the sky, envisaging the weather. The wind had
dropped. There was even a glimpse of the moon riding
behind the clouds. And now, a solemn and plangent token of
Oxford's perpetuity, the first stroke of Great Tom sounded.

## XXII

STROKE by stroke, the great familiar monody of that incomparable curfew rose and fell in the stillness.

Nothing of Oxford lingers more surely than it in the memory of Oxford men; and to one revisiting these groves nothing is more eloquent of that scrupulous historic economy whereby his own particular past is utilised as the general present and future. "All's as it was, all's as it will be," says Great Tom; and that is what he stubbornly said on the evening I here record.

Stroke by measured and leisured stroke, the old euphonious clangour pervaded Oxford, spreading out over the meadows, along the river, audible in Iffley. But to the dim groups gathering and dispersing on either bank, and to the silent workers in the boats, the bell's message came softened, equivocal; came as a requiem for these dead.

Over the closed gates of Iffley lock, the water gushed down, eager for the sacrament of the sea.

Among the supine in the field hard by, there was one whose breast bore a faint-gleaming star. And bending over him, looking down at him with much love and pity in her eyes, was the shade of Nellie O'Mora, that "fairest witch" to whose memory he had to-day atoned.

And yonder, "sitting upon the river-bank o'ergrown," with questioning eyes, was another shade, more habituated to these haunts—the shade known so well to bathers "in the abandoned lasher," and to dancers "around the Fyfield elm in May." At the bell's final stroke, the Scholar Gipsy rose, letting fall on the water his gathered wild-flowers, and passed towards Cumnor.

And now, duly, throughout Oxford, the gates of the Colleges were closed, and closed were the doors of the lodging-houses. Every night, for many years, at this hour precisely, Mrs. Batch had come out from her kitchen, to turn the key in the front door. The function had long ago become automatic. To-night, however, it was the cue for further tears. These did not cease at her return to the kitchen, where she had gathered about her some sympathetic neighbours—women of her own age and kind, capacious of tragedy; women who might be relied on; founts of ejaculation, wells of surmise, downpours of remembered premonitions.

With his elbows on the kitchen table, and his knuckles to his brow, sat Clarence, intent on belated "prep". Even an eye-witness of disaster may pall if he repeat his story too often. Clarence had noted in the last recital that he was losing his hold on his audience. So now he sat committing to memory the names of the cantons of Switzerland, and waving aside with a harsh gesture such questions as were still put to him by the women.

Katie had sought refuge in the need for "putting the gentlemen's rooms straight", against the arrival of the two families to-morrow. Duster in hand, and by the light of a single candle that barely survived the draught from the open window, she moved to and fro about the Duke's room, a wan and listless figure, casting queerest shadows on the ceiling. There were other candles that she might have lit, but this ambiguous gloom suited her sullen humour. Yes, I am sorry to say, Katie was sullen. She had not ceased to mourn the Duke; but it was even more anger than grief that she felt at his dying. She was as sure as ever that he had not loved Miss Dobson; but this only made it the more outrageous that he had died because of her. What was there in this woman that men should so demean themselves for her? Katie, as you know, had at first been unaffected by the death of the undergraduates at large. But, because they too had died for Zuleika, she was bitterly incensed against them now. What could they have admired in such a woman? She didn't even look like a lady. Katie caught the dim reflection of herself in the mirror. She took the candle from the table, and examined the reflection closely. She was sure she was just as pretty as Miss Dobson. It was only the clothes that made the difference—the clothes and the behaviour. Katie threw back her head, and smiled brilliantly, hand on hip. She nodded reassuringly at herself; and the black pearl and the pink danced a duet. She put the candle down, and undid her hair, roughly parting it on one side, and letting it sweep down over the further eyebrow. She fixed it in that fashion, and posed accordingly. Now! But gradually her smile relaxed, and a mist came to her eyes. For she had to admit that even so, after all, she hadn't just that something which somehow Miss Dobson had. She put away from her the hasty dream she had had of a whole future generation of undergraduates drowning themselves, every one, in honour of her. She went wearily on with her work.

Presently, after a last look round, she went up the creaking stairs, to do Mr. Noaks's room.

She found on the table that screed which her mother had recited so often this evening. She put it in the waste-paper basket.

Also on the table were a lexicon, a Thucydides, and some note-books. These she took and shelved without a tear for the closed labours they bore witness to.

The next disorder that met her eye was one that gave her pause—seemed, indeed, to transfix her.

Mr. Noaks had never, since he came to lodge here, possessed more than one pair of boots. This fact had been for her a lasting source of annoyance; for it meant that she had to polish Mr. Noaks's boots always in the early morning, when there were so many other things to be done, instead of choosing her own time. Her annoyance had been all the keener because Mr. Noaks's boots more than made up in size for what they lacked in number. Either of them singly took more time and polish than any other pair imaginable. She would have recognised them, at a glance, anywhere. Even so now, it was at a glance that she recognised the toes of them protruding from beneath the window-curtain. She dismissed the theory that Mr. Noaks might have gone utterly unshod to the river. She scouted the hypothesis that his ghost could be shod thus. By process of elimination she arrived at the truth. "Mr. Noaks," she said quietly, "come out of there."

There was a slight quiver of the curtain; no more. Katie repeated her words. There was a pause, then a convulsion of the curtain. Noaks stood forth.

Always, in polishing his boots, Katie had found herself thinking of him as a man of prodigious stature, well though she knew him to be quite tiny. Even so now, at recognition of his boots, she had fixed her eyes to meet his, when he should emerge, a full yard too high. With a sharp drop she focused him.

"By what right," he asked, "do you come prying about my room?"

This was a stroke so unexpected that it left Katie mute. It equally surprised Noaks, who had been about to throw himself on his knees and implore this girl not to betray him. He was quick, though, to clinch his advantage.

"This," he said, "is the first time I have caught you. Let it be the last."

Was this the little man she had so long despised, and so superciliously served? His very smallness gave him an air of concentrated force. She remembered having read that all the greatest men in history had been of less than the middle height. And—oh, her heart leapt—here was the one man who had scorned to die for Miss Dobson. He alone had held

out against the folly of his fellows. Sole and splendid
survivor he stood, rock-footed, before her. And impulsively
she abased herself, kneeling at his feet as at the great double
altar of some dark new faith.

"You are great, sir, you are wonderful," she said, gazing
up to him, rapt. It was the first time she had ever called him
"sir".

It is easier, as Michelet suggested, for a woman to change
her opinion of a man than for him to change his opinion of
himself. Noaks, despite the presence of mind he had shown a
few moments ago, still saw himself as he had seen himself
during the past hours: that is, as an arrant little coward—one
who by his fear to die had put himself outside the pale of
decent manhood. He had meant to escape from the house at
dead of night and, under an assumed name, work his passage
out to Australia—a land which had always made strong
appeal to his imagination. No one, he had reflected, would
suppose because his body was not retrieved from the water
that he had not perished with the rest. And he had looked to
Australia to make a man of him yet: in Encounter Bay,
perhaps, or in the Gulf of Carpentaria, he might yet end
nobly.

Thus Katie's behaviour was as much an embarrassment as
a relief; and he asked her in what way he was great and
wonderful.

"Modest, like all heroes!" she cried, and, still kneeling,
proceeded to sing his praises with a so infectious fervour that
Noaks did begin to feel he had done a fine thing in not dying.
After all, was it not moral cowardice as much as love that had
tempted him to die? He had wrestled with it, thrown it.
"Yes," said he, when her rhapsody was over, "perhaps I am
modest."

"And that is why you hid yourself just now?"

"Yes," he gladly said. "I hid myself for the same reason,"
he added, "when I heard your mother's footstep."

"But," she faltered, with a sudden doubt, "that bit of writing which Mother found on the table——"

"That? Oh, that was only a general reflection, copied out of a book."

"Oh, won't poor Mother be glad when she knows!"

"I don't want her to know," said Noaks, with a return of nervousness. "You mustn't tell anyone. I—the fact is——"

"Ah, that is so like you!" the girl said tenderly. "I suppose it was your modesty that all this while blinded me. Please, sir, I have a confession to make to you. Never till to-night have I loved you."

Exquisite was the shock of these words to one who, not without reason, had always assumed that no woman would ever love him. Before he knew what he was doing, he had bent down and kissed the sweet upturned face. It was the first kiss he had ever given outside his family circle. It was an artless and a resounding kiss.

He started back, dazed. What manner of man, he wondered, was he? A coward, piling profligacy on poltroonery? Or a hero, claiming exemption from moral law? What was done could not be undone; but it could be righted. He drew off from the little finger of his left hand that iron ring which, after a twinge of rheumatism, he had to-day resumed.

"Wear it," he said.

"You mean——?" She leapt to her feet.

"That we are engaged. I hope you don't think we have any choice?"

She clapped her hands, like the child she was, and adjusted the ring.

"It is very pretty," she said.

"It is very simple," he answered lightly. "But," he added, with a change of tone, "it is very durable. And that is the important thing. For I shall not be in a position to marry before I am forty."

A shadow of disappointment hovered over Katie's clear

young brow, but was instantly chased away by the thought that to be engaged was almost as splendid as to be married.

"Recently," said her lover, "I meditated leaving Oxford for Australia. But now that you have come into my life, I am compelled to drop that notion, and to carve out the career I had first set for myself. A year hence, if I get a Second in Greats—and I *shall*," he said, with a fierce look that entranced her—"I shall have a very good chance of an assistant-mastership in a good private school. In eighteen years, if I am careful—and, with you waiting for me, I *shall* be careful—my savings will enable me to start a small school of my own, and to take a wife. Even then it would be more prudent to wait another five years, no doubt. But there was always a streak of madness in the Noakses. I say 'Prudence to the winds!'"

"Ah, don't say that!" exclaimed Katie, laying a hand on his sleeve.

"You are right. Never hesitate to curb me. And," he said, touching the ring, "an idea has just occurred to me. When the time comes, let this be the wedding-ring. Gold is gaudy—not at all the thing for a schoolmaster's bride. It is a pity," he muttered, examining her through his spectacles, "that your hair is so golden. A schoolmaster's bride should—— Good heavens! Those ear-rings! Where did you get *them*?"

"They were given to me to-day," Katie faltered. "The Duke gave me them."

"Indeed?"

"Please, sir, he gave me them as a memento."

"And that memento shall immediately be handed over to his executors."

"Yes, sir."

"I should think so!" was on the tip of Noaks's tongue, but suddenly he ceased to see the pearls as trinkets finite and inapposite—saw them, in a flash, as things transmutable by sale hereafter into desks, forms, black-boards, maps, lockers, cubicles, gravel soil, diet unlimited, and special attention to backward pupils. Simultaneously, he saw how mean had been his motive for repudiating the gift. What more despicable than jealousy of a man deceased? What sillier than to cast pearls before executors? Sped by nothing but the pulse of his hot youth, he had wooed and won this girl. Why flinch from her unsought dowry?

He told her his vision. Her eyes opened wide to it. "And oh," she cried, "then we can be married as soon as you take your degree!"

He bade her not to be so foolish. Who ever heard of a headmaster aged three-and-twenty? What parent or guardian would trust a stripling? The engagement must run its course. "And," he said, fidgeting, "do you know that I have hardly done any reading to-day?"

"You want to read *now—to-night?*"

"I must put in a good two hours. Where are the books that were on my table?"

Reverently—he was indeed a king of men—she took the books down from the shelf, and placed them where she had found them. And she knew not which thrilled her the more —the kiss he gave her at parting, or the tone in which he told her that the one thing he could not and would not stand was having his books disturbed.

Still less than before attuned to the lugubrious session downstairs, she went straight up to her attic, and did a little dance there in the dark. She threw open the lattice of the dormer-window, and leaned out, smiling, throbbing.

The Emperors, gazing up, saw her happy, and wondered; saw Noaks's ring on her finger, and would fain have shaken their grey heads.

Presently she was aware of a protrusion from the window beneath hers. The head of her beloved! Fondly she watched it, wished she could reach down to stroke it. She loved him for having, after all, left his books. It was sweet to be his excuse. Should she call softly to him? No, it might shame him to be caught truant. He had already chidden her for prying. So she did but gaze down on his head silently, wondering whether in eighteen years it would be bald, wondering whether her own hair would still have the fault of being golden. Most of all, she wondered whether he loved her half so much as she loved him.

This happened to be precisely what he himself was wondering. Not that he wished himself free. He was one of those in whom the will does not, except under very great pressure, oppose the conscience. What pressure here? Miss Batch was a superior girl; she would grace any station in life. He had always been rather in awe of her. It was a fine thing to be suddenly loved by her, to be in a position to over-rule her every whim. Plighting his troth, he had feared she would be an encumbrance, only to find she was a lever. But —was he deeply in love with her? How was it that he could not at this moment recall her features, or the tone of her voice, while of deplorable Miss Dobson, every lineament, every accent, so vividly haunted him? Try as he would to beat off these memories, he failed, and—some very great pressure here!—was glad he failed; glad, though he found himself relapsing to the self-contempt from which Miss Batch had raised him. He scorned himself for being alive. And again, he scorned himself for his infidelity. Yet he was glad he could not forget that face, that voice—that queen. She had smiled at him when she borrowed the ring. She had said: "Thank you." Oh, and now, at this very moment, sleeping or waking, actually she was somewhere—she! herself! This was an incredible, an indubitable, an all-magical fact for the little fellow.

From the street below came a faint cry that was as the cry of his own heart, uttered by her own lips. Quaking, he peered down, and dimly saw, over the way, a cloaked woman.

She—yes, it was she herself—came gliding to the middle of the road, gazing up at him.

"At last!" he heard her say. His instinct was to hide himself from the queen he had not died for. Yet he could not move.

"Or," she quavered, "are you a phantom sent to mock me? Speak!"

"Good evening," he said huskily.

"I knew," she murmured. "I knew the gods were not so cruel. Oh man of my need," she cried, stretching out her arms to him, "oh heaven-sent, I see you only as a dark outline against the light of your room. But I know you. Your name is Noaks, isn't it? Dobson is mine. I am your Warden's grand-daughter. I am faint and footsore. I have ranged this desert city in search of—of *you*. Let me hear from your own lips that you love me. Tell me in your own words——" She broke off with a little scream, and did but stand with forefinger pointed at him, gazing, gasping.

"Listen, Miss Dobson," he stammered, writhing under what he took to be the lash of her irony. "Give me time to explain. You see me here——"

"Hush," she cried, "man of my greater, my deeper and nobler need! Oh hush, ideal which not consciously I was out for to-night—ideal vouchsafed to me by a crowning mercy! I sought a lover, I find a master. I sought but a live youth, was blind to what his survival would betoken. Oh master, you think me light and wicked. You stare coldly down at me through your spectacles, whose glint I faintly discern now that the moon peeps forth. You would be readier to forgive me the havoc I have wrought if you could for the life of you understand what charm your friends found in me. You marvel, as at the skull of Helen of Troy. No, you don't think me hideous: you simply think me plain. There was a time when I thought *you* plain—you whose face, now that the moon shines full on it, is seen to be of a beauty that is flawless without being insipid. Oh that I were a glove upon that hand, that I might touch that cheek! You shudder at the notion of such contact. My voice grates on you. You try to silence me with frantic though exquisite gestures, and with noises inarticulate but divine. I bow to your will, master. Chasten me with your tongue."

"I am not what you think me," gibbered Noaks. "I was not afraid to die for you. I love you. I was on my way to the river this afternoon, but I—I tripped and sprained my ankle, and—and jarred my spine. They carried me back here. I am still very weak. I can't put my foot to the ground. As soon as I can——"

Just then Zuleika heard a little sharp sound which, for the fraction of an instant, before she knew it to be a clink of metal on the pavement, she thought was the breaking of the heart within her. Looking quickly down, she heard a shrill girlish laugh aloft. Looking quickly up, she descried at the unlit window above her lover's a face which she remembered as that of the landlady's daughter.

"Find it, Miss Dobson," laughed the girl. "Crawl for it. It can't have rolled far, and it's the only engagement-ring you'll get from *him*," she said, pointing to the livid face twisted painfully up at her from the lower window. "Grovel for it, Miss Dobson. Ask him to step down and help you. Oh, he can! That was all lies about his spine and ankle. Afraid, that's what he was—I see it all now—afraid of the water. I wish you'd found him as I did—skulking behind the curtain. Oh, you're welcome to him."

"Don't listen," Noaks cried down. "Don't listen to that person. I admit I have trifled with her affections. This is her revenge—these wicked untruths—these—these——"

Zuleika silenced him with a gesture. "Your tone to me," she said up to Katie, "is not without offence; but the stamp of truth is on what you tell me. We have both been deceived in this man, and are, in some sort, sisters."

"Sisters?" cried Katie. "Your sisters are the snake and the spider, though neither of them wishes it known. I loathe you. And the Duke loathed you, too."

"What's that?" gasped Zuleika.

"Didn't he tell you? He told me. And I warrant he told you, too."

"He died for love of me: d'you hear?"

"Ah, you'd like people to think so, wouldn't you? Does a man who loves a woman give away the keepsake she gave him? Look!" Katie leaned forward, pointing to her ear-rings. "He loved *me*," she cried. "He put them in with his own hands—told me to wear them always. And he kissed me—kissed me good-bye in the street, where everyone could see. He kissed me," she sobbed. "No other man shall ever do that."

"Ah, that he did!" said a voice level with Zuleika. It was the voice of Mrs. Batch, who a few moments ago had opened the door for her departing guests.

"Ah, that he did!" echoed the guests.

"Never mind them, Miss Dobson," cried Noaks, and at the sound of his voice Mrs. Batch rushed into the middle of the road, to gaze up. "*I* love you. Think what you will of me I——"

"You!" flashed Zuleika. "As for you, little Sir Lily Liver, leaning out there, and, I frankly tell you, looking like nothing so much as a gargoyle hewn by a drunken stone-mason for the adornment of a Methodist Chapel in one of the vilest suburbs of Leeds or Wigan, I do but felicitate the river-god and his nymphs that their water was saved to-day by your cowardice from the contamination of your plunge."

"Shame on you, Mr. Noaks," said Mrs. Batch, "making believe you were dead——"

"Shame!" screamed Clarence, who had darted out into the fray.

"I found him hiding behind the curtain," chimed in Katie.

"And I a mother to him?" said Mrs. Batch, shaking her fist. " 'What is life without love?' indeed! Oh, the cowardly, underhand——"

"Wretch," prompted her cronies.

"Let's kick him out of the house!" suggested Clarence, dancing for joy.

Zuleika, smiling brilliantly down at the boy, said: "Just you run up and fight him!"

"Right you are," he answered, with a look of knightly devotion, and darted back into the house.

"No escape!" she cried up to Noaks. "You've got to fight him now. He and you are just about evenly matched, I fancy."

But, grimly enough, Zuleika's estimate was never put to the test. Is it harder for a coward to fight with his fists than to kill himself? Or again, is it easier for him to die than to endure a prolonged cross-fire of women's wrath and scorn? This I know: that in the life of even the least and meanest of us there is somewhere one fine moment—one high chance not missed. I like to think it was by operation of this law that Noaks had now clambered out upon the window-sill, silencing, sickening, scattering like chaff the women beneath him.

He was already not there when Clarence bounded into the room. "Come on!" yelled the boy, first thrusting his head behind the door, then diving beneath the table, then plucking aside either window-curtain, vowing vengeance.

Vengeance was not his. Down on the road without, not yet looked at but by the steadfast eyes of the Emperors, the last of the undergraduates lay dead; and fleet-footed Zuleika, with her fingers still pressed to her ears, had taken full toll now.

## XXIII

Twisting and turning in her flight, with wild eyes that fearfully retained the image of that small man gathering himself to spring, Zuleika found herself suddenly where she could no further go.

She was in that grim ravine by which you approach New College. At sight of the great shut gate before her, she halted, and swerved to the wall. She set her brow and the palms of her hands against the cold stones. She threw back her head, and beat the stones with her fists.

It was not only what she had seen, it was what she had barely saved herself from seeing, and what she had not quite saved herself from hearing, that she strove, so piteously to forget. She was sorrier for herself, angrier, than she had been last night when the Duke laid hands on her. Why should every day have a horrible ending? Last night she had avenged herself. To-night's outrage was all the more foul and mean because of its certain immunity. And the fact that she had in some measure brought it on herself did but whip her rage. What a fool she had been to taunt the man! Yet no, how could she have foreseen that he would—do *that?* How could she have guessed that he, who had not dared seemly death for her in the gentle river, would dare—*that?*

She shuddered the more as she now remembered that this very day, in that very house, she had invited for her very self a similar fate. What if the Duke had taken her at her word? Strange! she wouldn't have flinched then. She had felt no horror at the notion of such a death. And thus she now saw Noaks's conduct in a new light—saw that he had but wished

237

to prove his love, not at all to affront her. This understanding quickly steadied her nerves. She did not need now to forget what she had seen; and, not needing to forget it—thus are our brains fashioned—she was able to forget it.

But by removal of one load her soul was but bared for a more grievous other. Her memory harked back to what had preceded the crisis. She recalled those moments of doomed rapture in which her heart had soared up to the apocalyptic window—recalled how, all the while she was speaking to the man there, she had been chafed by the inadequacy of language. Oh, how much more she had meant than she could express! Oh, the ecstasy of that self-surrender! And the brevity of it! the sudden odious awakening! Thrice in this Oxford she had been duped. Thrice all that was fine and sweet in her had leapt forth, only to be scourged back into hiding. Poor heart inhibited! She gazed about her. The stone alley she had come into, the terrible shut gate, were for her a visible symbol of the destiny she had to put up with. Wringing her hands, she hastened along the way she had come. She vowed she would never again set foot in Oxford. She wished herself out of the hateful little city to-night. She even wished herself dead.

She deserved to suffer, you say? Maybe. I merely state that she did suffer.

Emerging into Catherine Street, she knew whereabouts she was, and made straight for Judas, turning away her eyes as she skirted the Broad, that place of mocked hopes and shattered ideals.

Coming into Judas Street, she remembered the scene of yesterday—the happy man with her, the noise of the vast happy crowd. She suffered in a worse form what she had suffered in the gallery of the Hall. For now—did I not say she was not without imagination?—her self-pity was sharpened by remorse for the hundreds of homes robbed. She realised the truth of what the poor Duke had once said to her:

she was a danger in the world. . . . Aye, and all the more dire now. What if the youth of all Europe was moved by Oxford's example? That was a horribly possible thing. It must be reckoned with. It must be averted. She must not show herself to men. She must find some hiding-place, and there abide. Were this a hardship? she asked herself. Was she not sickened for ever of men's homage? And was it not clear now that the absorbing need in her soul, the need to love, would never—except for a brief while, now and then, and by an unfortunate misunderstanding—be fulfilled?

So long ago that you may not remember, I compared her favourably with the shepherdess Marcella, and pleaded her capacity for passion as an excuse for her remaining at large. I hope you will now, despite your rather evident animus against her, set this to her credit: that she did, so soon as she realised the hopelessness of her case, make just that decision which I blamed Marcella for not making at the outset. It was as she stood on the Warden's door-step that she decided to take the veil.

With something of a conventual hush in her voice, she said to the butler: "Please tell my maid that we are leaving by a very early train to-morrow, and that she must pack my things to-night."

"Very well, Miss," said the butler. "The Warden," he added, "is in the study, Miss, and was asking for you."

She could face her grandfather without a tremour—now. She would hear meekly whatever reproaches he might have for her, but their sting was already drawn by the surprise she had in store for him.

It was he who seemed a trifle nervous. In his "Well, did you come and peep down from the gallery?" there was a distinct tremour.

Throwing aside her cloak, she went quickly to him, and laid a hand on the lapel of his coat. "Poor grand-papa!" she said.

239

"Nonsense, my dear child," he replied, disengaging himself. "I didn't gave it a thought. If the young men chose to be so silly as to stay away, I—I——"

"Grand-papa, haven't you been told *yet?*"

"Told? I am a Gallio for such follies. I didn't inquire."

"But (forgive me, grand-papa, if I seem to you, for the moment, pert) you are Warden here. It is your duty, even your privilege, to *guard*. Is it not? Well, I grant you the adage that it is useless to bolt the stable door when the horse has been stolen. But what shall be said of the ostler who doesn't know—won't even 'inquire' whether—the horse *has* been stolen, grand-papa?"

"You speak in riddles, Zuleika."

"I wish with all my heart I need not tell you the answers. I think I have a very real grievance against your Staff—or whatever it is you call your subordinates here. I go so far as to dub them dodderers. And I shall the better justify that term by not shirking the duty they have left undone. The reason why there were no undergraduates in your Hall to-night is that they were all dead."

"Dead?" he gasped. "Dead? It is disgraceful that I was not told. What did they die of?"

"Of me."

"Of you?"

"Yes. I am an epidemic, grand-papa, a scourge, such as the world has not known. These young men drowned themselves for love of me."

He came towards her. "Do you realise, girl, what this means to me? I am an old man. For more than half a century I have known this College. To it, when my wife died, I gave all that there was of heart left in me. For thirty years I have been Warden; and in that charge has been all my pride. I have had no thought but for this great College, its honour and prosperity. More than once lately have I asked myself whether my eyes were growing dim, my hand less steady. 'No' was my answer, and again 'No'. And thus it is that I have lingered on to let Judas be struck down from its high eminence, shamed in the eyes of England—a College for ever tainted, and of evil omen." He raised his head. "The disgrace to myself is nothing. I care not how parents shall rage against me, and the Heads of other Colleges make merry over my decrepitude. It is because you have wrought the downfall of Judas that I am about to lay my undying curse on you."

"You mustn't do that!" she cried. "It would be a sort of sacrilege. I am going to be a nun. Besides, why should you? I can quite well understand your feeling for Judas. But how is Judas more disgraced than any other College? If it were only the Judas undergraduates who had——"

"There were others?" cried the Warden. "How many?"

"All. All the boys from all the Colleges."

The Warden heaved a deep sigh. "Of course," he said, "this changes the aspect of the whole matter. I wish you had made it clear at once. You gave me a very great shock," he said, sinking into his arm-chair, "and I have not yet recovered. You must study the art of exposition."

"That will depend on the rules of the convent."

"Ah, I forgot you were going into a convent. Anglican, I hope?"

Anglican, she supposed.

"As a young man," he said, "I saw much of dear old Dr. Pusey. It might have somewhat reconciled him to my marriage if he had known that my grand-daughter would take the veil." He adjusted his glasses, and looked at her. "Are you sure you have a vocation?"

"Yes. I want to be out of the world. I want to do no more harm."

He eyed her musingly. "That," he said, "is rather a revulsion than a vocation. I remember that I ventured to point out to Dr. Pusey the difference between those two

things, when he was almost persuading me to enter a Brother-
hood founded by one of his friends. It may be that the world
would be well rid of you, my dear child. But it is not the
world only that we must consider. Would you grace the
recesses of the Church?"

"I could but try," said Zuleika.

" 'You could but try' are the very words Dr. Pusey used to
me. I ventured to say that in such a matter effort itself was a
stigma of unfitness. For all my moods of revulsion, I knew
that my place was in the world. I stayed there."

"But suppose, grand-papa"—and, seeing in fancy the vast
agitated flotilla of crinolines, she could not forbear a smile—
"suppose all the young ladies of that period had drowned
themselves for love of you?"

Her smile seemed to nettle the Warden. "I was greatly
admired," he said. "Greatly," he repeated.

"And you liked that, grand-papa?"

"Yes, my dear. Yes, I am afraid I did. But I never
encouraged it."

"Your own heart was never touched?"

"Never, until I met Laura Frith."

"Who was she?"

"She was my future wife."

"And how was it you singled her out from the rest? Was
she very beautiful?"

"No. It cannot be said that she was beautiful. Indeed,
she was accounted plain. I think it was her great dignity
that attracted me. She did not smile archly at me, nor
shake her ringlets. In those days it was the fashion for
young ladies to embroider slippers for such men in
holy orders as best pleased their fancy. I received
hundreds—thousands—of such slippers. But never a pair
from Laura Frith."

"She did not love you?" asked Zuleika, who had seated
herself on the floor at her grandfather's feet.

"I concluded that she did not. It interested me very greatly. It fired me."

"Was she incapable of love?"

"No, it was notorious in her circle that she had loved often, but loved in vain."

"Why did she marry you?"

"I think she was fatigued by my importunities. She was not very strong. But it may be that she married me out of pique. She never told me. I did not inquire."

"Yet you were very happy with her?"

"While she lived, I was ideally happy."

The young woman stretched out a hand, and laid it on the clasped hands of the old man. He sat gazing into the past. She was silent for a while; and in her eyes, still fixed intently on his face, there were tears.

"Grand-papa dear"—but there were tears in her voice, too.

"My child, you don't understand. If I had needed pity——"

"I do understand—so well. I wasn't pitying you, dear, I was envying you a little."

"Me?—an old man with only the remembrance of happiness?"

"You, who have had happiness granted to you. That isn't what made me cry, though. I cried because I was glad. You and I, with all this great span of years between us, and yet— so wonderfully alike! I had always thought of myself as a creature utterly apart."

"Ah, that is how all young people think of themselves. It wears off. Tell me about this wonderful resemblance of ours."

He sat attentive while she described her heart to him. But when, at the close of her confidences, she said: "So you see it's a case of sheer heredity, grand-papa," the word "Fiddlesticks!" would out.

"Forgive me, my dear," he said, patting her hand. "I was very much interested. But I do believe young people are even more staggered by themselves than they were in my day. And then, all these grand theories they fall back on! Heredity . . . as if there were something to baffle us in the fact of a young woman liking to be admired! And as if it were passing strange of her to reserve her heart for a man she can respect and look up to! And as if a man's indifference to her were not of all things the likeliest to give her a sense of inferiority to him! You and I, my dear, may in some respects be very queer people, but in the matter of the affections we are ordinary enough."

"Oh grand-papa, do you really mean that?" she cried eagerly.

"At my age, a man husbands his resources. He says nothing that he does not really mean. The difference between you and other young women is that which lay also between me and other young men: a special attractiveness. . . . Thousands of slippers, did I say? Tens of thousands. I had hoarded them with a fatuous pride. On the evening of my betrothal I made a bonfire of them, visible from three counties. I danced round it all night." And from his old eyes darted even now the reflections of those flames.

"Glorious!" whispered Zuleika. "But ah," she said, rising to her feet, "tell me no more of it—poor me! You see, it isn't a mere special attractiveness that *I* have. *I* am irresisitble."

"A daring statement, my child—very hard to prove."

"Hasn't it been proved up to the hilt to-day?"

"To-day? . . . Ah, and so they did really all drown themselves for you? . . . Dear, dear! . . . The Duke—he, too?"

"He set the example."

"No! You don't say so! He was a greatly-gifted young man—a true ornament to the College. But he always seemed to me rather—what shall I say?—inhuman . . . I remember now that he did seem rather excited when he came to the concert last night and you weren't yet there . . .

You are quite sure you were the cause of his death?"

"Quite," said Zuleika, marvelling at the lie—or fib, rather: he had been *going* to die for her. But why not have told the truth? Was it possible, she wondered, that her wretched vanity had survived her renunciation of the world? Why had she so resented just now the doubt cast on that irresistibility which had blighted and cankered her whole life?

"Well, my dear," said the Warden, "I confess that I am amazed—astounded." Again he adjusted his glasses, and looked at her.

She found herself moving slowly around the study, with the gait of a *mannequin* in a dressmaker's show-room. She tried to stop this; but her body seemed to be quite beyond the control of her mind. It had the insolence to go ambling on its own account. "Little space you'll have in a convent cell," snarled her mind vindictively. Her body paid no heed whatever.

Her grandfather, leaning back in his chair, gazed at the ceiling, and meditatively tapped the finger-tips of one hand against those of the other. "Sister Zuleika," he presently said to the ceiling.

"Well? and what is there so—so ridiculous in"—but the rest was lost in trill after trill of laughter; and these were then lost in sobs.

The Warden had risen from his chair. "My dear," he said, "I wasn't laughing. I was only—trying to imagine. If you really want to retire from——"

"I do," moaned Zuleika.

"Then perhaps——"

"But I don't," she wailed.

"Of course, you don't, my dear."

"Why, 'of course'?"

"Come, you are tired, my poor child. That is very natural after this wonderful, this historic day. Come, dry your eyes. There, that's better. To-morrow——"

"I do believe you're a little proud of me."

"Heaven forgive me, I believe I am. A grandfather's heart—— But there, good night, my dear. Let me light your candle."

She took her cloak, and followed him out to the hall table. There she mentioned that she was going away early to-morrow.

"To the convent?" he slyly asked.

"Ah, don't tease me, grand-papa."

"Well, I am sorry you are going away, my dear. But perhaps, in the circumstances, it is best. You must come and stay here again, later on," he said, handing her the lit candle. "Not in term-time, though," he added.

"No," she echoed, "not in term-time."

# XXIV

FROM the shifting gloom of the staircase to the soft radiance
cast through the open door of her bedroom was for poor
Zuleika an almost heartening transition. She stood awhile on
the threshold, watching Mélisande dart to and fro like a
shuttle across a loom. Already the main part of the packing
seemed to have been accomplished. The wardrobe was a
yawning void, the carpet was here and there visible, many of
the trunks were already brimming and foaming over. . . .
Once more on the road! Somewhat as, when beneath the
stars the great tent had been struck, and the lions were
growling in their vans, and the horses were pawing the
stamped grass and whinnying, and the elephants trumpeting,
Zuleika's mother may often have felt within her a wan
exhilaration, so now did the heart of that mother's child rise
and flutter amidst the familiar bustle of "being off". Weary
she was of the world, and angry she was at not being, after
all, good enough for something better. And yet—well, at
least, good-bye, to Oxford!

She envied Mélisande, so nimbly and cheerfully laborious
till the day should come when her betrothed had saved
enough to start a little café of his own and make her his bride
and *dame de comptoir*. Oh, to have a purpose, a prospect, a
stake in the world, as this faithful soul had!

"Can I help you at all, Mélisande?" she asked, picking her
way across the strewn floor.

Mélisande, patting down a pile of chiffon, seemed to
be amused at such a notion. "Mademoiselle has her own
art. Do I mix myself in that?" she cried, waving one
hand towards the great malachite casket.

247

Zuleika looked at the casket, and then very gratefully at the maid. Her art—how had she forgotten that? Here was solace, purpose. She would work as she had never worked yet. She *knew* that she had it in her to do better than she had ever done. She confessed to herself that she had too often been slack in the matter of practice and rehearsal, trusting her personal magnetism to carry her through. Only last night she had badly fumbled, more than once. Her bravura business with the Demon Egg-Cup had been simply vile. The audience hadn't noticed it, perhaps, but *she* had. Now she would perfect herself. Barely a fortnight now before her engagement at the Folies Bergères! What if—no, she must not think of that! But the thought insisted. What if she essayed for Paris that which again and again she had meant to graft on to her repertory—the Provoking Thimble?

She flushed at the possibility. What if her whole present repertory were but a passing phase in her art—a mere beginning—an earlier manner? She remembered how marvellously last night she had manipulated the ear-rings and the studs. Then lo! the light died out of her eyes, and her face grew rigid. That memory had brought other memories in its wake.

For her, when she fled the Broad, Noaks's window had blotted out all else. Now she saw again that higher window, saw that girl flaunting *her* ear-rings, gibing down at her. "He put them in with his own hands!"—the words rang again in her ears, making her cheeks tingle. Oh, he had thought it a very clever thing to do, no doubt—a splendid little revenge, something after his own heart! "And he kissed me in the open street"—excellent, excellent! She ground her teeth. And these doings must have been fresh in his mind when she overtook him and walked with him to the house-boat! Infamous! And she had then been wearing his studs! She drew his attention to them when——

Her jewel-box stood open, to receive the jewels she wore

to-night. She went very calmly to it. There, in a corner of the topmost tray, rested the two great white pearls—the pearls which, in one way and another, had meant so much to her.

"Mélisande!"

"Mademoiselle?"

"When we go to Paris, would you like to make a little present to your fiancé?"

"Je voudrais bien, mademoiselle."

"Then you shall give him these," said Zuleika, holding out the two studs.

"Maid jamais de la vie! Chez Tourtel tout le monde le dirait millionaire. Un garçon de café qui porte au plastron des perles pareilles—merci!"

"Tell him he may tell everyone that they were given to me by the late Duke of Dorset, and given by me to you, and by you to him."

"Máis——" The protest died on Mélisande's lips. Suddenly she had ceased to see the pearls as trinkets finite and inapposite—saw them as things presently transmutable into little marble tables, bocks, dominos, absinthes au sucre, shiny black portfolios with weekly journals in them, yellow staves with daily journals flapping from them, vermouths secs, vermouths cassis . . .

"Mademoiselle is too amiable," she said, taking the pearls.

And certainly, just then, Zuleika was looking very amiable indeed. The look was transient. Nothing, she reflected, could undo what the Duke had done. That hateful, impudent girl would take good care that everyone should know. "He put them in with his own hands." *Her* earrings! "He kissed me in the public street. He loved me" . . . Well, he had called out "Zuleika!" and everyone around had heard him. That was something. But how glad all the old women in the world would be to shake their heads and say: "Oh, no, my dear, believe me! It wasn't anything

249

to do with *her*. I'm told on the very best authority," and so
forth, and so on. She knew he had told any number of
undergraduates he was going to die for her. But they, poor
fellows, could not bear witness. And good heavens! If there
were a doubt as to the Duke's motive, why not doubts as to
theirs? . . . But many of them had called out "Zuleika!"
too. And of course any really impartial person who knew
anything at all about the matter at first hand would be sure
in his own mind that it was perfectly absurd to pretend that
the whole thing wasn't entirely and absolutely for her. . . .
And of course some of the men must have left written
evidence of their intention. She remembered that at The
MacQuern's to-day was a Mr. Craddock, who had made a
will in her favour and wanted to read it aloud to her in the
middle of luncheon. Oh, there would be proof positive as to
many of the men. But of the others it would be said that
they died in trying to rescue their comrades. There would be
all sorts of silly far-fetched theories, and downright lies that
couldn't be disproved. . . .

"Mélisande, that crackling of tissue paper is driving me
mad! Do leave off! Can't you see that I am waiting to be
undressed?"

The maid hastened to her side, and with quick light
fingers began to undress her. "Mademoiselle va bien
dormir—ça se voit," she purred.

"I shan't," said Zuleika.

Nevertheless, it was soothing to be undressed, and yet
more soothing anon to sit merely night-gowned before the
mirror, while, slowly and gently, strongly and strand by
strand, Mélisande brushed her hair.

After all, it didn't so much matter what the world thought.
Let the world whisper and insinuate what it would. To slur
and sully, to belittle and drag down—that was what the
world always tried to do. But great things were still great,
and fair things still fair. With no thought for the world's

opinion had these men gone down to the water to-day. Their deed was for her and themselves alone. It had sufficed them. Should it not suffice her? It did, oh it did. She was a wretch to have repined.

At a gesture from her, Mélisande brought to a close the rhythmical ministrations, and—using no tissue paper this time—did what was yet to be done among the trunks.

"*We* know, you and I," Zuleika whispered to the adorable creature in the mirror; and the adorable creature gave back her nod and smile.

*They* knew, these two.

Yet, in their happiness, rose and floated a shadow between them. It was the ghost of that one man who—*they* knew—had died irrelevantly, with a cold heart.

Came also the horrid little ghost of one who had died late and unseemly.

And now, thick and fast, swept a whole multitude of other ghosts, the ghosts of all them who, being dead, could not die again; the poor ghosts of them who had done what they could, and could do no more.

No more? Was it not enough? The lady in the mirror gazed at the lady in the room, reproachfully at first, then—for were they not sisters?—relentingly, then pityingly. Each of the two covered her face with her hands.

And there recurred, as by stealth, to the lady in the room a thought that had assailed her not long ago in Judas Street . . . a thought about the power of example . . .

And now, with pent breath and fast-beating heart, she stood staring at the lady of the mirror, without seeing her; and now she wheeled round and swiftly glided to that little table on which stood her two books. She snatched Bradshaw.

We always intervene between Bradshaw and anyone whom we see consulting him. "Mademoiselle will permit me to find that which she seeks?" asked Mélisande.

"Be quiet," said Zuleika. We always repulse, at first, anyone who intervenes between us and Bradshaw.

We always end by accepting the intervention. "See if it is possible to go direct from here to Cambridge," said Zuleika, handing the book on. "If it isn't, then—well, see how one *does* get there."

We never have any confidence in the intervener. Nor is the intervener, when it comes to the point, sanguine. With mistrust mounting to exasperation Zuleika sat watching the faint and frantic researches of her maid.

"Stop!" she said suddenly. "I have a much better idea. Go down very early to the station. See the stationmaster. Order me a special train. For ten o'clock, say."

Rising, she stretched her arms above her head. Her lips parted in a yawn, met in a smile. With both hands she pushed back her hair from her shoulders, and twisted it into a loose knot. Very lightly she slipped up into bed, and very soon she was asleep.

CHRISTOPHER ISHERWOOD

# Prater Violet

Set in London in the mid-1930s *Prater Violet* explores the relationship between Viennese film director Friedrich Bergmann, brought to London by Imperial Bulldog Pictures to direct a film, and Christopher Isherwood, hired to write the script. Against the background of the plight of Austria and the rise of fascism, the novel counterpoints the true role and limits of the artist with the fatuous nature of the film Bergmann is directing, a sickly and sentimental period romance.

At once a comic portrait of the film industry and a serious analysis of the relationship between art and life, this book marked a turning point in Isherwood's writing – the first to be written after his spiritual conversion. But above all it endures as one of the most accomplished short novels of the century – a sophisticated, witty book with a subtle and questing inner depth.

'The best prose writer in English' Gore Vidal

# CHRISTOPHER ISHERWOOD

# A Single Man

'George, the middle-fiftyish English don at the Californian university, has lost his boyfriend, killed in a motor crash. He carries on with his life, making faces at the children in the nearby houses, lecturing on Aldous Huxley, gossiping with other members of the teaching staff, drinking too much with a fellow expatriate who has been abandoned by her husband. All the time he is tormented by his urges: the sight of a blonde young man playing tennis, a chance meeting with one of his students for whom George has been nursing a passion which leads to drunken nude bathing. Mr Isherwood has not written anything as good as this for a long time. It is all very sad and yet at times wildly funny . . . The description of the Californian scene is bitter, nostalgic, yet at the same time tinged with love'
David Holloway, *Daily Telegraph*

'In *A Single Man*, published in the mid-sixties, [Isherwood] produced what seems now the most accurate and far-sighted of all the novels written in and about that difficult decade' *Books and Bookmen*

'A testimony to Isherwood's undiminished brilliance as a novelist' Anthony Burgess, *The Listener*

CHRISTOPHER ISHERWOOD

# All the Conspirators

Isherwood's theme, in a novel which clearly shows his early influences, was to recur in his later work: the destruction of the son by the evil mother. In the Kensington of the 1920s – silver frames, inlaid bureaux, charming sitting-rooms – the "conspirators", Philip and Joan, fight to throw off the oppressive power of their mother.

In Isherwood's own words, *All The Conspirators* is the story of "a trivial but furious battle which the combatants fight out passionately and dirtily to the finish, using whatever weapons come to their hands."

'This first novel is a key to Isherwood and the twenties. It is as mature, as readable, as concentrated as anything he has written since'   Cyril Connolly

'The best prose writer in English'   Gore Vidal

# CHRISTOPHER ISHERWOOD

# Goodbye to Berlin

The narrator of *Goodbye to Berlin* is called "Christopher Isherwood" ("Herr Issyvoo"). His story, in this novel, first published in 1939, obliquely evokes the gathering storm in Berlin before and just after the rise to power of the Nazis. Events are seen through the eyes of a series of individuals: his landlady, Fraülein Schroeder; Sally Bowles, the English upper-class waif; the Nowaks, a struggling working-class family; the Landauers, a wealthy, civilized family of Jewish store owners, whose lives are about to be ruined.

Wry, detached, impressionistic in its approach, yet vividly eloquent about the brutal effect of public events on private lives, *Goodbye to Berlin* has provided the inspiration for a highly successful stage play, *I Am a Camera*, and the stage and screen musical, *Cabaret*. It has long been recognized as one of the most powerful and popular novels written in English in this century.

'Mr Isherwood is revealed as a genuine humorist. The book as a whole throws a vivid light on the historical background of Hitler's rise to power' *Yorkshire Post*

'How to render in fiction what seemed more grotesquely fictional than anything that could be imagined? Isherwood . . . took the oblique view, suggesting by his own brand of resonant understatement the full extent of the political emptiness and personal despair that lay beneath the brittle surface' *Books and Bookmen*

ALEJO CARPENTIER

# The Lost Steps

A composer, fleeing an empty existence in New York
City, takes a journey with his mistress to one of the few
remaining areas of the world not yet touched by civiliz-
ation – the upper reaches of a great South American
river – on the pretext of collecting primitive musical
instruments. As he strikes deeper into the jungle, he
imagines that he is travelling back in time, retracing the
lost steps of mankind to a point where the work of so-
called progress may be undone. *The Lost Steps*,
Carpentier's most celebrated novel, describes his search,
his adventures, and the extraordinary decision he makes
in a village that seems truly to be outside history.

'Carpentier's prose shines with extraordinary brilliance
. . . The story starts in New York City, and the descriptions of the City, and of the journey and the revolution-
torn South American town where the travellers rest
before setting out for the jungle, are masterly'
*New Yorker*

'A brilliant and enviable accomplishment'   *Commonweal*

'Alejo Carpentier transformed the Latin American
novel. He transcended naturalism and invented magical
realism . . . We are all his descendants'   Carlos Fuentes

ALEJO CARPENTIER

# The Chase

'Alejo Carpentier transformed the Latin American novel. He transcended naturalism and invented magical realism. He took the language of the Spanish Baroque and made it imagine a world where literature does not imitate reality but, rather, adds to reality. It is good to know that *The Chase* is in English at last. We welcome back our father and his bounty; we owe him the heritage of a language and an imagination. We are all his descendants' Carlos Fuentes

'A hypnotic performance, weaving strands of religion, art and politics around the core of a swift psychological thriller . . . Into this slim anecdote Carpentier crams a huge vista of sensations and ideas. T. S. Eliot once dreamed of an art to unite metaphysics and the smell of cooking. In its dense entanglements of sense and intellect that, almost exactly, is what *The Chase* delivers' *Observer*

'As well-constructed a novel as one is likely to read . . . Having finished reading *The Chase* the reader is strongly advised to turn to the beginning and start again. Foreknowledge brings to the surface hitherto unperceived marvels and intricacies conceived by this undoubted genius' *Literary Review*

'The translation is so good that you think Carpentier must have written in English to begin with . . . Ten out of ten all round' *The Times*

PETER HANDKE

# The Afternoon of a Writer

'This brief tale of the after-work hours of one of those nameless writers (he walks into town, out of town, has a drink or two, walks home and goes to bed, alone) applies such an intense sensibility to his paragraphs that we seem to enter a supernatural dimension . . . With a phenomenal intensity and delicacy of register [this] little book captures the chemistry of perception and of the perceptions' transformation into memory and language. We are there with the writer, behind his eyes and under his skin'  John Updike, *New Yorker*

'Widely regarded in Europe and America as the most important writer since Beckett, Handke remains criminally neglected in Britain. Yet the Austrian's latest work is a beautifully rendered novelette which resonates with a rare power . . . In his most subtly and quietly realized work to date, Handke illuminates the writer's struggle with language. In doing so, he highlights his own mastery of the written word and reinforces his position as the last of the great Modernists'  *Blitz*

'Scrupulously translated by Ralph Manheim'
*New York Times*

HELEN SIMPSON

# Four Bare Legs in a Bed

'Absolutely brilliant . . . the only book this year that's made me sick with envy'   Julie Burchill

'These stories of sex pack a truly original pungency . . . kicking off belly-laughs or melting you with an apt phrase, Simpson makes a delectable debut'
*Mail on Sunday*

'She can be sparingly tragic and unsparingly funny . . . a unique writer'   Ruth Rendell

'Outstanding . . . You should read her'   *The Times*

'Dazzlingly original . . . Simpson's black-hearted humour is something to relish'   *Sunday Times*

'Stories told in such succulent prose that you wince at their brevity . . . a most exceptional debut'
*Evening Standard*

'Deserves all the literary prizes she will get'
*Daily Telegraph*

# DONALD BARTHELME

# **Sixty Stories**

'The most innovative short story writer since Borges . . . his writing is characterised by wit and invention, by craftsmanship and impudence. It is imposssible to do justice to the rich variety of these stories: he takes his thoughts for a walk through innumerable landscapes, and the results are refreshing, infuriating, delightful' *Independent*

'He is a writer's writer, someone who explores the potentials and limitations of modern fiction, and who – at his best – shows the nature and difficulty of our own creativity as few writers ever do. He is also a reader's writer, a fount of story-telling, filled with invention and excitement . . . As good a compendium of the state of contemporary writing ans its pleasures as you could wish to find' Malcolm Bradbury, *Sunday Times*

'Donald Barthelme is the American master of the short story, the short story in italics, double-distilled and heady' Lorna Sage, *Observer*

'He occupies a special place in the art of the short story where only Borges may dare to tread' Andrew Sinclair, *The Times*

'Of the stories that now comprise the essential Barthelme canon, some are delirious frivolities, some ache with a poignancy that more conventional tactics might well find unutterable; but every tale is scalding' *Times Literary Supplement*

# GILBERT ADAIR

# Love and Death on Long Island

'A latter-day and very English reworking of the *Death in Venice* theme . . . it is a little gem of a book, beautifully written and constructed, superbly characterised. What disturbs is the sheer elegance of Adair's prose style – most of us had probably forgotten that English could be written so well . . . A *tour de force*'
Anne Smith, *Literary Review*

'[It] is in a direct line from *Lolita* and (as the title implies) *Death in Venice* and comparisons with Nabokov or Mann are not out of place. Brief, pure, intense, and as almost ludicrously desperate as all tales of impossible love must be . . . with perfect poise and poignance, in a shimmering, cold prose, Adair puts across the impossibility of fulfilment, the heat and humiliations of passion. The writing is masterly, the conjuring of contrasting worlds a triumph'
Isabel Quigly, *Financial Times*

'Quibbles vanish beside the force of his slyly erotic and erudite prose in this beautifully executed literary pastiche' *Independent on Sunday*

'A concoction which is as memorable as a night in the stalls of the human psyche ought to be'
Tom Adair, *Scotland on Sunday*

EVA FIGES

# The Tree of Knowledge

'In fact, Milton's daughter was discovered in poverty and then kept by the charity of the curious. Her grandfather was ruined in the Civil War. He never paid John Milton for his daughter's dowry, and she was persecuted for the want of it. A woman without property had no prospects, except marrying an old man with desires no lower than his stomach. With a humane comprehension of right speech, Eva Figes makes Milton's daughter breathe again, and deliver a homily against male oppression, which her father would never have admitted, for all his talk of freedom for men and the right of divorce. This is the apple of wisdom that the serpent of experience has given to this new Eve, who cannot regain the paradise that men like her father have lost for her' Andrew Sinclair, *The Times*

'This is a woman's version of literary history, a deeply felt response to the smug argument that "genius" is something to be pampered and cosseted . . . As a commentary on the domestic and intellectual deprivations suffered by women during (and not only during) this period, *The Tree of Knowledge* is totally compelling: but its ambitions go further than that. It is not simply about "knowledge" in the sense of learning because, as the final chapter makes movingly clear, Deborah Milton has been denied not only her education but the very right to give voice to her knowledge of herself' Jonathan Coe, *Guardian*

# A Selected List of Classics Available from Minerva

While every effort is made to keep prices low, it is sometimes necessary to increase prices at short notice. Mandarin Paperbacks reserves the right to show new retail prices on covers which may differ from those previously advertised in the text or elsewhere.

The prices shown below were correct at the time of going to press.

| | | | | |
|---|---|---|---|---|
| ☐ | 7493 9934 1 | **Adam, One Afternoon** | Italo Calvino | £4.99 |
| ☐ | 7493 9923 6 | **If on a Winter's Night a Traveller** | Italo Calvino | £5.99 |
| ☐ | 7493 9702 0 | **Berlin Novels** | Christopher Isherwood | £6.99 |
| ☐ | 7493 9828 0 | **Dubliners** | James Joyce | £4.99 |
| ☐ | 7493 9830 2 | **Portrait of the Artist as a Young Man** | James Joyce | £4.99 |
| ☐ | 7493 9829 9 | **Ulysses** | James Joyce | £5.99 |
| ☐ | 7493 9952 X | **The Castle** | Franz Kafka | £5.99 |
| ☐ | 7493 9955 4 | **The Trial** | Franz Kafka | £6.99 |
| ☐ | 7493 9158 8 | **A Dance to the Music of Time 1** | Anthony Powell | £9.99 |
| ☐ | 7493 9159 6 | **A Dance to the Music of Time 2** | Anthony Powell | £9.99 |
| ☐ | 7493 9160 X | **A Dance to the Music of Time 3** | Anthony Powell | £9.99 |
| ☐ | 7493 9161 8 | **A Dance to the Music of Time 4** | Anthony Powell | £9.99 |

All these books are available at your bookshop or newsagent, or can be ordered direct from the address below. Just tick the titles you want and fill in the form below.

Cash Sales Department, PO Box 5, Rushden, Northants NN10 6YX.
Fax: 01933 414047 : Phone: 01933 414000.

Please send cheque, payable to 'Reed Book Services Ltd.', or postal order for purchase price quoted and allow the following for postage and packing:

£1.00 for the first book, 50p for the second; **FREE POSTAGE AND PACKING FOR THREE BOOKS OR MORE PER ORDER.**

NAME (Block letters) ............................................................................................................................

ADDRESS .............................................................................................................................................

..............................................................................................................................................................

☐ I enclose my remittance for ..........................

☐ I wish to pay by Access/Visa Card Number ☐☐☐☐☐☐☐☐☐☐☐☐☐☐☐☐

Expiry Date ☐☐☐☐

Signature ..............................................................................................................................................

Please quote our reference: MAND